THE SAME
Time

Brona Mills

Edited by Theo Fenraven
Edited and Proofread by Emily A. Lawrence of Lawrence Editing
Cover design by Murphy Rae of Indie Solutions
www.murphyrae.net
Formatted by Elaine York of Allusion Graphics
www.allusiongraphics.com

Permission obtained from Arthur Aron to reproduce parts of his work: The Experimental Generation of Interpersonal Closeness: A Procedure and Some Preliminary Findings by Arthur Aron, Edward Melinat, Elaine N. Aron, Robert Darrin Vallone and Renee J. Bator (April 1st 1997) Sage Journals 1997 Vol 23, Issue 4 Page(s) 363-377 http://journals.sagepub.com/doi/abs/10.1177/0146167297234003

This is a work of fiction. Names, characters, businesses, places, events and incidents are either the products of the author's imagination or used in a fictitious manner. Any resemblance to actual persons, living or dead, or actual events is purely coincidental.

First Published 2018

Warning: Due to some mature subject matters, such as explicit sexual situations and coarse language, this story is not suitable for anyone under the age of 18.

THE SAME

Time

Book two of The Time Series, *The Same Time.*

This book can be read as a standalone,
although it will contain spoilers if you haven't read book
one, *A Time for Everything.*

This book is heavily intertwined with book one,
and is recommended to be read in order.
You can purchase book one here:
www.amazon.com/Time-Everything-book-ebook/
dp/B071N9Y7MT/
www.amazon.co.uk/Time-Everything-book-ebook/
dp/B071N9Y7MT/

ACKNOWLEDGEMENTS

So much thanks needs to go out there, not only for the continued support while writing this book, but for the support after the release of book one, from people that I've never even met. Thank you for reading. Thank you for loving the book. Thank you for sending me such lovely words of support.

To my husband and family, for continuing to support me with all the spare time that is needed to take on such a huge task – thanks for giving me all the hours ☺

As always the friends and beta readers from my workshop helped make this what it is, and helped calm me down when things felt like they were never working. Thank you ☺

To my ARCs and typo party participants! This was invaluable. To have so many people on hand willing to give their time and feedback at an early stage was what managed to fine tune the final piece.

A special thanks to Arthur Aron for giving his permission to include word for word his research questions featured in The Experimental Generation of Interpersonal Closeness: A Procedure and Some Preliminary Findings. It was important to me, and to the story that these questions be used word for word, as the study is intended to be used. Full citation and links are on the copyright page, or you can click here. http://journals.sagepub.com/doi/abs/10.1177/0146167297234003

The work Arthur and the co-authors did was so fascinating that I had to include it in my novel. The first draft of this novel did have the entire 36 questions and answers included throughout, but through editing to fit with the story it had to be cut. You, the reader can view the full, unedited first draft of the scene by following the link at the end of the book, as it will contain spoilers.

Prologue

Monday, February 29, 2016
Cedars-Sinai Medical Center
Los Angeles, California.

When my dad was in his coffin, I could see his soul had already gone. All that remained was a body. David looks like that now. Lying in bed, hooked up to machines, a nurse bent over him. 'He got here ten minutes ago,' I tell Mike. 'They can't wake him up.'

CHAPTER

Twenty-two years ago
Saturday, June 11, 1994
Cedars-Sinai Medical Center
Los Angeles, California.

Pain runs through my core, and I grab my stomach.

'This insurance card has expired,' the receptionist says.

I steady my breathing and nod. 'My new employer, Cici's Boutique, picked up the payments. Maternity is on it. Call and check.'

She studies the card and smiles like she feels sorry for me. 'Take a seat, and I'll get you when the paperwork is sorted.'

Hell, even *I* feel sorry for me. I thought I'd be resting in a private hospital with nurses to pass me crushed ice and a husband to hold my hand.

Leaning on the reception counter, I breathe through the contraction, trying not to draw the attention of the only other person in the waiting room. The pain passes, and I waddle to a seat in my too tight jeans, which have been unbuttoned for the last two months.

The man attempts to make eye contact with me, so I keep my gaze on the swirly-yellow linoleum floor and fiddle with my T-shirt.

'You in labour?'

His British accent instantly makes him sound trustworthy. Ha, a trustworthy man. I bite back a smile and nod but don't raise my head. He leans toward me. He's older than me, well over the age of thirty, perhaps approaching forty. Heck, everyone in a labour and delivery ward feels older than me, but lots of people have kids at twenty-one. I just hope he won't look down on me. *I* would have judged me.

People with money hide their age well. His brown chequered shirt and jeans are designer. They might even be next season, but I don't recognise who. I've fallen behind on keeping up with the European designers these past few months.

An expensive watch catches the light as he rests his arms on his knees. I check out his shoes. Must be next season's. Despite being a little ragged around the eyes and sporting a few days of stubble—which of course he manages to make attractive—he's totally hot for an older man. He's the type to have a hot wife who only gained ten pounds during her pregnancy and is probably off labouring in a glamorous way.

'You alone?' he asks.

One loud sob bursts from my throat, and the tears follow. I throw my hand over my mouth to stop any more weeping from escaping and calm my breathing before the next contraction comes. The man rises from his seat and timidly sits next to me. It takes two attempts for him to one-handedly pull a stubborn tissue free from the box on the magazine table.

4

'I didn't mean to pry. I meant while you waited on someone. Not alone in the bigger-world sense of things.' He hands me the tissue and leans back.

'I can't reach my mom,' I confess. 'Someone's trying to find her for me. She's probably been thrown out of her favourite martini bar.' I check my watch and tuck the faded leather strap back under the clasp. 'Pamela should be en route to a much cheaper and more tolerant-of-drunk-people place by now.'

He nods.

There's not much you can say to that. I twist in the plastic, screwed down seat and give him my full attention. How is it people who have everything in life seem to have a sparkle in their eyes? I used to have that shine, until Nathan knocked it out of me. Literally. 'Sorry for the tears. Must be the hormones.' Or fear of the enormous task ahead of me.

Another contraction rips through me. I bite my tongue and hold my breath to stop from screaming. I throw my hand out and he catches it, allowing me to squeeze his fingers until they turn white.

'Don't hold your breath. You'll pass out.'

I hiss between puckered lips and count. Twenty seconds later, I'm coming back down to normality. He relaxes with me as I loosen my grip on his hand and finally let go.

'Are you here with your wife?'

'No.' He chuckles. 'I'm a little out of sorts right now.'

I raise my eyebrow, waiting for more information.

'Car crash.' His face falls. 'I was driving.'

'You look okay.' I check him over, head to toe. He's not holding himself or moving like he's in pain. Perfect face doesn't have a scratch on it. Arms and shoulders, all good–I always notice the strength in a man's upper body, right down to their hands and fingers, which I was squeezing the life out of. Chest, good. Long legs. Heat fills my cheeks. Shit, I just checked him out. I close my eyes momentarily. Hopefully he'll think it's being in labour that has me blushing.

'I am. I think.' He shakes his head. 'We were chasing my friend's wife.'

I stop breathing and lean away from him.

He turns to me, holding his hands up defensively. 'Completely in a non-stalker kind of way. She was in trouble, and we were trying to help her. Turns out we made things worse.' He drops his head and stares at his hands. 'I made things worse.'

Dread rolls around my stomach. 'Is she dead?' I whisper.

'No, I don't think so,' he rushes. 'But nearly. A few other people too. I just want the people I care about to live, you know.'

'That's normal,' I say with the least amount of sarcasm I can muster. 'Why are you in the waiting room of the labour and delivery ward?'

'I sort of ended up here.'

'Sometimes I subconsciously end up at Chanel of Beverly Hills.' I snort and rub a hand over the non-designer, cotton shirt that covers my belly. 'It's embarrassing when I remember I can no longer afford to be there.' I smile.

He snorts out a laugh and walks to the water fountain. Even that thing looks older than me.

'The places we visit often are in our subconscious. We don't remember getting there, as things we do out of habit are stored in a different part of the brain from our memories.' He frowns, passing me a cup of water. 'I guess people are the same. If we think about them enough, spend most of our lives with them, when we get lost, we navigate towards them, like a homing beacon of sorts.'

I raise my eyebrow at his bland definition of my shopping blunders. 'You come to maternity wards often? Just sort of navigate to them now and then? How many kids do you have?'

'None.' He smiles tightly. 'I have a stepson, though. My wife letting me be a father to him is the best thing that ever happened, even after the divorce.'

He swallows thickly, and I gulp my water, the plastic cup crackling and shrinking in my grip.

'I think I was meant to be there—to make a difference in their lives.'

The receptionist interrupts us and tells me I can move to a semi-private room. The man stands and picks up my backpack. 'Let me help you get settled in until your mom gets here.'

Another contraction hits me. I grab hold of his arm to steady myself. The pain passes twenty-seven seconds later. 'I'm Stella.' I offer my hand for shaking. The Brits are into all that formal stuff. I remember from when I used to work for my dad.

He takes my hand and shakes it firmly. His smile is forced. 'David.'

Nine hours into my labour, I'm grateful to the universe for sending me this complete stranger. David passes crushed ice and helps me aimlessly wander around the sterile looking room between contractions. He talks about everything and nothing—from how easy it is to drive on the left hand side of the road to how he predicts that TV shows will be attracting mainstream Hollywood actors in the future. It's mostly his voice distracting me from the pain that's intensifying as the hours pass. Every time the door opens I expect to see my mom.

'Pamela's still not here.' I rock from side to side on the edge of the bed.

'Why do you call her Pamela?'

'Everyone needs a nickname.' I take the opportunity to change the subject. 'Even you. David's such a formal, English name. No one ever try to Americanise you? Shorten it to Dave, Davey? Hot Dave?' I snicker.

'No.' He scrunches his nose.

Shit, I just got shot down flirting with a guy while I was in labour. A married guy—divorced, whatever. Divorced David. That's what I should call him. 'Can I call you DD?' *Totally hot DD?* 'All the cool kids use initials.' I pull my hair back with a tie, and he hands me a cold washcloth for my neck.

He shrugs, like he knows there's something more I'm not telling him, or maybe he's run out of things to say to me.

I groan and answer the question I'd avoided. 'I only call her Pamela when she's frustrating me.' I push off the starched white sheets and busy myself with the buttons that adjust the top half of the bed. 'We've had a few tough months, that's all. Once the baby gets here, she'll be back. I know she will.'

'Don't worry. Sometime in the future everyone will have built-in GPS and social media on their phones. You'll be able to track her down much easier.' He winks.

'Sometime in the future, I just hope she's sober.' I drop the control panel on the pillow.

'She will be. You have to give her time to deal with whatever this is.'

8

'This is history repeating itself.'

'How so?'

'She was pregnant young too. Had to depend on my dad, even when she wished she didn't have to.'

'I don't see you depending on the dad here.'

'Only 'cause Pamela knew how bad things got. She gave up everything we had to get rid of him.' I grimace but not from pain. 'My mom lost our home to get me out of this mess.' I run my hand over my belly. 'Do you know the best part? It actually worked.' I smile. 'Sorry, I know this is a bit much, sharing life details and labour pains with someone you've only met. Although I've been doing most of the oversharing.'

'The lifeboat scenario.'

'The what now?'

'When you spend a concentrated amount of time with someone you don't know in a high stress situation. You end up sharing personal information you normally wouldn't.'

'Well, sorry you're in my lifeboat.' I force a grin as I manoeuvre around the bed, trying to ease the back pain.

'Any time, Stel'.' He smirks.

'Oh, you think you're funny, do you?'

'Come on, all the cool kids are doing it.' He grins.

That smile is going to do some damage one day. DD stretches out his back. 'We should get the midwife to bring you one of those birthing balls. It's supposed to ease the pressure.'

'How the hell do you know that? Pick up women in labour often, do you?'

His smile fades. 'My wife was pregnant once.'

I stop at the foot of the bed, shooting him a look.

'I always wanted kids. Even though we were raising my stepson, I wanted to be there from the beginning too.' DD

9

takes time undoing his cuffs and rolling the sleeves back. 'I always felt bad she was alone the first few years with him.' He brings another cup of crushed ice to me. 'I wished I could've been there to help her when she needed it.' He pauses. 'I read everything on pregnancy and birth and the crucial first year. I wanted to be prepared, so she'd know I wasn't going to leave her to do everything on her own.'

I feel sick asking, but I need to know. I crunch the ice chips, preparing to speak. I've heard too many stories about last minute emergencies, cords being wrapped around the baby's neck, unforeseen complications, still births. I'm standing on the edge of the cliff, waiting to see if everything is going to be okay in my child's birth. What else do I need to add to the list of worries? 'What happened?' The cool trail of water soothes my throat.

'She had an abortion. It eventually ended our marriage.'

I rub my belly, like my unborn child could be harmed by the word.

He glances at my hand. 'In the beginning of the pregnancy she was happy. Something changed, and she didn't tell me until after she did it. The worst part was she seemed a little sad too.'

'You couldn't forgive her?'

'She shut down and wouldn't let me help her. She said she didn't want any more kids. That she didn't want to rely on anyone anymore. I knew she was lying. I think that's what drove me away in the end, the fact she wouldn't be honest with me.' He places his hand on my lower back and rubs out a knot that's formed. 'Everything I came up with to justify her actions was so much worse than the truth.'

'You got the truth from her?'

'A few months ago. About fifteen years too late.'

'Fifteen years ago? How old are you?'

He chuckles. 'We were married young.'

'Why did she do it?'

'Because she trusted me.' He looks at me, his eyes red with unshed tears. 'She made the right decision, and it kills me that I hated her so much all those years.'

My son is placed on my pounding chest. Gown open at the top, I'm shaking, and the muscles in my back and arms are agony, trying to unclench the tension of pushing. It's like I've gone a round in the boxing ring.

'Your friend wants to come in and see you when you're ready,' the OB nurse tells me.

'Can you send him in now?' I don't take my eyes off my son, burrowing his face into me. He's small and wrinkly and slightly blue. I wrap him closer in case he's cold, out here in the big bad world for the first time.

The door opens, and instead of hoping for Pamela, I smile when DD slowly pads in. 'Is it okay to see him?'

'They told you it was a boy?' I'm a little disappointed. I wanted to make the *It's a boy* declaration to someone.

He nods and crosses the room. I catch sight of the blood-soaked sheets, which the nurses tidy away. He doesn't notice. He can't take his eyes off my baby.

'Does he have a name yet?' DD sits on a stool and rolls over to the bed.

'Not yet. I thought I was having a girl. I don't know why. Maybe I'll name him after my dad.'

'Would he like that?'

'Who, the baby or my dad?'

DD laughs and rests his chin on the bed's side bar. 'Either of them.'

'Probably neither of them.' I chuckle. 'How about you? Did you have names picked out?'

'No. I was so caught up in the pregnancy, I didn't get as far as the baby-name books.'

I slump back, emotions overtaking me again. 'I'm going to be a terrible mother,' I sob. 'I never even thought to pick out a boy's name.'

He slips his hand into mine. 'In a few days you won't be as overwhelmed with everything.'

'I didn't even read any books. How the hell can I do this? You were so much more prepared than me, and you didn't even get your baby. How is that fair?' I cry.

His eyes redden. He looks down at my baby. 'Max.'

'What?'

'You should call him Max. It's a good name, and no one can ever shorten it to something awful.' He scrunches his nose.

'I like it.' I stare at Max, and it's perfect. He's perfect. I can do this. I can be a mom. Just me and Max. We'll do okay. 'Why are you still here? Shouldn't you be with your friend and his wife?'

'I'll leave once you're okay. That's how it works for me.'

He pulls a soft toy giraffe out of his pocket and squeezes it. 'I saw this downstairs in the gift shop. I checked the tags. It's suitable from birth. Thought it was cool 'cause it's more like a teddy so he'll be able to grasp onto it soon enough. Might even be able to chew on it when he's teething.'

I smile. 'You got him his first teddy.'

He nods. 'You could call it GeGe. Keep the whole nickname thing going.'

Max is a day old, and DD still hasn't left us. I'm pretty sure he slept in the waiting room, because he showed up first thing this morning wearing the same clothes.

'You can use the shower if you want.' I gesture at the bathroom door. 'The other woman checked out last night after you left, so there's no one sharing. My wash bag is in there. If you're quick, the nurses won't even notice.'

'Some hot water might be nice.' He goes to the tiny en suite. 'It's been a tough few days. Don't suppose you have a razor in there?' He smiles and his face lights up.

I snort, 'I haven't seen a razor in months. But my friend Cici packed my bag so feel free to use any pink razors or mango body butter if you find it.'

He looks relieved as he enters the tight bathroom. I'm not sure if it's the thought of showering, or that I haven't called him out on the fact he's spent two days in the hospital taking care of someone he doesn't know. The water from the shower batters down on the tiled floor, and I hear the disturbance of the drops as DD steps into the flow.

Someone steps into the doorway and I turn.

'Think I wouldn't show up to visit my son, Stella?' Nathan says. His skin is tanned, and I know he must have blown all our money on a beach somewhere. His lips pull back in a sinister smile. It never used to be sinister. It used to be attractive. *He* used to be attractive. Now I can practically see the inner beast—the fangs and saliva dripping from his snarl.

'You're not supposed to be back.' I twinge my stitches getting out of bed and wince.

'Should've told that to your friends. A lot of calls were made trying to find Pamela. I told you I still had friends here, watching you.'

'You need to leave.' I reach for the bassinette, not liking how close it is to the door, but Nathan beats me to it.

He wheels the basket towards himself.

I freeze, terror running all the way from my heart to my toes.

'He's my son too. Aren't you going to let me meet him?'

'Don't touch him,' I yell. I dive forward and slide the crib away from him with my elbow, while I reach around Max's precious body and lift him to safety. Nathan lets me take him. I cross the room to the window, putting as much distance between us as I can. Despite being the same height as me, he always feels taller. Like his overbearing presence makes me shrink.

'Thought we could take a trip. You, me, and the kid. Somewhere south of the border. Start a new life down there. Families know how to behave in Mexico, do as they're told.' He raises an eyebrow.

'I'm not going anywhere with you.'

'You will if I take the kid.' He steps forward.

'I don't have anything else to give you,' I whisper. 'You've already cleaned us out. Just leave us alone please. Leave.'

The bathroom door opens, and DD takes in the scene before him.

I must look pathetic, huddled in the corner, as Nathan stands straight and smug.

'Who the hell are you?' Nathan practically spits. His confidence falters as he takes DD in.

'I thought you were out of the picture?'

Nathan laughs, but I can hear the nerves under it. 'She told you that? Damn, that bitch will say anything to get a sugar daddy to look after her.'

'I'm a family friend,' DD says, not breaking a sweat. 'We all know someone like you is easily bought, so here's what I'm going to do . . .' He rolls his shirt sleeve up.

Nathan tenses.

DD unfastens his watch and holds it out. 'Cost fifty-grand new.' He tilts the watch and the light catches it, sending an expensive sparkle along the linoleum floor. 'I'm not sure how much you could get at a pawn shop, but if you ask around, you could probably get twenty-five, maybe even close to thirty.' He thrusts it at Nathan. 'There's a good one in Beverly Hills.'

Nathan takes the watch and inspects it.

Ha, like he could tell if it was a fake.

DD takes advantage of his momentary lapse to throw Nathan against the wall. 'There's one condition, asshole.' He punches Nathan in the gut then grabs his throat, squeezing. 'Don't come back.'

Nathan nods, and when DD loosens his grasp, backs up to the door. 'At least I got what I was owed.' He turns to me. 'I'll be keeping an eye on you,' he snides before darting away.

My tears fall when DD turns to me.

'Are you okay?'

'Why the hell are you helping me?'

The sunlight brightens the room, and I have to raise my hand to look at him. Something is wrong though. The light is too bright, and the window is behind me. DD takes three long strides towards me, and the light comes with him.

'I'm about to disappear. I might even be going home now. You need to know that when he comes back I'll be here, okay? I've shown up every time you need me. I'll always be here for you.'

'What?'

15

'I did all I could for now. One day we're going to make him leave for good.' He runs his thumb under my eye and wipes away a tear. 'I keep going farther into your past, but you're safe now. I think I got them all.'

'All of what?'

'The times you died.' The light surrounding him gets brighter and a shrill noise fills the space between us. 'Don't be scared. You're an awesome mom, and the strongest little mouse I've ever met.'

The light and the noise evaporate, sucking him inside. The contrast with the regular lighting makes the room appear dark until my eyes adjust.

Pamela rushes through the door, calling my name. She's wearing jeans and a pressed shirt, and her hair is tied back in a simple ponytail. Her make-up looks a day old. I wonder if she managed to shower and change in the middle of a three-day binge.

'I saw Nathan leaving the elevator.' She's pale and looks tense.

'Don't worry about him. I had some help.' I loosen my grasp around Max and walk to the bed, glancing at the spot behind me DD disappeared into. 'Sit down and you can hold him.'

My mom's face crumbles. 'Oh, Stella, I'm so sorry I wasn't here for you. You shouldn't have had to do this on your own.'

'I didn't. Someone showed up out of nowhere to help me.'

CHAPTER

Two

Three years later
Friday, April 4, 1997
Lakewood, Los Angeles County, California

I'm on my knees on the kitchen floor, holding my head in my hands. My hair covers my face, and I revel in the small form of escapism. I drag my hands down my eyes, trying to wipe away the exhaustion that started at 5:00 a.m. It's been a shitty morning, and there are still another thirteen or fourteen hours until bedtime. I take a deep breath. I can have a better day tomorrow. I can sort out my life—tomorrow.

'Mommy, what you doing?' Max waves his spoon in the air.

He must think I'm playing because he jumps on my back. 'Go, horsey, go,' he yells.

'Get off me,' I snap.

Max slides off my back, fetches the paper towels, and kneels beside me. 'Can I help clean?'

I rip a sheet from the roll. 'Don't touch the broken pieces, or you might cut yourself. Grab the trash can for me.'

I gather the broken cereal bowl and dump it in the trash. It clinks off Pamela's empty wine bottle.

The shower cuts off upstairs, and I push down the urge to bang on the door and ask her to hurry up. If I miss this bus, I'll be late again. I finish cleaning the kitchen, wipe down the countertops, and rummage through the fridge, making sure there's food for lunch.

'I do feed him, you know.' Pamela crosses the small space to the coffee pot and fills a mug.

'Just checking.'

'You know, if I could've had my grandkids first, I would've.' Pamela grins into her coffee. 'They're so much more fun.' She grabs Max off the floor and tickles his side as she twists him upside down.

I slam the fridge closed. 'It's not like we can afford for me to stay home too.'

She places Max on his feet, and her face softens. 'I was only making a joke, Stella. I know you look after us all.'

I dart down Rodeo Drive, balancing Cici's coffee cup in one hand, smooth the wrinkles in my pencil skirt and attempt a wave at Tony, Chanel's security guy.

Crap, two guys are watching Cici's Boutique, waiting on the bench near the entrance, framed by overflowing flower beds. They look like two models, about to be placed in a magazine. Their attention is on the door. If I've made customers wait, Cici will be pissed. At least I polished the glass doors before I left last night; last thing they need to be staring at is fingerprints while they wait for us to open. I slow, digging into my purse for the keys. I smile politely when the man on the right catches my eye, but I quickly turn to unlock the door.

'We're looking for Cici.' He bounces to his feet. 'We were told we could find a friend through her. Stella Lewis.'

I stiffen. Nathan's run out of money again. He warned me he'd have people watching. I don't know what I expected of any thugs Nathan might send to scare me. But this guy should know who he's here to threaten, not ask people on the street to identify his target. My heart speeds up and I don't turn fully around when I answer. 'We don't hand out employee information,' I manage evenly. 'Who sent you?' I twist the key in the lock.

'I'm Michael, and this is David. We know Stella, sort of,' he mutters.

Like hell you do.

Michael's not very intimidating. He should probably work on that. He's too attractive to be a professional thug, and lacks the confidence. Nathan obviously can't afford to hire scary people.

'Huh. Look, I don't know what he promised you, but I never got any money. Why else would he leave? You should go too, or I'll call the cops.'

I put my weight on the glass door to push it open.

'Sorry for the confusion,' the other one says.

It's DD's voice. Smooth and grating around the edges, all at the same time. The way he rolls some of his R's and clips them in other words. It makes the butterflies in your stomach that you thought had died long ago churn back to life. His voice is calming and soothes your ears, through to your brain, and slides down your throat, making the rest of your body stand to attention.

He grins and extends his hand to introduce himself. It's not him. It looks like him alright. His hair is dark and his skin is tanned. His smile crooks slightly to the right, where he has one dimple. His face is the same, but he's a hell of a lot younger than I remember. A younger brother maybe, or . . . oh shit, a son. He had a son, right? No, that was a stepson. He wouldn't look like his younger twin.

'I'm David Wembridge. This is Mike Knight. I think there's been a misunderstanding. We're not here for anything untoward.'

Untoward.

Un.To.Wa.Rrr.D. I punctuate each syllable in my head. The Rs are rolling.

Heat runs through me, as three years of dreaming about the man releases a desire for him I wasn't even sure was real.

I stare at his offered hand. It's the same hand I clung to when I couldn't stand on my own. The same hand that passed me fresh blankets to wrap Max in the first night he was born, when I hadn't burped him properly and he threw up in his bassinette. There's strength in those fingers and shading of blue veins over the back of his hands, leading to his solid arms. It's the same hand but younger.

He grins and drops his hand.

Fuck, I forgot to shake.

'We've just flown in from England, and a friend of ours told us to meet up with Stella. We have some business to discuss with her, and we weren't sure how else to contact her. If we could give you our contact information, maybe you could pass it along to Cici when she gets here,' David says.

Stella.

He's never said my name before. I wish my name had an R in it so it would roll around his tongue, like he didn't want to finish saying it.

He's looking at me like I'm a stranger. He doesn't remember me. Why does he look my age? Why isn't he floating around in a ball of white light?

'What do you want to talk to Stella about?' I narrow my eyes, knowing it will be interpreted as irritation, when really I want to see if the distorted glare from the sun surrounding this guy will make him look more or less like DD when I saw him departing.

'It's sort of private,' Mike interrupts.

'I'm Stella,' I snap. *And I was talking to DD, not you.* 'Tell me what you want and don't waste my time. I have to get inside and start work.'

'*You're* Stella?' Mike squeaks like a guinea pig, killing his attractiveness.

DD sighs.

God, I hope that's in disapproval of his friend's reaction and not disappointment that I'm Stella.

'We're here about your acting agency. I know you're the best,' Mike says. 'I'm an actor, and I just moved here. I need you to represent me.'

I deflate. I turn to the door, ready to go inside. When I worked for my dad's agency, I yearned for my own career. No need to rely on a man or a husband for security. But one glimpse into the real Hollywood life, the cut-throat business and fake loyalties, and I'm glad about my current job title. No way in hell am I going back to that world. 'I'm not an agent. I'm a sales assistant.'

I go inside and lock the door, not even looking at younger, hotter, possible DD. If it's really him, he'll be back. Because he said when he returned, it would be to save me from Nathan.

My quick stop at the grocery store after work has set me back twenty-six dollars and a half-hour delay getting home. It's nearly eight forty-five and Max is bouncing like a puppy at the door, waiting for me. I hate arriving home this late. The monthly inventory at the store delayed me another hour, which left me no spare time to go to the library as I intended and look for those paranormal books again.

I scoop Max up in my arms as I step through the front door into the living room. He smells fresh out of the bath, and his soft pyjamas mould to my skin when he clings to me. Pamela says her goodnights as she jogs up the stairs. Juggling the grocery bag, I make it the five steps through the room to the kitchen, landing everything, including Max on the counter. Max tells me about his day with Pamela while I unpack the groceries. His chat consists of some truth and some make-believe moments of play time where dinosaurs attacked them, and they hid under the kitchen table.

I'm only half paying attention, replaying meeting DD this morning. I kept expecting him to return to the store, so I could ask him what the hell was going on. Max's voice is getting louder as he tries to hold my attention. I need to get Max wound down and into bed. Two hours of work await me, and I want it completed for Cici before morning. I need to show Cici exactly what I've got planned for the boutique redesign. Finally put my years of high-end shopping and spending to use.

'Mommy, you're not listening again,' Max says.

'Sorry, baby.' I open my arms and Max jumps into them. We sidestep my purse and heels. 'Let's go watch TV in bed. I'll come back and get you a snack and I can work in bed next to you.'

'Don't tell Granny. She won't let me eat in bed,' Max whispers in my ear.

'Okay,' I whisper back.

I put Max on his bed, against the back wall of our bedroom, and turn on his nightlight. Before I've crossed the room to the single dresser the TV sits on, Max has pattered his tiny feet over the floorboards and jumped into my bed.

'Go on then, you might as well get under the covers.' I undo my skirt and pull my pyjamas out of the closet, mentally taking note of what I can wear tomorrow. It's the one good thing about having a small closet; I can pick out a full outfit, shoes, and a bag in one glance. Once Max is settled with his favourite movie of the month, I go around the house locking up. At the bottom of the stairs, I only have to stretch to check the front door is locked while I use the banister to swing around in full circle towards the kitchen for the back door.

The house may be small, but it's damn expensive. It's about the same size as the pool house at the home I lived in when I was Max's age, when my parents were still together. A badly decorated, greyer, duller version of the pool house, with one shared bathroom and no pool.

When I get back, Max is throwing pillows in the air. 'I want you to watch this with me.'

I climb on the bed and motion for him to sit back down.

'No books. Put your work away and watch this with me.'

'Okay, no books.' I slide the files onto the nightstand and lean back, aching with the relief of resting. *Don't fall asleep.*

I wrap my arms around Max and touch the side of his head. He's losing the look of a toddler and turning into a boy. A boy who's starting to take on the same shape as his father. The pale skin was inherited from both sides of the gene pool, but the dark hair and brown eyes are Nathan's. It's an unwelcomed, constant reminder of our brief relationship that tells me I was stupid enough to fall for a nasty man and Max will never have a good man to call his dad. Someone who'd be so good, they would sweep in and save a complete stranger, someone who might even turn into a guardian angel one day.

Once Max has fallen asleep, I transfer him to his bed and get my catalogues together. *Don't work past midnight.* I trawl through the paperwork, making notes as I go and highlighting the clothing that would sell well. I make a separate pile of the things I like, but the recommended retail price makes the margin of profit too small, leaving it for Cici to make the decision. By eleven o'clock, there isn't much left to go through. I can finish the rest on the bus in the morning, as long as I manage to get a seat.

After washing my face, I stare in the mirror at the lines forming around my eyes. When did I get so old looking? My blonde hair is dull. I tug on the frayed ends. I can blow dry it in the morning to style it, but it could use a condition at the salon. Hair and makeup products are so darn expensive. At twenty-four, I shouldn't have to worry about which cheap brand of makeup covers the scars on my face as well as the wrinkles around my eyes.

CHAPTER
Three

Before the lunch rush, Cici asks me to organise the boxes of material we bought to replace the changing-room curtains three years ago. Now that Cici can put more money into the store, she wants to address our original plans. I've moved the boxes aside and have them arranged by content and colour. I'm making a list and taking picture samples when she calls me from downstairs.

'Stella, I need you.'

I finish the photograph I was taking, slide the box back to its new place, and trot down the stairs. Slipping through the curtains that hide the chaos of the store room, I smooth my outfit and straighten my hair. Looking up, I see Mike with Cici. Why is David not with him? 'I told you yesterday I'm not interested in anything you have to say.'

'I just want to have a chat, see what I can offer you.' Mike fidgets, nearing the door as he speaks.

'Stella,' Cici hisses. 'Don't speak to such a nice young man in that manner. It's your break now anyway, so go on out with him and don't be so rude. He's British. They don't stand for any of that impoliteness.'

I glance at my watch. 'It's not even twelve-thirty. I don't go on lunch till two.'

'Take half an hour now and you can take the rest later.' Cici points at the door. 'I won't have any arguments in front of the customers. It's unprofessional.'

'There's a Starbucks down the street,' I mutter in Mike's direction. 'Let's make this quick.' I storm out. My hostility has more to do with the lack of David, if it really *is* David, or some other paranormal explanation version of him. The short walk to Beverly is silent as Mike falls in step with me.

'Is it always so bright here?' Mike asks. His English accent, despite being stronger than David's, makes him more appealing than the average wannabe actor.

'Wait till summer. It will be hot before noon.'

'It's not just the sun. It's everything.' He digs his hands in his pockets. 'The palm trees and flowers. Damn, even the pavements are vibrant.'

'Sidewalks,' I tell him.

In Starbucks, I order a low-fat, decaf, iced frap with hazelnut syrup and half a serving of whipped cream with toffee syrup. Might as well indulge since this schmuck is paying.

Mike takes our drinks to a couch, allowing me to sit first. Damn manners on those Brits. I sit on the edge of the couch. There's no way I'm staying long enough to get comfortable. Mike sits opposite. For about twenty minutes, he explains how he and David came to LA on a recommendation from a friend while Mike looks for acting work.

I wish I knew what the hell was going on. I thought David and I were connected, like he was somehow my saviour. I'm

26

going to have to stop at the library on the way home and find more books on the paranormal to try and make sense of this. I only read one book once I was discharged from the hospital. Max took up so much time, weeks had passed before I realised I hadn't actually read them all, and then I was fined for late return. I didn't have the mental energy to check them out again.

Mike never gives me any indication of knowing anything unusual about David or him knowing me before. He's too busy trying to convince me how great an agent I could be in the future if only I utilised all the things I learned from my dad. I'm knocking down all his ideas and answering more on autopilot than anything.

'I know your dad was hot stuff or whatever in the movie business. This could work out.'

Mike's comment makes my blood boil and probably sparks the first real response I've had this whole meeting. 'My dad was *hot stuff* until he lost it all. I mean everything. He divorced my mom, and we lived on state welfare while he tried to rebuild his life.' But it was the second time his business failed, years later, when I really suffered. 'I was pregnant and scared. You know what he did then? Gave it all away to his fucking mail-order bride. When he died, she got everything. The only good thing was that everyone who was in my life for the money went away too.'

I lean closer, so he'll really hear me. 'You really want people to screw you over for your money? 'Cause this is the right place and the right career path to go down. Friends are rare in life, and when you're young and rich and vulnerable, everyone wants a piece of you.'

He coughs. 'Look, if this is going to work out, let's be straight with each other. I'm going to be a success, and everyone will know who I am. My movies are going to be box-office successes, and Oprah is going to have me on her show many times. Guys are going to want to be my friends, and girls are going to want to get in my bed, and I might even acquire a stalker or two, so I need an agent who can handle it all.

'I need to know who to audition for. I need to be told what to do and how to improve. Proper guidance, not someone who shows up once a year to see how I'm doing. I need to know whose ass to kiss and where I can find that ass.'

'Well, look who just turned into a diva,' I mock. 'I gotta love the confidence. If you can do half of what you say, we'll be home free.'

'So you're in? I can do this, Stella. I just can't do it on my own.'

'Maybe.' If I had a fraction of the earning's Mike thinks he's going to have, I wouldn't have to stress about every bill that comes my way.

Cici catches my attention in the doorway. I jump up and she rushes to me. Her usual care-free demeanour is gone.

'What's wrong?'

'Max was in an accident. He's at St. Mary's Medical Center.'

I snatch up my purse and head for the door. My heart is racing, the thumps driving my feet forward. The blood pumping in my ears means I can hardly hear Cici talking behind me.

'Your mom rang the store. He fell in the park and split his head open. I have a cab outside. I billed it to the store, just get to the hospital.'

CHAPTER
Four

By the time I make it to the hospital, Max has stopped vomiting. We're moved from the ER waiting room to a curtained off bed. Two different doctors visit us and spend a lot of time looking into his eyes and discuss the vision black spots that Max is describing. Cici arrives an hour after me. She gets coffee and chocolate and tells me I need the sugar to get the colour back in my face. She lets me sit on the only chair and puts her arm around me when I cry.

We're taken for a scan, and once the results come back as normal, Pamela says she'll meet us at home. There's a large gash on the side of Max's head, which I was assured looks worse than it actually is. There's a lot of blood on the gauze when the nurse changes the dressing.

'Head injuries bleed more,' the nurse tells me. 'We need to keep him for a few hours for observations, but the doctor is happy.'

Cici holds my hand while I hold Max's, and the nurse changes the bandages on his head. It's not as bad as it could have been for the height of the jungle gym he fell from. But he has a large bump and a gash that needs to be tended to for a few days.

I lean over to Cici and whisper, 'I can't believe Pamela left.'

'It's not like she abandoned him, dear. The doctor's given him the all clear.'

'She's his grandmother. You'd think she'd wait and go home with us.'

'Pamela's finding life tough right now. She puts on a good act, but I say the guilt of being the one who was looking after Max today when he fell was enough to push her over the edge. You know she doesn't like being around too many people. She just needed to get a breather. Don't blame her, Stella.'

'I wish she'd be more grown up and get a job. A great, well-paying job that will help pull us out of this hole.' But it was me who lost my mom her home, so I guess I kind of owe her. 'I can't let go of this feeling, like I've reached my limit, that stage before you explode.

'When I arrive home at night, Pamela takes that as her cue to disappear. It's like she doesn't want to see me. I think she blames me for losing the last thing she managed to salvage from her life.'

'Oh, Stella, no. She managed to keep the most precious things in her life. Sometimes, people go through things that makes them difficult to be around, but believe me, she's finding it difficult being herself right now too.'

I take a deep breath. 'What was she doing while he fell anyway?'

'Stop,' Cici scolds. She's rarely so harsh, so I know I've crossed a line with my over-the-top Pamela-bashing.

'Granny was crossing the monkey bars when I fell.' Max answers the question I never should have muttered. 'She only made it two bars over before she laughed and dropped to the ground. I was trying to get down quick to show her how to do it proper.'

'It's okay.' I soften, squeezing Max's hand. I lean over to Cici. 'It feels good to vent. It's not like I would've said it to her face.'

'She's your mother. She knows what you're thinking. Maybe that's why she left.' Cici drops my hand. 'Maybe she's tired of disappointing you, but you know what? No matter what she does, or how perfect she could become, you'd still have hostility towards her.'

I glance at the nurse, who pretends she can't hear us. 'I'm disappointed in her lack of sobriety. Not her,' I whisper in Cici's ear so Max won't hear.

'For her, it's the same thing. Perhaps if you started treating her like you want her to behave, she might live up to that expectation.' Cici nods at Max. 'You have a three-year-old you use reverse psychology on all the time. Try it on your mother. What have you got to lose?'

The nurse finishes with Max and hands me a printed sheet listing the dangers signs to look for after a head injury. God, there's no way I'm going to relax enough to sleep tonight. I'll be checking on him every five minutes. 'Just as well he sleeps in my bed most nights anyway.'

The nurse smiles. 'I need to get the doctor to sign off, then you can be on your way.' She unrolls a collection of Spiderman stickers and lets Max choose which one to place on his T-shirt before she closes the curtain and leaves us alone.

I slide onto the bed with Max and pull him into me. He snuggles into my arms while we wait.

'What did that English guy want?' Cici asks.

I immediately think of David. 'I don't know, I haven't seen him in years,' I mutter.

'You know him? I got the impression he was new in town. He looked so . . . green.'

Shit. 'Not really. I . . . em. He wants me to be his agent,' I blurt, knowing it will redirect the conversation.

Cici smirks. 'He did tell me that. Why do you think I made you go for coffee? You could make a living being an agent, and you know what you're doing. It would beat surviving on the salary you make from the store.'

I open my mouth to protest.

Cici holds up her hand. 'I pay you. I know exactly what you make and how hard it must be to support three people. I'm just sorry I'm not in a position to bring you in as partner or at least pay you more.' A blush starts at the base of Cici's throat and quickly flushes up her neck.

'Cici, is everything okay?'

'No need to worry yet. Things at the store aren't going as well as I expected, so if this opportunity is real, as your friend and as your parents' friend, I urge you to grab it. You can work both jobs for a while until you start making money as an agent. You have your dad's drive and smarts. You ran the office for him. He taught you everything. You could do this with your eyes closed. You need that one opportunity, that one push to make you do it.'

'That's basically what Mike said.' I shift in the bed to face Cici head-on. 'He said he had a friend in England who told him about me, that I was going to be the biggest agent in Hollywood. You don't think maybe he sort of knows what's going to happen, do you?' Oh my god, it sounds ridiculous out loud.

Cici answers before I can backtrack. 'If anyone ever saw you work for your dad, of course they recognised the talent and potential you have. You, Stella Lewis, can achieve great things. You only have to believe in yourself.'

'Mike said it wasn't my fault Dad's production company went bankrupt.' I gulp.

Cici takes my hand. 'Did you think it was?'

I nod. 'I was the only other person working there. It was as much my responsibility as his.'

'You were eighteen. It wasn't your fault.' Cici's face hardens. 'I've known your parents longer than you've been alive, and one thing Simon Lewis never did was let anyone else influence his business. He took control, too much sometimes. Everything that ever happened to him was a result of his own decisions. And you know what else?'

I shake my head.

'He loved you.' She smiles.

I shake as I hold back a sob and cover my mouth, not wanting Max to stir from his slumber.

Cici squeezes my hand. 'He was a director first and foremost. He added an agency department to an already failing production company. He was good at what he did in all areas, but it was too much on his own. He was already in difficulty when you got there, and he knew it. And that two-bit whore never got as much for it as she let on.' She winks at me. 'Your dad gave you a job so he could share his life's work with you. Show you how the business worked, in case you ever wanted to make it your career. He made you work so you could see the negatives that come with so much success and responsibility and you could always make an informed decision in your career.'

I take a deep breath. 'Just because his business was failing, and his new wife was a bitch, I still needed him. I still wanted him around . . . do you think he had it planned?'

'I don't think it's healthy to speculate too long on why someone takes their own life, or if anything could have stopped it. Sometimes saving someone is only temporary. All you need to know is that if he could have overcome it, he would have stayed for you.'

I know he didn't choose to leave me, but sometimes I miss him so much, the anger takes over and all I can concentrate on is how selfish he was at the end. 'I used to dream about having a career with an income like my dad's. I would never have to depend on anyone—especially a man. Cici, I think I could do this. And Mike might be a great first client who just fell into my lap. He wants me specifically. He's going to pay me a higher percentage, and cover a day's childcare so I can work on my day off. I could make at least fifteen percent from him. He's hounding me after all. Even when I told him how much hard work it's going to be starting with nothing.'

'He must have heard how great you were.' She stands and gathers her purse. 'I'm going to stretch my legs and find a soda. You want anything?'

I shake my head and shrug off her compliment. 'It's not like I'd have anything to lose by giving it a shot. Once you've lost it all, the only way is back up, right? All I'd have to do is make a few phone calls. Speak to some people who owe me favours, if they're still around. If I put in some real effort, worked a few weeks, couple months, I could even land him a regular TV spot. He's hot enough to be a regular, and he looks like he works out, plus the English accent is going to kill some ovaries in auditions. Fifteen percent of a SAG minimum on a recurring TV role could get us all out of the hole.'

'Sounds like it might be the opportunity you've been waiting for. Work from the store on your day off until you get to know him. You can use the upstairs office.'

'Thank you. You do more for me than my own mother.'

'No, I don't,' she says. 'It so happens at this stage of your life, I have access to the things you need. But I only have a business and my home because your parents were good friends to me when I needed it. Now I get to repay that help through you. So the thing I'm going to ask you to do in repayment is start treating your mother how you treat me. Be kind to her. Be nice to her. If you stop thinking about all the things you wished she didn't do, she might surprise you.'

Cici holds her car door open for me when I climb in with Max in my arms. She takes the written instructions the nurse gave us out of my hand and packs them safely in my purse. Max has fallen asleep in my arms, and I stroke his hair, taking special caution around the bandaged area above his ear.

'Why the hell was Mike in the waiting room with you when I came out?'

'He wanted to see that everything was okay. You're mad he came to check on you?'

'Just wondering why David didn't bother to come with him.'

Cici raises her eyebrow. 'And why haven't I ever heard of David?'

I sink back in my seat. I never told anyone about David. They would have thought I was crazy, and I didn't need any more pressure after having a child. Whomever Mike's friend David is, he's not my DD. DD wouldn't want me to go back into a life I hated. He'd *ask* me what I wanted to do. Counsel me about my life choices. That's what guardian angels do, right? Maybe—just maybe, David is only a version of DD that could guide me. Maybe the other version of him died in that car crash he spoke about, or when he disappeared into thin air. Maybe here, he gets to live a little and help me at the same time?

'What were you and Mike talking about? You jumped out of your seat like your ass was on fire, that gossiping ass of yours.'

'Stella,' she scolds. 'I consider you and Pamela my family. And one thing I don't gossip about is family.'

I smile meekly at her. 'Sorry, I know that.'

'I didn't tell him anything he didn't already know. You interrupted right as I was about to divulge what colour of underwear the personal trainer was wearing when he snuck out of Marjorie Considine's bedroom window when her husband came home from France early.'

I snicker. 'You would think cheating with a personal trainer was supposed to be all hot and muscles and sex on legs. That guy could do with the services of a personal trainer himself.'

Cici looks at me in the mirror. 'Now who's a gossip?'

I chuckle again, and the brief escape from my worries is relaxing. I lean my head back and close my eyes.

I hug Max closer to me when the car pulls up outside my townhouse. I climb out, holding him tight. Inside, I toss the hospital receipt Cici paid for on top of the bills on the table by the front door. Good health insurance shouldn't be a luxury. If I had a great job, like my dad had always planned for me, I wouldn't have to constantly worry about a fall in the park, or play catch up on utilities.

Pamela is asleep on the armchair, fully dressed and clutching a tissue. I take Max upstairs to my bed. 'Back in a sec, baby boy,' I whisper.

Downstairs I pick up the empty wine bottle and the glass at the foot of Pamela's chair and head for the recycling bucket. Fuck it. I'm sick of clearing up after her. I throw a blanket over her. She'll be out cold till morning. I lock up for the night and take the empty bottle upstairs with me, depositing it on her bedside table. She'll find it when she gets up.

I tiptoe into my room and grab my pyjamas from under my pillow.

'Why you crying, Mommy?' Max asks.

I dash the tears off my cheeks, climb in behind Max, and curl myself around him. 'I'm not, baby. Go back to sleep. We're home now.' And one day soon, we'll be home free.

CHAPTER
Five

I see David across the street through the boutique window. Even from a distance, and despite the annoying reflection off the glass, I recognise his walk. He commands attention in the way he carries himself, from the sway of his hips and the confidence of what he must carry between them.

Shit, don't look at his junk, Stella.

His head is high, not intimidated walking down one of the richest streets in America. The expensive clothes he wears are more subtle than other guys our age. He's not wearing designer labels to show off his money. He focuses on the store and he doesn't react when two girls pause behind him and giggle, staring at his ass as he crosses the street to the store. He's coming to see me. *Please, be coming to see me.*

I wait at the door, ready to greet him, like I would any customer. Hell, if the store were empty, I'd probably dart outside, shake him, and scream at him for not remembering me, for not being *my* David. I pull the door open gently as he pushes from the other side.

He grins when he sees me. He's probably flashed that pantie-dropping expression at a million girls, but this smile doesn't have any bullshit about it—I can spot the bull shitters—he looks happy to see me, or to be here—I'm not sure which.

'Hi.' He slides his sunglasses on top of his head.

My eyes linger on his short brown hair that's just starting to grow out. I'd like to give it a tug while my tongue is inside his mouth. Fuck, I have to stop thinking like this around him. I never thought like this with *my* David.

Sure, DD was super-hot too, but being older and married meant the pull I felt toward him was more like friends—not friends, that feels like too loose a connection. Soulmates, maybe? We just clicked the moment we met. He snuck up on me, and in those two days in the hospital, climbed into the hole in my chest and filled it with friendship that was missing in my life. *This* David looks the same, only that he might give me a good fucking too. Shit, I did it again.

'You going to speak, or are you just waiting for me to repeat myself?'

'Sorry, what?' Double fuck.

'I said I wanted to leave you my number.' He waves a cell phone.

See . . . fucking. My heart falls like cement into my stomach, cooling off the fantasy I had brewing. It's not my DD at all.

'Geez, Mighty. You don't need to look so pissed that I offered you my number.' He narrows his brow.

'Mighty?'

He grins. 'Just thought a cute little nickname might get your attention.'

'Mighty isn't cute or little.'

'Is when he's a mouse, or you. You could be a girl mouse.'

39

'Have you ever flirted before? Because calling a girl vermin is really not the way.'

David opens his mouth, then closes it again. 'I wasn't flirting—well, not intentionally.' He gulps.

'So you go around stores, handing your number out to people?'

'No, I told you. I wanted to give you our number so you can speak to Mike about representation.'

Oh crap, I missed that part when I was in hair-pulling fantasy. I chew on the inside of my lip and nod.

'Great. I'll tell him you're going to call. Later today or tomorrow would be best.'

Shit, I didn't mean to agree to that.

'Why are you guys sharing a burner phone?' I cross my arms.

David smiles. 'We can't really afford to be in L.A. We've had to cut down on expenses, and Mike's family aren't in a position to help him. We're pooling everything we have just to survive for the time being. He's a good guy, and he needs this opportunity. We know how good you are, Stella, and this could make a difference to everyone. Give it a shot. Talk to Mike again, okay?'

'I'll think about it.'

He tilts his head, waiting for more.

'I promise to call, but I need to think things through, okay?'

'Okay.'

I give him the notepad we leave by the cash register, and he writes down their contact details.

'So what's with the nickname?' I ask, filling the silence.

'Thought it suited you, that's all.'

'I look like a mouse?'

'No, you look deceiving.'

'Two-faced? Huh, guess you really weren't flirting.'

'That's not anywhere near what I said or meant.' He frowns.

'Then what did you mean?'

'You're cute.' He drops his gaze to the paper. Could this man's confidence be wavering? 'And small, but when you met us the other day, you looked fierce. Like you had a hell of a lot more strength than people would think. You're not just a total knock-out with designer handbags.' He hands me the pad.

Even his writing is sexy. It's bold and confident, like him.

He takes a candy bar from his back pocket and sets it on the counter.

'What's that for?'

'Your son. Mike told me he was hurt yesterday.' He slides his sunglasses down and walks out the door.

I'm frozen to the spot, staring after him.

Please, David, remember me.

'Wow,' Cici speaks behind me.

I swat away a tear and turn to see her gaping at me. 'Not like you to be stuck for words.' I deflect.

'Honey, if I were stuck for words, I wouldn't be able to tell you that hunk of a man is going to fall in love with you.'

'I don't even know him. Not really.'

'You don't need to know someone to love them, Stella. Some people were born a match. He might be yours. Call your mom in here. We have to talk about your new job.'

It takes Pamela the rest of the day to get to Beverly Hills. When I called, she had put Max down for a nap and wanted

41

to let him rest before feeding him lunch, packing up a bag of toys and food, and riding the two busses over. If it wasn't for my giddiness about seeing Max in the middle of the day, I would've told Cici to come home with me after closing instead.

We huddle in the back storeroom, and Cici draws the curtain halfway so she can see if the other sales assistant needs a hand. She empties a brown box, turns it upside down for Max to play with, and gives him some crayons.

'Stella, I know how much you were hurt when you worked in the industry before. We all were. You lost a lot of friends,' Pamela tells me.

'I lost my so called friends when we lost money. If I do this, the only thing I need to worry about is the people I let into my life in the first place.' I look around the packed store room. With the three of us leaning against opposite walls, and Max on the floor, there's barely enough space to shuffle our feet, let alone pace in frustration. 'When my life went to shit'—I take Cici's and my Mom's hands—'you two were the only ones who helped me. So this isn't about getting back to the glitzy life.' I gaze at Max. 'It's about this little thing here. He deserves a better life than I can give him right now.'

'We're doing okay.' Pamela stands straighter.

I suck in a breath. 'We're not. We owe two month's rent, and I can't catch up. I've missed three utility bills. I'm juggling them each month, giving each one a little money. We can't keep going. The only places we can afford to live are not places I want Max growing up in.'

'You should've told me,' Cici says.

'You're not in any position to help. You pay me more than the other girls, and my commission is always topped up even if I don't meet my sales targets. I know the hospital bill last night went on your credit card. Don't tell me you have anything to give me, 'cause I think you're in trouble too, and it's because of me. I've been given an opportunity at a job that could get me out of this and pay you back. I'd be an idiot not to take it. I still have a lot of contacts and favours I could call in. With a lot of work and a strategy plan, media attack, résumé polishing, and audition tutoring, all Mike will need is one big break, and we'll be moving. He's hungry enough.' I let out a deep breath. There's always the chance neither Mike nor I will make any money for a while.

My mom slips her hand in mine. 'You remind me so much of your father when he was younger. He had so much drive and talent. He taught you well.'

I smile at her.

'I only wish he'd taught me too.' Her shoulders slump and I recognise the self-deprecating thoughts crossing her face. 'I wish I could help you, but things right now . . .'

'I understand they're bad, but maybe we can all work together if I manage to pull this off.'

'Stella.' Pamela meets my eye, determination in her tone. 'There isn't a doubt in my mind you can make a success out of anyone. Half the work your dad's company retained was actually due to you pulling the strings in the office. In the later years, anyway.'

I snort. 'Yeah, and look how that worked out.'

'Your father invested his money badly. Or whored it away.'

'Sh,' I scold her, tilting my head to Max.

'Hell, I bet you could even get that David a career too.' Cici chuckles. 'They are lookers, the pair of them. Must be

43

something in the water over there. Remind me to retire in England.'

'Last week you said Barbados. You're going to have to pick between the weather or the men.'

'Well, isn't my life just full of difficulties.' She winks.

The three of us laugh, and I pick Max up off the floor and squeeze him tight. 'You really think I can do this?'

'You were born doing this,' Mom tells me.

Sunday, April 22, 1997
Lakewood, California.

'How are you getting on?' Mom asks from the kitchen doorway.

'Good.' I clear some notes off the other chair, and she sits next to me. 'Thank god Cici lets me take her laptop home in the evenings. I've most of the ground work already established.' The dead of the night is a calming time for me to get through some work. Especially since Pamela has been putting Max to sleep. With the TV off and the kitchen already wiped down for the evening, there's nothing stopping me from working till midnight.

'It's only been two weeks. You don't mess around, do you?' She smiles. 'Max is asleep.'

'Thanks for helping out in the evenings too,' I say. 'This really is team work, getting this business up and running.'

She nods. 'When your dad and I were married, and his career was in full swing, I used to feel bad that I couldn't help out. I wanted to be useful, so I'm glad I can help you this time around.'

44

'You've always helped me.' I tap the top of her hand, not quite at the hand squeezing and hugging stage yet. 'Even if I never told you, I should have. The only reason I'm able to work the hours I do is because you look after Max.' I swallow hard. 'Thank you.' It's the first time I've said those words to her in years.

'You're welcome.' She pats my leg. 'You want some coffee?' She gets up and flicks the switch on the machine.

'God, yes.'

'You know, one thing your dad did let me do was decorate his office. I was really good at it. When you're ready, let me know, and I'll see what I can do.'

I shrug. 'Dad had a lot more spare cash than we're going to have for a while.'

'There are lots of things you can do on a budget, if you're willing to get your hands dirty.'

I look at her hands. 'I know you don't get manicures anymore, but do you really want to get them dirty?'

'Why not?' She smiles and this time it reaches her eyes. 'In the meantime, can you do me a favour?'

'Sure.'

'Tell me what you're doing.' She sits again and scoots the chair closer to me. 'I want to know exactly how this all works.'

I chuckle. 'Well, I haven't pulled it off yet.' I shove the laptop to the end of the table and pull up a document. 'I'm drafting emails so I can send them when I arrive at the boutique tomorrow morning and connect to the store's Internet. I'll check for replies at lunchtime and before I leave for the day.'

I open a folder and show my mom the contents. 'We've had headshots taken for free, thanks to Joanne. She's an established photographer, who started her career with me through Dad's agency. Once I finalise Mike's résumé, she'll print them in exchange for publicity once I have my new website up.'

'How do you get a website?'

'Isaac is going to help with that.'

She shrugs. 'Why Cici divorced him, I'll never know.'

'You never know what goes on in people's relationships.'

'That's true.'

'I've contacted the girls who used to work with Dad, and a couple of interns I used to know, who are now assistant producers for casting directors.' I've worked so much on this, as well as in the boutique, I only get to see Max briefly in the mornings and evening. 'How about the day after tomorrow, we pack a picnic and spend the whole day in the park? Max needs to get his confidence back on the jungle gym.'

'I'd like that.' She squeezes my hand.

CHAPTER
Six

Upstairs in Cici's office, after a disastrous practice audition Mike read for me, I realise the only mistake I made these past few weeks of starting my agency business was not checking to see if Mike could act. He's not terrible, but he's not mind-blowing either. He's average. Average we can work with, but it's going to take time. With all the favours I'm going to have to call in, I'm *spending* all that I have.

He'll need acting workshops, maybe even a voice coach to control his wavering inflections. He's going to have to chase this harder, because I can't quit. Not now I've glimpsed a life where I wasn't worried about paying bills or buying school supplies. Shit, Max hasn't even started school yet, and there's no way I can afford it if this doesn't work. Mike needs to be shown what *making it* can look like in this part of the world.

'I think we've done all we can for today. Can I borrow this?' I hold up the book he read from.

'Sure. I haven't read it in a while anyway.'

That fucker. Sheer tiredness and the ridiculousness of him admitting his lack of preparation has me laughing rather than giving him hell. I smack him on the side with the damn book, but miss, and he takes most of the hit with his arm. 'Don't ever go to an audition unprepared again.'

'No problem.' He chuckles, rubbing his arm.

Good, I hope it hurt.

'Consider that a permanent reminder,' he tells me.

I mentally check my wallet to see if I have enough cab fare to get to my dad's old house near Bel-Air. I have this month's rent I was going to deposit in the bank, but this could be a make or break moment for us. I hit his arm with the book again. 'Come on. There's something I want to show you.' Out on the street, I hail a passing cab and give the driver my old address in Beverly Hills. I don't know who needs to see this more, Mike or me.

We scale the wall around the back of the gated community, and I buzz the intercom of my old home to make sure Whore-bride isn't there. When no one answers the door I take it as an invitation to climb the property wall near the main gates to get a better look at the place. Once we're perched on the flat brick top, I explain to Mike about the life and home I used to have here.

'How big is this?' Mike asks.

'About fifteen thousand square feet. Six bedrooms, eight bathrooms, a game room, media room, cinema room, gym, gourmet kitchen, eight-car garage, yada, yada . . . you get the drift. Oooh, secret kids' room right there off that corner bedroom.' I gesture to the right, remembering all the times I used to hide there, pretending to be my dad and making my dolls line up and audition for me. He even bought me my own camcorder when he caught me playing one day. 'And a pool house out back that is bigger than where we live right now.'

I don't necessarily want this life back, but I want the security that money brings. Knowing all the bills can get paid at the same time.

I gulp. My next admission might bring tears that I won't be able to control. 'I have a child, and there is a good chance I could be homeless one day. I used to worry about manicures and hairstyles and having designer toilet paper in the guest bath.' I wiggle my fingers in Mike's face. 'I have to apply my own nail polish for work.'

'Imagine.' He gasps.

I'm glad he gets my humour and doesn't see me as an ex-rich bitch moaning about the life I lost. 'It used to be the kind of thing I thought should be illegal. Now I think it's disgusting that a house this size has one gold digging whore living in it.'

'Why did they build it with more bathrooms than bedrooms?'

I laugh. I might like this guy as much as David. Maybe not that much, but this is definitely someone I can work with. 'I don't know, it's what they do out here.' I take Cici's advice and think about the things my mom does for me, rather than focusing on the negatives. 'Despite everything that's gone wrong in my life, my mom's alarm goes off at six and she looks after Max while I work. At least we have one wage coming in, right?' I lean back on my hands and bounce my legs off the wall. 'I wish the evenings weren't so strained. I get home around eight at night, then the real work begins. She frustrates me sometimes with everything that we've been through. I wish she could hold it together a little better.' Her old habits are sneaking back. She retreats to her room when she gets the chance. She pulls back from contact and conversations. I thought we'd turned a corner, but I guess she's finding it difficult, especially since we have nothing to show for all the extra work we're doing. 'Everyone said it would be hard to raise a kid on your own, but I never realised how endless it is. It's tiring. And expensive. Everything you need for a kid is so damn expensive, and that's before we even get to do any of the fun stuff.

'I've reached my limit of struggling. I've gotten to the stage right before a little bit of sanity leaks out of your brain. I'm tired of living paycheck to paycheck, of telling Max we can't afford some things in the grocery store.' I catch the tears before they consume me. 'I'm twenty-four and I'm just exhausted, Mike.'

He puts his arm around me, but I straighten and push him away. I don't need comfort. Comfort will make me relax and I'll succumb to the emotional exhaustion. I don't need to have someone tell me this will be okay. I need to work.

'Why did you bring me here?' he asks.

'To show you what you could have if you're willing to do what I tell you. Because I can do this. I can get us to a stage where we don't need to worry about the price of milk.'

'Excuse me?'

'I said I can do this.'

'No, the milk.'

'It's just something my dad used to say. Some people worry about the price of milk. Now I know exactly what he means. I can be a damn good agent.' I take a deep breath. 'And I'm going to buy this house again. No matter what, I want it back.'

CHAPTER
Seven

I call Mike from the boutique phone, a sneaky part of me hopes that David answers instead.

'Hello.'

I bite my lip to control a grin when I hear the smile behind the hypnotic English accent. The warm, strong smile that made me feel safe the night I became a mother.

'Stella?' David asks.

Shit. Why do I forget to speak around him?

'Eh, hi.'

'I thought we got disconnected.'

I swear I can hear him smile. 'Sushi,' I blurt, then cover my eyes in embarrassment.

'Did you call to shout random food groups at me, 'cause I gotta say, you would have gotten a better rise out of me if you'd said pizza.'

God, how I hope to get a rise out of him. *Stop it, Stella. How old are you?* 'I'm calling to bribe Mike with sushi. Both of you, if you want.'

'Are there more details to this, or are we going to show up and get hit in the face with raw fish?'

I roll my eyes. *Form a coherent sentence, Stella.* 'I need some help clearing out Cici's garage. I have a lot of my dad's company files and things I can use to set up a home office, but going through it and packing up the boxes will take a while. Cici is working tomorrow but is lending me her car. Isaac's going to help too. If Mike's offer to help me get things set up is still good, I thought I'd swindle him some free sushi. It's expensive. We're all broke. Isaac always picks up the tab. I thought the luxury would be a good bribe.'

'Is Isaac your boyfriend?'

'He's Cici's ex-husband, but he's around a lot. We're probably going to fill both of their SUVs. I can pick you guys up.'

'Okay, we're in.'

'Don't you want to check with Mike first?'

'Nah, he was being serious when he said he'd help out, so there's no need. Plus, he's never had sushi before. It'll be funny when manners get the better of him and he has to eat a free dinner.' He chuckles.

'Oh my god, that's so mean.' My gasp turns into a light chuckle.

'We're broke. It'll be the best entertainment since we've got out here. Text me the details, Mighty.'

I swallow the lump in my throat as heat passes through my core. 'Will do.' I place the phone on the cradle and chew my lip, attempting to curb the smile that's trying to split my face open.

Cici comes over from the lingerie display grinning. 'Was that Mike? Is he going to help you?'

'It was David. They both are.' I correct her and then realise my mistake.

Her eyebrows rise. 'Thought so. You were beaming that whole conversation.'

'I haven't known him long. I told you.'

'Long enough, dear.'

'Long enough for what?' I squint my eyes. She better not be insinuating I need to get laid, even if I do.

'Long enough to put a genuine smile back on that pretty face of yours.' She squeezes my chin, and I swat her hand away. 'Don't worry, I'll get Isaac to get the scoop for me.' She winks.

I glance around the store and then at the clock. 'Do you think it's going to pick up before the end of my shift?'

'Got somewhere to go?'

'I don't have a waxing appointment, before you ask.'

She laughs. 'That's not even what I was going to ask, but since you got off the phone with Mr Dreamy, and that's the first thing that popped into *your* head, maybe you should make one.'

I blow my bangs out of my eyes. 'I have some things I want to check online before I leave tonight, and I'd hate to be late home to Max again.'

'Go ahead, dear. If it gets busy, I'm sure I can handle it. I do own the place, you know.'

'Thank you.' I take a spare notepad and pen from under the counter. 'You can dock me the last hour. I really want to get a jump on some things.'

'Don't worry about it, girl. I'm happy you're not fretting about the store being quiet for once. Normally, you're pacing the door, ready to pull customers in from the street.'

I gape at her. 'I am so not that bad,' I squeal.

'You kind of are.'

Above the boutique, in the office that is slowly being taken over by excess stock, I tap on the desk until the computer connects to the Internet. In the search engine box, I type the name of the books I checked out of the library the first time DD disappeared on me. Each search brings up some variation of ghosts and paranormal activity. I click into a few, but nothing matches what happened to me. After an hour of searching paranormal lights and people who disappear into thin air, my fingers are sore from scrolling and reading the first few pages of websites. I need to catch the bus, or I'll be late home. There are two more websites on this page. I'll skim those and then run to the bus stop.

The next one I click in has a picture at the top of the site that catches my attention. It's a panoramic full-length picture, stretching from one end of the page to the other, with some universal stars or glows around the edge. In the centre is a large, blinding light, which softens around the edges.

My heart beats fast. It's not exactly what DD looked like when the bright light showed up and stole him from me, but it's the closest representation I've seen. I scroll down and read book titles with subject matters that mean very little to me: disruption of time, perceptions of universal reality, changing your history.

I hover over the 'Contact Us' link at the bottom, then click. I'm redirected to another page that pops open an email enquiry box. What the hell am I going to say? The email address is for e.bennett@ucla. At the bottom of the page is an address to the Physics and Astronomy building on campus, right here in LA. I jot down the details and click back to the welcome page. Professor Ethan Bennett and his son Liam Bennett are listed as the website's administrators. I sink back in the chair. I think I just found a lead. I tear the page off the notepad, haul ass down the stairs, and run the whole way to the bus stop.

CHAPTER
Eight

David slides our lunch wrappers to the edge of Cici's desk and stacks a pile of scripts and reference books in front of me. Cici's office is spacious. The half now claimed by me is becoming a well-organised work space.

'You don't need to help me with this.'

'I'm not helping you, I'm helping Mike.' He folds down an empty packing box and stacks it with the others by the door.

'You already helped clear my dad's things out of Cici's garage. Trust me, the manual labour was enough.' I tried my best to ignore him yesterday while they were packing, but he totally busted me checking him out when he was lifting some of the heavy boxes. The way his biceps flexed under the weight of the files was hypnotic. I had to leave the room when he caught me staring.

I straighten my back. I never thought I'd have lower-back problems at this age, but I guess labour and looking after a baby, then a toddler, then a three-year-old energy ball can do that to you.

'It's okay. I need a break from research anyway. My head was getting too full.'

'Can a head get too full?'

He chuckles. 'Sometimes. Mostly, I think you need a break to let all the new information settle neatly in your brain. Usually I run or work out at the gym. Otherwise, important stuff might get knocked out of the way.'

'Important stuff like?'

'Speaking in coherent sentences.' He grins. 'Ever been so wiped out that your words get all jumbled, and you don't even have the energy to laugh at yourself?'

I smile. 'Yes. They call that baby brain.'

'Ha, well, I'm suffering from baby brain.'

'College too much for you?' I ask. 'Maybe you should see about dropping some subjects or settling in before you decide on your major.'

'I've already finished my degree. I'm completing a fellowship here.'

'What? How old are you?'

'Twenty-one, same as Mike. University works differently in the UK, and since my grades were high, I managed to continue my fellowship here. I have a thesis outlined, and I even got funding for an assistant next semester. That's why my head hurts. I want to get everything exactly where I want it before the funding kicks in. I don't want to waste Liam's time and energy on basics I can set up myself.'

I sit on the edge of one of the sturdier packing boxes. 'Holy shit. What are you studying?'

He dips his head and tries to hide his grin. 'The research title is *Proving Unbalanced Time*. It's about missing time caused by leap seconds in atomic clocks. It's basically physics, but I'm furthering some initial research Ethan Bennett started in the early '90s on the theories and probabilities of bending our own perceptions of reality and allowing changes to be made in our previous decisions, manifesting itself physically in our time reality. His son Liam is the one funded to assist me.'

'Change your history,' I recall from the website.

His face splits into a grin. 'Spot on, Mighty. Basically I'm studying time travel. For real. In a fully funded science department at a highly respected university. It's every geek kid's dream come true. Well, my geek kid dream.'

Holy fuck. I swallow hard. Forget finding a lead. I just hit jackpot. 'You're going to time travel?' The epiphany clears the confusion and worries of the past three years of my life.

He narrows his eyes. 'You have a lot of faith in me. No, I'm going to put together a great argument about how one day, for one person, under the right circumstances, it might be theoretically possible. Then, I'm going to see if I, or someone . . . can work out if it can be harnessed and controlled. I've made some pretty good progress in a short amount of time. I have a good source of raw data to tap from. There's just some time restraints on the source.' He sighs.

'You don't need to be quick. It's time travel, right? It doesn't matter when it gets figured out.'

David brays a full belly laugh before forcing his face straight. 'Are you a time travel geek, Stella?'

I ignore his jibe. 'But if you ever figured it out, would you do it? Travel through time to change something in the past—in someone's life?'

'I don't know. I hadn't thought about it like that. I look at it from an outside perspective, a facilitator rather than a participant. I'm not even sure it's controllable, like if you can choose a person or a specific time to go to. What about you?'

He leans forward. 'If you had the opportunity, what would you change?'

'I have a lot of regrets in my life, but I wouldn't change them. The interference would be too much. How would you ever know what things were okay to influence?'

'You mean the ripple effect? I know. Change something small, and all hell could break loose somewhere else. But there has to be a flip side, like an opportunity to save someone or make things better. What if you *don't* change things? How do we know they won't be better? You think your life is better even with your mistakes?'

'I have Max. Everything I ever did wrong in life gave me him.'

'That's what I'm working on. How can we tell what is meant to be? What are the things we can change without affecting the bigger picture in individuals' lives or the overall course of the universe? Some people should only know certain things about their future. Too much information for the wrong person at the wrong time can have devastating effects.'

'*Humph*, who would have thought? Hot and smart.'

David raises his eyebrows.

I jump from the packing box like my ass is on fire. 'I mean, hanging around with Mike and looking like that.' I raise my arm up and down in front of him. 'The two of you together turn heads. Everyone is going to assume you're an actor too—or a model or something.'

'Well, I'm getting all the compliments today, aren't I?'

'Actually, that was an insult.' Like hell it was. He's hot, and he knows it. I don't want to be another girl who inflates his ego.

'How is that an insult?' He leans over the desk.

'Because a good guy—one as smart as you—should be getting compliments on being exactly that. Good guys don't always have to finish last, you know.'

He smiles wider now. 'You think I'm a good guy?'

'You're going to a lot of trouble to help your friend. And you're going to a lot of trouble to help *me* help your friend. You've spent a lot of time with me over the past few days, and you've not made me feel uncomfortable or hit on me.' I don't know why I want him to think I prefer him not to hit on me. 'Well, not in a creepy way.'

'Duly noted. If I'm ever to hit on you, I'll make sure it's uncreepy.'

I stretch over the desk, getting close to his face. 'That's not even a word, smartass.'

'Oh, I like it when you call me that.' He chuckles.

'Why? Girls usually take one look at your abs and ignore the rest you have to offer?' I tease.

His smile falls a little. 'Pretty much.' He recovers his grin. 'They're pretty awesome abs, although now I know you've been paying way more attention to all the lifting and carrying I was doing yesterday.' He pops a cold french-fry in his mouth and gathers up the wrappers.

'I have to start work.' I turn away from him and head for the stairs.

'I'll walk you out. Call me tomorrow if you need any more help.' He follows. When we reach the bottom, he places his hand on my arm before I go through the curtains. 'Hey, I'm going to take a risk here and ask you out on a date.'

I stare, ready to protest.

'Before you answer, I know you think it's probably a bad move to mix business and pleasure, but remember it's you and Mike who are working together, not you and me. Since you've noticed I actually am a person, under this totally hot supermodel package . . .'

I roll my eyes.

'I'm being honest, based on your willingness to set me up with a modelling contract.'

I laugh, feeling lighter than I have in years. 'That's not even remotely what I had in mind.'

'Ha-ha. So you had something in mind?'

I start to roll my eyes again, but he holds his hands up and catches my attention halfway.

'As I was saying, since you seemed to be more interested in me, I thought maybe we could go on a date.'

'How do you figure I'm more interested in you?'

'Because you never looked at me so intently until I started speaking about my work. It interested you. *I* interested you. Not the looks, but the person. Not many girls want to know about my studies, which kind of sucks, because science has always been a big part of my life.' He shrugs. 'It's why I joined the gym when I was fourteen; realised pretty quickly that it's only fit geeks that get dates.' He smirks.

I can't help but chuckle. 'I suppose your pretty face helps?'

His eyes widen. 'I'm so not pretty. Girls are pretty. You're pretty.' He takes a confident step forward, his breath close to mine. 'You're going to have to call me something way more manly if this is going to work.'

'You're getting ahead of yourself. I haven't even agreed to a date.'

'Then agree, and I'll make sure it's a first date to remember.'

My heart stops. *Oh please, David, don't be that guy with me.* My face must have fallen, as his eyes widen in panic.

'Hey, that's not what I meant. I wasn't being the creepy flirty guy. I was being the nice flirty guy. What I meant was, let's do something different. No movies or dinner or walks along the pier.'

I tilt my head. 'Then what the hell are we going to do? Sit in your car and chat all night?'

'No, smartass, I don't have a car.' His eyes dart to the right. 'I should get one, though. We've been here for weeks.' His attention is back on me. 'How about we do something that's really getting to know each other.'

'Like?'

'We could go to my lab. I could show you around campus, show you my work. What I've done so far.'

I relax. 'That actually sounds nice.'

'Maybe afterwards, we could pick up Max and go for lunch.' He holds the curtain to the shop floor open for me, like it was the most natural thing to include my son in our plans.

'You want me to bring my son on our first date?'

'He's a major part of your life. I want to get to know you better. Seems like a great idea.'

'You know, most people don't introduce their children to the people they're dating for months.' I get off my chair and stand in front of him.

'I know, but we're not most people, are we? Besides, we work together, sort of. Obviously we're not going to tell him it's a date. I'm your friend.'

I swallow hard. 'Let me think about that one.'

'But you're okay with the first part?'

'Yes.' I smile, happy to be making a date with David. He's not divorced and broken. He's the same age as me, crap he's actually a couple of years younger. He seems to be interested in me, and I'll have an opportunity to figure out if he's going to grow into a forty-year-old man who figures out how to time travel and comes to help me in my time of need. What guy has ever done that?

Our date is arranged for the weekend. It's Thursday. I can't wait till Saturday. I want to spend time alone with David, get to know him, see if he really is the man I knew before. I know he is—he has to be. He's studying theory on time travel, for crying out loud. But personality wise, is he the same? People change over time. I want this to be real, because I don't want to figure out that those two great days in my life were just a hallucination or a mental breakdown. And most of all, I want to know if this David could be the friend I miss. If he's the sort of person to sleep two days on a hospital chair to make sure I had someone to help me the first time I changed Max's diaper and he peed on his own face, and I freaked out at already being a shit mother. If he's the type of person who's here? Oh my god, he's here. The bell above the door chirps, announcing his arrival, and snaps me out of my daydream.

'Hi.' David smiles and comes over to the cash register where I'm restocking the compact mirrors.

'What you doing here?'

He holds up a set of keys. 'Giving you a ride home.'

'You got a car?'

He shrugs. 'Your comment about making out in my car all night made me want to trade up from taking you on a date on the bus.'

I tilt my head, waiting for him to explain. 'I said chatting all night.'

He grins and I can see him chew the inside of his lip. 'Seriously. I wanted a car. We should probably have one for getting Mike to auditions and stuff. I called my parents. They sent over some money.'

'Ah, a rich kid. I did wonder about you.'

'Really?'

'The expensive clothes, the sneakers, and now a car. You fit right in here on the Westside.'

'Calm down, Mighty. You haven't seen it yet.' He shoves the keys back into his jeans. 'What time you finish?'

'Now.'

'Thought so. I dropped Mike at work, and he mentioned your commute home was torture. Thought I'd take the new wheels for a spin.'

'You want to drive me over to Lakewood, then drive all the way back to UCLA?'

'Why not? Come on, take advantage of my good mood. Next week the novelty will be gone, and you'll be stuck on the bus again.' He grins.

'You really know how to woo the ladies, don't you?'

Outside Starbucks, I halt in front of the car. 'You're right, it's not young Hollywood at all.' I stare at the fifteen-year-old Toyota.

'Why do you think I didn't park on Rodeo? Just 'cause my parents can afford to help out doesn't mean they're idiots. They sent me enough money to get a functional, reliable, second hand car. I'm not going to be driving around in a convertible any time soon.'

He doesn't sound annoyed, simply stating a fact. Like he knows it might happen one day. He opens the door for me, and I get in. Once in the driver's seat, he adjusts the mirrors and puts the car in reverse. 'You know, we need a cool name for the car.'

'You don't have to name a car.' I scoff. 'It's lame. Only sleazeballs name their car Lucy and Baby and things.'

He chuckles. 'I don't want a sleazeball name,' he confirms. 'I said a cool name. What you got for me?'

'You want me to name your car?'

He shrugs. 'Just make it something unique. Something reliable.'

Unique, reliable? I can't really suggest David, now can I? 'GeGe.'

'GeGe?'

'GeGe the giraffe is Max's stuffed animal. It's reliable, in the sense it was the go-to thing to calm him down. He chewed on it when he was teething. Rubbed it on his eyes when he was tired. It was always with him. Got us both through some tough nights.'

He turns and smiles at me. 'GeGe it is.'

CHAPTER
Nine

David and I lean over the desk in his office, which is slowly taking on the resemblance of a lab workspace. The office has been rearranged, and the place is packed with equipment and whiteboards of information. He shows me the vast printouts of data he's prepared for his new lab assistant, due next week. I really need to see if I can meet Ethan before his son starts working for David.

David is excited and talks quickly when he gets to a part where he has made the most progress on the speed of light, the measurable size of a leap second and the impact of leap-day births on the perceptions of our year.

Everything is organised and labelled, sometimes twice. When he can't find the time graph that explores how our clocks' recording limitations control our perceptions on the control of time, he searches for the location number on his computer. While he types, he explains the immeasurable impact adding a leap second is having on the way we view time. He pulls the hard copy graph from a labelled box file. Since becoming a mother, I've learned to appreciate organisation. I like to be able to find things without the impending feeling the world will crash around me if I drop the ball even a little.

'See, this was the problem when I was in high school. I couldn't find shit. Maybe if I were more organised, I wouldn't have gotten so frustrated with studying.'

David grins. 'I've been known to go mad if anyone touches my shit.'

I stroke a pile of notes and raise an eyebrow, daring him.

He chuckles. 'I'll let you get away with it, but if you're looking for me to throw you across the desk, I'll have to spend five minutes filing first.'

I keep my smile in place, but my gut clenches.

'It was a joke.' He leans forward. 'Sorry. I know my mouthing off doesn't impress you. I finally found a girl who wants to know about my passions. I'm not going to scare you off. Hopefully I won't scare you off. It's going to take a little adjustment on my part.'

'It's okay.'

'It's not okay, 'cause it makes you back off.'

'I don't want you to think because I have a kid, I'm an easy lay.'

He steps towards me. 'That's not what I think. I'm not an asshole. I used to behave like one because I could get away with it. I could practically ask a girl for sex, and most of the time I'd get it. And it made me kind of sad, especially if I liked her. So I kind of have a no sex rule if I'm looking for something more.'

He wraps an arm around my waist, and I rest my outstretched hand onto his hard-as-a-rock chest.

I run my hand down his muscles, feeling his abs through his shirt. I rest my fingers on his belt buckle.

He moves in and kisses my lips then pulls back slightly and waits for me to react.

My heart beats fast, and I open my mouth and lean into him, letting him kiss me longer. He slides his tongue in my mouth, and I moan, tightening my fingers on his belt when I really want to unbuckle it.

He coils his arm around my waist and crushes himself against me, breathing deeply, sucking for air as he kisses and nibbles his way around my lips. He continues kissing across my cheek and jaw, up to my ear, kneading his hands through my hair.

'We need to stop,' I breathe.

He looks me in the eye. 'You okay?' His voice is hoarse.

'Yes, but if you keep doing that, I'm going to make you mess up that desk of yours.'

His eyes fall shut. 'Fuck. I know you're not using me, Stella. But I need to wait. I know it's this stupid thing I need to get over.'

'You're telling me you're insecure? It's fine. It's probably for the best anyway. There's a good chance I've forgotten what the hell to do anyway.'

He opens his eyes and tilts his head.

'I have a three-year-old child. I haven't had time to date, and there's not a lot of people who want to go near a single mom.'

'Are you saying you've not been with anyone in three years?'

'He's three and a half, and the nine months I was pregnant, I did everything to avoid sex.'

'Nothing? Like, nothing in more than four years?'

'Jeez, David. Let it go.'

'Hm, I think we need to work on some reminding.' He tugs me out of the lab, locking the door behind us.

'Where are we going?'

'Somewhere better than an office.'

David takes me to his dorm building and squeezes my hand when we enter the hallway. We take quick steps up the stairs, passing a couple of students on the way, and he takes his keys from his back pocket.

'Did you mean it when you said you wanted to ruin my desk?' He opens the door and pulls me inside.

My heart thuds. I glance across the room at the one single bed. 'No roommate. Pretty convenient.'

He places two fingers under my chin and tips my face up. 'I like you, Stella.' He kisses my mouth and quickly moves to the side of my face and down my neck, making goosebumps break out over my body. 'I really want to kiss you.' He nibbles my ear. 'Head to . . . toe.'

I tense and hold my breath, not wanting my speeding heart to give away my anticipation.

He stops. 'You don't want it to go too far?'

I shake my head, before I've even realised I've turned him down.

He relaxes, like maybe I told him he could fuck me all night. I panic. Maybe he misunderstood me.

'How about I help you out with your dry spell.' He tightens his hands on my hips and backs me against the door. 'We'll leave the sex until we know neither of us is going to run out in the morning.' He nibbles the side of my mouth.

'So you're happy I turned you down?'

He bites his lip, keeping back a grin. 'Kind of weird, right?'

'Not really.' I smile.

'Besides, I don't think you turned down my first offer.' He flashes a killer smile that lights up his whole face. He lowers his mouth to the top of my shirt, edging his lips under the fabric. 'Let me know if you want to stop,' he whispers.

I throw my head back, and it bounces off the door.

He stops kissing me. 'You'll let me know, right?'

'Yes.' My voice is rough, the tingling from his kiss already travelling down my body.

David attacks my mouth with more urgency. We both fall against the wall. He moves down a few inches and grabs my thighs. It's rough and gentle, and I can't keep my enthusiasm to myself. I grind against him, and he picks me up. I wrap my legs around him and he takes us across the room. On the bed, he leans over me. The seconds give me time to catch my breath and relax in the promise of what he's about to give me. He pushes my dress up, baring my panties and belly. Laying his mouth over my stomach, he tugs my dress off over my head. He pauses and looks me over, his hard dick pushing against his jeans as he straddles me.

I reach for his zipper, but he takes a hold of my hand. 'Not a good idea.'

I frown.

'If you start touching me, I won't be able to concentrate.'

'You need to concentrate?' I tease him.

'I need to make sure neither of us gets carried away.' He places my hand on his shoulder and I slide my hands over his biceps. He lowers himself down me, kissing around my thighs as he slips my panties down my legs, then flicks his tongue over my clit.

My back arches, and I gasp at his confidence to go straight for the kill. I moan and drop my knees to the bed. He settles between my legs, giving my feet a light squeeze and he manoeuvres them where he wants them.

I sigh out years of tension and run my fingers through his hair in a caress when I want to give it a sharp tug, drag him up to me and let him drive inside me.

There's a noise at the other end of the room, his door opens, and the light from the hallway spills inside. David has already leaped off the bed and I startle.

'Wait,' he screams, shouldering the door before it fully opens.

I scramble around the floor for my dress and pull it over my head before looking for my panties.

David has the door resting on his hip, blocking the view of whoever is on the other side. 'You can't come in here.'

'God, man,' Mike replies.

Of course it's Mike. David might not have an official roommate, but where else could Mike afford to stay but on his friend's floor? I find my panties and unroll them to yank them over my feet.

'I'm really sick of this shit,' Mike continues. 'It's one thing to bang a new girl every week, but do you have to bring them here when we're sharing a room? Can't you go to their place?'

My face flushes. I can't believe I fell for this. What makes you want to sleep with a hot guy more than him telling you he wants to wait until you're in love with him? I'm a total sucker.

David grunts. 'Shut the fuck up, man.' He looks back at me, but I put all my attention into getting my heels back on. 'Go for a walk and give me five minutes to sort out the shit you got me in.'

'Stop picking up psycho bitches, and you won't have to deal with throwing them out after you've banged them,' Mike chirps.

David slams the door on him and faces me. 'Would you believe me if I told you that was all in the past?'

I try to hide the hurt behind a smile as I reach for to the door.

'Stella.' He takes my arm as I pass him. 'I never hid my past with you. I told you exactly what I was like in college.'

'You're still in college, David.'

'I meant college in England. I told you I slept around.'

I continue to the door.

'Past tense,' he tells me.

I pause at the threshold. 'How many girls have you had in this room?'

'A couple,' he breathes. 'None since I realised how much I like you.'

'What, four days ago when you asked me out?' I laugh and open the door.

Don't cry until you make it to the safety of your own bed. I'm good at hiding tears until I'm alone. A few steps down the hall, David's door closes and locks behind me. Nice. I hold my head up. No one will know I'm doing the walk of shame at ten o'clock at night.

I flinch when I see David in the corner of my eye, and my heart doubles in speed. 'You scared the shit out of me.'

'Sorry.' He puts his hands in his pockets and falls in line beside me.

'For what part?'

'For scaring you.'

'And not for being an asshole?'

'This has been a misunderstanding, but I'm sorry for taking things too far tonight. You don't believe me when I tell you how much I like you. That I won't lie to you. Then we need to slow down.'

'Slow down?' I spit. 'What the hell do you think is happening right now?' I shove the main door open and step into the cool breeze.

'Getting you home.' He hands me a jacket I never realised he was carrying.

Fuck. Despite not wanting to look at him right now, I'd much rather not make my way back across town alone.

CHAPTER

In the elevator, I twist my hands together, nervous about the possibility of bumping into David. I've spent the last three days holed up in the library reading Ethan Bennett's book, and don't need to bump into David now.

Ethan's offices and labs are on the basement level of UCLA's Physics Department, just like David's office. Once out of the elevator, I follow the yellow and brown hallway all the way to the back of the building, the same path David brought me on a few nights ago. The coincidence that Ethan's office is directly opposite David's is not lost on me. I knock on Ethan's door and am met with a younger man than I expected. His black hair is pulled back into a hair-tie and his shirt is rolled up, exposing his arms fully covered in tattoos. Vibrant coloured ink runs from his wrists all the way up and under his sleeves and when my gaze reaches his face, his ice blue eyes complement the colours he's artificially added to his body.

'Professor Bennett?' I ask.

He smiles and his lethal expression is transformed into a friendly face. 'Not yet. I'm Liam Bennett, his son.' He points to the book sticking out of my bag. 'Please don't tell me you're some weird stalker fan who wants my dad to sign your book?'

'No,' I yell, then lower my tone. 'Not weird. I did show up in the hope of meeting him.' I hold the book in the air. 'There are some interesting things in here and I wanted to know how things were progressing.' I look over his shoulder into the office, but there's no one else inside.

He folds his arms and leans on the doorjamb. 'You want to know how his research is going? Are you a fan who has a crush on my dad?' His tone is slightly sarcastic, but I can't help but notice the serious question there.

I cast a glance at the door behind me and hope David can't hear people talking in the hall. 'I thought I might be able to discuss some theories with him.'

Liam relaxes and lets the door fall open. 'Ah, you're a student.'

'No.' I put my hand out. 'I'm Stella.' I hear a crash of something behind David's door, and losing my nerve, I step back. 'Never mind.' I retreat down the hall then stop. 'You know, you don't have to tell him I was here. No need to let the guy think he has a weirdo crushing stalker following him around.'

Liam laughs. 'Wait up.' He closes the office door and locks it. 'I'm heading out for coffee.' At the elevator, Liam turns to me. 'Are you the director's daughter?'

I try not to react. Despite my brief stints with the entertainment industry, I was never in a position to be recognised by the public.

'Thought so.'

Apparently my lack of reaction also works as confirmation.

'Well, since we're acquainted, you should join me for coffee.' The elevator pings open on the first floor.

'That's okay. I've embarrassed myself too much already today.'

He faces me full-on. 'Stella. One thing I've learned working alongside my dad is when someone shows up as nervous as you, who isn't a student or a fan, it's normally because they've had an unusual experience. Something along the lines of what my dad is trying to prove.'

I try to remain nonchalant. 'His theories are a little crazy.'

'But they brought you here. So let's compare notes on what we've seen, shall we?'

Liam pays for the coffees, and we take them out to the grass area to sit in the sun. Having men pay for things like coffee and dinner again makes me uneasy. If I let myself enjoy these little treats too often, I might get trapped into depending on someone. We sit side by side on a bench and I sip my coffee but can't shake the bitter sick feeling at the back of my throat.

'I'll start the confessions, shall I?' On the edge of the park bench, Liam looks around. 'When I was ten, we were on a family vacation in England, and I got lost. Kind of. We were having lunch in one of those tourist pubs, and I went to the bathroom. On the way, I started seeing spots of light. I used to get blinding migraines when I was a kid, so I thought one was coming on. I splashed water on my face and waited in the bathroom a few minutes. The headache never came, but the lights settled in my eyes. I went back out to my parents, but they weren't sitting at the table where I left them. So I sat down and waited.

'The table had been cleared and bussed, so I had nothing to do but people-watch. The group at the table next to me were having a small party, and there was a girl there, who was the most beautiful woman I'd ever seen. She was older, like thirty maybe, but I remember thinking she looked cool.' He glances at me. 'She had purple strands in her hair, and I knew she wasn't the type to live the regular life of a grown-up. She still wanted to have fun. Like some soft punk wanna be. I wanted to be like her. Then a guy joined the group who caught all her attention. So much so, she never even saw me staring.'

I nod, knowing what it's like to lose your whole self in someone so quickly.

'Then they disappeared into thin air. Or I disappeared—I'm not sure which. Maybe both.'

My skin tingles, and I shift on my seat. I thought if I ever met someone who knew what I'd experienced, I'd be excited or relieved. Instead, I'm nervous. 'What do you mean?'

'I mean exactly what my dad talks about in his book. The descriptions and theories he's formulating are based on my experiences as a kid. And what happened afterwards.'

'What happened?' I lean forward.

'Nah, you have to tell me your story first. I know who you are, but I need to make sure we're on the same page.'

At least I can test my theories on someone who's not David. I can ask all those questions I need the answers to. He wrote the fricking book that has the closest experiences I had. 'A man came to me once. Saved my life. It wasn't something dramatic, like saving me from a runaway train, but sometimes even the subtlest offerings of help can change someone's life. I was in a dangerous situation, and he helped me avoid it. Then he disappeared into a ball of white light. He seemed to be expecting it, like he'd done it before. He said every time he left, he went farther into my past. That he'd be

77

back, but he thought he got them all. For him, he'd already been in each stage of my future that he needed to be.'

'What did he get?'

'All the times I died,' I whisper.

Liam's face turn ashen. 'Are you serious?'

'Please don't tell anyone. I mean, even if you think I'm crazy or don't believe me. I've never said it out loud before, and I know how crazy it sounds. Maybe I was having a reaction to the drugs.'

'Drugs?' His expression falls.

'I was in labour when he was there.'

'Hm, yeah, that could be it. The brain is a terrifying thing that can alter perceptions of what we see.'

'He left the next day. Maybe the way I thought I saw him disappear was only a reaction to the stress of giving birth.'

'What drugs do they give you in labour, and how much do you think you had when you saw this?'

I shake my head. 'It was the day after I gave birth. They'd already stopped giving me prescription drugs the day before. All I was getting was over the counter painkillers for the stitches.'

Liam looks at me like I've shared too much.

'Sorry, didn't mean to give you all the details.'

'When things changed around me in the restaurant, when the light came back, the people at the next table disappeared first. They were embodied in this strong light. The restaurant faded in and out around me. I glanced around and realised it didn't look exactly like I remember when I got there with my parents. My attention returned to the Cute Punk Girl. She wasn't slipping away with the rest of her friends. It was like she was being pulled in a different direction. She was in trouble, and none of her friends noticed. Next thing I know, I'm at the table and the food is back. My dad's coat is on the chair next to me. The place is quieter, and my dad is shouting my name from the other end of the restaurant. When I ran up to my parents, it was clear the staff and a few customers had been looking for me. I got the typical hugs, followed by a lecture about running off. But I hadn't. I was sitting at that table the whole time.'

'Do you think you travelled through time? That's what your dad talks about in his book'

He shrugs. 'Like you, I never said anything for a long time. Not until we had a visitor a few years later. This time, my dad saw it too. It helped to have someone else witness and let you know you weren't crazy. One of the Cute Punk Girl's friends appeared out of a bright light and landed in my dad's office. He spent the rest of the day with us, filling us in with scraps of information. Because he said that too much information at the wrong time would have disastrous effects. He told us he'd been travelling through time for a while. That we'd meet him in our timeline, before any of this started for him, but we had to keep the specifics of it all secure. He doesn't want to know anything until the time's right for him. He gave us a letter and told us not to pass it on to the right people until 2015.'

'What did it say?'

He opens his arms up and leans back against the bench. 'I wanted to read it right after he left, but my dad, the rational thinker, said we mustn't tamper with destiny. My dad locked the letter in a safety deposit box. I don't even know which bank he used. Honestly, the more I've learned with him over the years, the more I think he's right. After the time traveller left, we started studying together. He switched his teaching focus and published the book, like we were told to do.'

I look down at Ethan and Liam's book. 'He told you to write this?'

'He said some important people would find their way to us once the book was out there.'

'And did they?'

'You're here, aren't you?'

I huff. 'I don't think I'm the person he was talking about.'

Liam shuffles in his seat. 'Wherever I went when I was a kid, the people at the dinner table were talking about Hollywood. I stopped staring at the Cute Punk Girl and listened 'cause we live in LA. It sort of felt like home. Some director's daughter and grandson were murdered by her ex-husband. They heard it on the news. Only said her name was Stella.'

I swallow a lump in my throat, knowing that DD's warning about Nathan coming back is something I should be taking more seriously. 'Still doesn't mean it's me,' I whisper.

'Wherever I travelled to that day in England wasn't real. The time traveller told me how he'd found himself in an alternate version of his future. The same place I visited when I was a kid. I travelled to an alternate future and saw what could happen.'

'I was dead.'

'The guy made the decision to leave and return things the way they were supposed to be. He didn't give me and my dad specific details before he left. He just said he needed to check on Stella and Max one last time.'

Tears escape my eyes and I don't wipe them away.

Liam leans closer. 'Don't be scared, Stella. I found the time traveller in this timeline. My dad and I think we finally have a breakthrough. We don't know exactly what brought him to LA, or what his true research goals are, but my dad has set up his funding. He's much younger than when we met him, but he knows a lot of things already.

'My dad insists we don't interfere with his knowledge of time travel, yet. That we don't cause any ripple changes. How easy it is to trigger one of those alternate futures where you or someone else might be dead. Imagine if we bombard him with too much information, and it throws him off the correct path for his discoveries.'

'How do you know you haven't sparked an alternate future already, just by meeting him?' *Could I have already pushed him off his original path?* I lean back. What if I've already pushed him so far off the path of his original life and the wife and white picket fence he was supposed to have?

'I'm not sure, but the important part is, I found him.'

'So did I. Which means it's time for him to save me again,' I croak.

CHAPTER
Eleven

The smell of roast chicken and homemade stuffing hits me as soon as I open the front door. Max is playing with his dinosaurs in front of the TV, and Pamela is at the stove. I don't think I've seen her cook since I was a kid. Not like this. I ruffle Max's hair on the way to the kitchen. 'Smells good. You didn't have to cook for us. I know it's a long day for you too, especially since I'm putting in extra hours with Mike.' Cici's right. When I treat her better, she acts better in return.

She smiles and steals my nose when I pass her. 'I love to cook.'

'You do?' I scoff. 'Since when?'

She continues stirring gravy at the stove. 'I lost a bit of myself for a while.'

I pull out a chair at the table and sit. 'Mom, something's happened.'

She turns around; I have her attention. 'What's wrong, Starbar?'

A piece of my dad's determination returns with the nickname. 'Nathan might be back soon.' My voice doesn't waver like I expected it to.

She places a hand over mine and sits. 'How do you know?'

'I have a warning of sorts in place. It's not a guarantee, but things are starting to look like he might come back. I wanted you to know. I need you to be vigilant when you have Max and let me know if anything seems out of place. Even little things.'

'Of course.' She smiles. 'I want to be there for you. It means a lot you want to share things with me.'

'I need your full understanding, Mom. I'm not telling you this to keep you in the loop. I'm telling you because he's dangerous. So when you're out, you need to pay attention in case anyone is watching you. Here at the house, keep the doors locked and don't answer unless you know the person.'

'Oh, Stella,' she cries. 'It's going to be okay, honey.'

Her tears seem to be of sympathy for me, rather than worry about the situation she's wrapped up in by being my mother.

'We're going to have to move,' I tell her.

'Move?'

'I'm working on it. We've been here for a while, and all my old friends know where I live. Nathan could find us easy enough if he comes back. I want to switch apartments. It won't be far. I need to be close to the boutique, and this is too expensive for us anyway. I'm going to ask Mike to come in on it with us, David too. They've been sharing a room, and with them pitching in for rent, we might be okay. It will cut down on travel time for Mike and I working together.'

'Okay. We can start looking today.'

She says it as naturally as if I'd suggested trying a new brand of bread or switching to two-percent milk. I thought she'd freak out about the financial implications of moving—

first and last month's rent, final payments on utilities, connections at the new place, renting a U-Haul. We can't even afford packing boxes and tape, but there's no panic, there's no saying we can't do this. She's resolved. 'If he ever finds us, we need to leave the city. We need to pack our bags and go far away.'

She nods. 'I'll be ready.'

'You'll come with me?' I ask softly.

Her eyebrows shoot up. 'Of course I'll come. I'll never leave you and Max.'

The pressure and information from today weighs down on me and I burst into tears. David's been here a couple of months. What if Nathan is already here too, watching me from afar? I thought once I met someone like Liam, who knew what I knew, it would all be over. That finding out the answers would help me sleep better at night, rather than leave me with more questions. What if I drop my guard and feel safe because part of DD is already here in David? Then Max might have to grow up knowing his father killed his mother. What the hell kind of fucked up situation would that be? Mom wraps her arms around me, and I cry into her shoulder.

Wednesday, July 16, 1997
Westwood, Los Angeles

'We can't afford this.' The five of us glare at the apartment building. It's in a good part of town, in a nice building. Unless there are no floorboards or drywall inside, we're not moving in anytime soon. Despite downgrading from a townhouse to

84

an apartment and sharing bills, I'll still be overstretched if I also want to make payment on my rising debt.

'We totally can afford it,' David says. 'They want first and last, and a security deposit as well as utility deposit, so the outlay upfront is expensive, but you and Pamela's share of the rent is slightly over half what you pay now.'

'So our rent is less, in a better neighbourhood, it's close to work, and you guys are chipping in on the bills. What's the catch?'

'It's through the university. They have apartment allowances for fellowship students and their families. We're practically family, right?' David throws an arm around Mike's shoulder and holds open the building door until my mom, Max, Mike, and I are all inside.

'Where are we going to get the upfront money?' Mike asks. 'I've still not earned much yet.'

The hall carpet is clean, and there are pictures hanging at intervals on the walls.

'We can sell GeGe.'

Max stops in his tracks, staring at David.

'The car, not the giraffe,' David assures him.

'You can't sell your car for an apartment,' I squeak.

David stops me from following the others through the apartment door. 'I don't need it. This place is close to the university and close to your work.'

'You used to live on campus. How is this better for you?' I ask.

Max screams, and I lean in the apartment doorway. He's running through the place, trying to find his new room. The apartment smells new. It's not huge, but our furniture will probably fit. The kitchen and living room are open plan, and there are two hallways leading off them in opposite directions.

'I needed the car to meet you in Lakewood. I never wanted you to worry about getting home if I took you out on a date.'

My mouth slacks.

'The apartment is more important,' he tells me.

Moving us to this place, where no one from my old life knows me, might save me from Nathan without David even realising it.

'Besides, Liam is working out great. Means I can concentrate on other areas. I can leave early and work from home. If we live together, it means we can hang out while we get work done. No better way to get to know someone than live with them, right?'

David grabs hold of my pinkie and tugs me through the rest of the apartment. He's been doing that a lot. Small gestures that let me know he's still interested in me. Opportunities to spend time together, even if it's just working side by side or grabbing a coffee together once he drops Mike at work.

Pamela leads the way around the apartment. A large bedroom and bathroom are off to the right. 'Mike and David should take this one, since they need two beds,' Pamela tells me. 'The bedrooms on the other side of the apartment will do us fine.'

'There's only one bathroom.' Mike shrugs. 'Sorry, ladies. Going to have to cut down on your beauty routine.'

'Oh, honey.' Pamela shoves him. 'You're dealing with natural beauties here.'

Max pulls me down the hallway. 'Come on, I want to choose our room.'

Mike picks Max up and turns him upside down before turning him right ways and tossing him to David in the living room, like he weighs nothing more than a football. My heart stops for a beat until David catches him and lifts him on top of his shoulders.

Max giggles and kicks his legs. 'Again,' he screams.

'No,' I yell. 'I can only take that once a day.'

David winks at me. 'Don't worry, Mighty. We won't let our lunch fall to the ground.'

'I'm not your lunch,' Max screams. 'Can we go to the park now?'

'Yes, let's *all* go for a race across the monkey bars,' David jibes.

Mike heads to the door with David and Max, talking about which store to stop at for lunch supplies.

CHAPTER
Twelve

Six months later
Wednesday, December 24, 1997
Beverly Hills, California.

Mike and David have become a twosome at the store
these past few months. When I'm rehearsing with Mike late
in the evening, David comes by to help pack up and go over
our schedules. On the late nights with no rehearsals, like
tonight, David collects me on Rodeo Drive, before we meet
Mike on Beverly and catch the bus home together.

David opens the door to Starbucks for me and lets me
inside first. Mike is sweeping the floor and gives us a curt nod
when we enter. 'You didn't need to come over here and help
me close the Boutique, David. I was planning on catching the
bus with Mike anyway. It's Christmas Eve, for god's sake.'

'Exactly. I wanted you to be able to finish early tonight.'

I lean against a bar stool at the door while Mike mops his
way over to us.

'I have a problem,' he tells us. 'I think I accidently invited
Sophie to January's premiere.'

'Yikes,' David says.

'Oh god, Mike.' I scan the coffee shop for sight of Sophie. 'This is your first movie premiere. What if she makes a scene? Some things you can't recover from this early.'

'I'm more concerned about her pouncing on me, like she does every guy who walks into this store. It's your fault anyway.' He turns to me. 'You said to find a date.'

Sophie walks through a door marked STAFF at the back of the barista counter.

'Hi, guys.' She winks and places her hand on Mike's shoulder. 'Did he tell you he invited me to his movie premiere?'

'We were just getting the details, Soph',' David says and my stomach tightens at him giving someone else a nickname.

'It's super exciting. Imagine one of my employees, in a movie.'

'Who would have thought?' I cross my arms and lean against the table. 'A LA barista who's really an actor?' I retort.

'I know. I mean, I always thought I could spot the actors and directors who came in here, and turns out we have a shining star right under my nose. The stories I could tell.' She smiles.

Stories you could sell, more like it.

'I only have a couple of small scenes,' Mike tells her. 'I haven't even seen the final cut.'

'Yeah, there's a possibility he might not even be in the final movie at all.' I snap at Sophie, but Mike's hurt expression reels me back in. 'I mean, of course you are.' I hop onto the stool. 'We need to get going, Mike. Lots of gifts to be wrapping and mulled wine to be drinking at home.'

When we board the bus, Mike sits in the empty seat in front of me, and David takes the aisle seat next to me and pulls out his phone. I dig around in my purse for the book Mike leant me. 'Sorry for the delay.' I hand him the tatty copy of *Break the Piece*. 'Had a busy social life recently.'

David's eyes dart to mine and I know instantly he's wondering if I've been dating someone. Serves him right.

'Busy social life how?' Mike asks.

God, Mike, no need to call me out in front of the guy. 'I've had to read other things first.'

'Like what?' David asks.

Damn him and his interest.

'Nothing important.'

He narrows his eyes at me. He knows I'm lying. 'Suit yourself.' He turns back to his text messages.

'Never mind him,' Mike says. 'He's been in a foul mood ever since I cock-blocked him at the start of summer.'

'Shut up, dude.' David darts forward and thumps Mike in the arm.

'Ow, that hurt.' Mike smacks David on the head with the script he was reading.

'Stop it,' I yell. 'I have to be a mother all day. I don't want to babysit you two.'

David gulps. 'Sorry.'

'Sorry, Stella,' Mike says. 'I'm not used to David having his heart broken, is all.'

'What?' I snap.

'Drop it, Mike,' David warns.

'Who the hell was she, anyway?' Mike glares.

My heart palpitations relax. At least David never told him it was me.

'No one.'

'Oh, it was someone alright. You should've seen him.' Mike turns to me. 'All upset over having a girl run out on him.'

'If you go around bullshitting enough girls into bed, you're bound to get rejected now and again,' I toss out.

'Oh, he's been rejected lots of times, believe me,' Mike chuckles.

David smacks Mike in the ribs.

'I said I was sorry, Dave. If you want to tell me who it is, I can let her know I was the one being an ass.'

I lean forward. 'What do you mean?' I ask too eagerly because David puts his phone away.

'Yeah, Mike. Why don't you tell Stella how you came home in a huff and shot your mouth off?'

Mike pinches the bridge of his nose. 'I had a bad day, and I wanted to get to bed. David told me he had a date with someone, and I flipped. I was so annoyed, I just wanted her to leave, so I said something I knew she'd hear.' Mike opens his eyes and turns to David. 'It was shitty of me, but I didn't realise you actually liked her. I told you I'd call her and explain.'

'You made the stuff up?'

'No, it's true. Well, it *was* true. I may have made out that it happened more recently than it did.'

I flick my gaze back to the stack of papers in my lap. 'David asked you to tell her that?'

'He won't even tell me who it is. So now I know he actually likes this one, which makes me feel bad 'cause I screwed up his first attempt at having a real girlfriend.'

I scoff. 'It was their first date. You don't know that they would've had a relationship.'

'No, but I know David.' He presses the stop button on the hand rail and stands. 'And he's scared he won't get this one back.'

Once off the bus I tighten my coat around myself. 'I need to go to the store down the street, pick up some spare batteries for the morning.' I back away from the bus stop in the opposite direction. 'You guys go ahead and I'll meet you at home.'

Both Mike and David turn in the direction of the store with me, but David taps Mike on the arm. 'I'll walk her. You go ahead home.'

'Fine by me.' Mike digs his hands in his pockets and jumps on the spot. 'No one ever said it would be cold in LA in December. I get first dibs on banana bread from Pamela.' He grins and jogs away.

'Lay off the bread,' I call after him. 'You have a red carpet to walk after the holidays.'

David leans against the railings. 'Will you at least speak to me about this? I've been giving you time to get to know me properly so you know I'm not lying to you.'

I nod and walk down the street to the store, knowing I want more than speaking. I just don't want to be left heartbroken. I don't need a causal fuck from the twenty-year-old player-version of the man I want to fall in love with.

'You didn't tell Mike to say that on the bus?'

David scoffs next to me. 'You know better than anyone he can't perform under pressure.'

I giggle, and his face hardens.

'I'm not seeing anyone else. I haven't seen anyone since I met you. I want to fix this and take what we had further. I used to sleep around.' He kicks at stones on the ground. 'I met a few girls I thought were interested in more than what they heard about me around campus, but the moment I offered up sex, they normally took it. It kind of became like a game for me. See if anyone was interested in more.'

'So if she took you up on the offer, you politely declined and went back to licking your wounds?'

He fights to keep a grin from breaking out. 'No, I'd still fuck her, but that would've been it. A few dates maybe, but it was always about sex. Nothing longer than a couple of weeks. Four max, then I'd move on.'

'What would they have heard around campus about you?'

He gulps. 'I'd rather not say.'

'So what you're telling me is, if I have sex with you, you won't date me longer than a few weeks. But if sex is off the table, you'll want to go on another date with me?'

He pauses in front of the store. 'Well, when you say it like that, it sounds really wrong, but I swear I'm not some creep.'

'How long would I have to wait?'

'Excuse me?'

'I like you, David. What if we get to date three or four or more and I want to have sex, how long are you going to make me wait?'

'I'm not sure. I normally don't think these things through.' A blush colours his cheeks.

'No, you do a really good job to get a girl interested in you, then you throw her away for being too promiscuous?'

'God, I don't mean it like that.'

'It sounds like you have double standards. You fuck a lot of women but think badly of them for letting you.'

'Just the ones who seek me out. They're using me. It's not the same.'

'Why would women seek you out?'

''Cause I'm good in bed. That's what they tell their friends, and when you're twenty and know how to give a good fuck and make a girl come three times before you do, girls want to try you out.'

'This isn't really how I thought this conversation was going to go.' I enter the store, the automatic doors opening and announcing our arrival, and David follows.

'Stella, wait. I'm sorry. That sounded bad, but I wanted you to know I'm used to girls using me, and I know that's not you. We had such a good time together, and I've enjoyed getting to know you these past months. I don't want to ruin this. I've never had a date where I've felt like I was hanging out with a friend.'

'I had a good time too, and that's why I was mad. You were ready to judge me, based on all the other women you've been with.'

'I'm not judging you.'

'But if I'd had sex with you that night, you would have. And you know what's funny? I wanted to, and not because of some girls saying you were good in bed. We seemed to connect. Maybe that would've been something great if we were in bed together.'

He takes a step toward me, backing me into a quiet corner near the door, and I raise my hand. He places his hands on my hips, and instead of pushing him away, I let my hand rest on his chest.

'I would have been apprehensive that you were using me, like a lot of people have in my past, but I wouldn't have judged you. I would have clung to you and dated you. But you heard something about my past that freaked you out. I've

94

been giving you time to realise I'm waiting for you. Maybe you'll let me show you that we could be good together. That we can date and you might let me sweep you off your feet.'

I close my eyes and inhale his scent as I lean towards him. I remember his taste, and I want him again. His grip on my hips tightens when he realises I'm going to kiss him. Before I make contact, I open my eyes. I run my hand over his jaw, through the day old stubble that's there. He's watching me, not daring to close the space until I nudge his lips open with mine. He moans and pulls me flush against him, deepening the kiss I barely started.

CHAPTER
Thirteen

The last two weeks, David's been spending all his free time with me. Even now, in the kitchen behind me, he's chopping and prepping dinner, while I catch up on an hour's work.

He's been a perfect gentleman, not even attempted to take things past kissing, and honouring my request to keep our burgeoning relationship secret for now. I don't want Max to know about us until I know for sure there's a possibility of something long term. And the more I think about what a future with David, or DD might be, the more scared I am about committing to something that's either going to end in divorce as predicted, or ends sooner while David figures out that I'm not actually the one for him and meets his real wife who will end up breaking his heart.

I also didn't want Mike's work to suffer—wondering if his best friend and agent were going to break up. And Pamela, I didn't want her to think David was the reason we all moved in together.

I chew on the tips of my fingers and set aside Mike's new contract sitting in front of me. Isn't there a saying, if a relationship needs to be kept secret, you shouldn't be in it?

Shit. I don't want anyone making up their own reasons as to why we kept this a secret. I need to speak to David, see how he'd feel about telling Max about us. Guess it's time he can take us on that joint date he keeps asking for.

I tap my pen on the kitchen table, the reps getting faster as my concentration drifts. Staring at the same page of my dad's business manual, I rub my head, trying to get my focus back. I normally have my A-game on when I pull this folder out. I fell in love with it when I read it the first time. I used to lie in bed reading how to close a business deal. He spent a lot of time putting this together for me. It's sectioned, like a college textbook, into the basics of running a business and accountancy information, complete with names and numbers of professionals he trusted in the business. Finding and training talent. How to empower people to succeed. Training people in specific areas of the entertainment industry; acting, presenting, writing, and producing. He wasn't just a director. He wanted to be everything. He had his fingers in many pies, including overseas property rentals and a small collection of convenience store franchises in San Fran. He laid it all out in front of me. After he declared bankruptcy for the second time, I threw the manual at the back of my closet and told myself it was all a pile of shit.

Five years later, I have a better understanding of how much money I need to survive. I need to separate his failures from his knowledge. His business ultimately failed through bad investments and pushing his ceilings too high. If I keep this small, keep my client list tight, I can make a living from this. I don't need to earn millions right away, like he wanted to. First, I just have to make rent.

'You thinking of taking up drumming lessons over there, Mighty?'

I drop my pen and hold back a grin so he can't hear it in my tone. I hate how much he affects me. I'd rather have the upper hand in a relationship, and I'm failing terribly. 'Sorry.' My mouth betrays me and I grin like a fucking idiot. I love it when he calls me that. Hell, he could call me anything and I'd love the undivided attention it creates.

'Do you need any more money to tide you guys over for a bit?'

'What?' I spin in the chair to face him.

'Mike said you guys ran out of petty cash. I'm going to call home and make up some shit about replacing lab tools and ask my parents to top up the account before next month's allowance.'

I sigh. 'David, I don't want money from you or your parents.'

'Relax, Mighty.'

I hear his amusement, and it makes me smile.

'My parents can afford to send me an extra few hundred here and there. Honestly, I used to spend more throwing parties in Cambridge. They're getting a better deal now I'm halfway around the world.'

'Thanks for the offer.' I soften. 'But I don't need anything.' I look at my file folder that contains a pile of unpaid bills from the townhouse I'm still trying to catch up with.

'Is that why we all moved in together?'

'It's a friendship and business deal. Believe me, it was not my first choice to ask someone I dated once to move in with me, my mother, my son, and the man I was making a possible non-lucrative business deal with.'

'Ah, nothing to do with sharing bills? You really want to see me coming out of the shower naked, right?'

I chuckle. 'It is tempting, imagining water dripping off your muscles . . . ' I stop laughing and try to hide the fact I've turned myself on with the picture.

He laughs. 'You can't say shit like that to me. We're taking things slow, remember?'

'Two weeks is slow when you spend every evening together.'

'Stella,' he whispers.

'Have I ever told you I love it when you say my name?' I lean over the back of the chair and flash him a grin.

'Fuck.' His voice is hoarse. 'This is getting off topic.' He clears his throat and is back to business. 'I'm going to give Mike an extra hundred for you—'

'Don't,' I cut him off.

'It's petty cash for your business,' he says sternly. 'In case you need to pay for anything unexpected.'

I think I'm finally in a place where I trust that he cares about me. That he's not a low life cheating scumbag. That he'd never hurt me, not physically anyway. I only hope he doesn't hate me when he realises I may have kept him from someone else.

'Time for a break. Dinner's ready.' David serves up plates of steaming-hot chicken pasta, and I carry mine and Max's to the couch.

'He's not been on yet, Mom,' Max tells me.

David joins us, and we settle in to watch Mike at the premiere interviews.

'Did you tell Mike about us yet?' I ask.

David looks at Max, sitting between us, his attention on the TV, then at me. 'You said you wanted to see how things went before we told anyone.'

'He knows you're seeing someone, though?'

He shakes his head. 'If I told him, he'd want to meet her—you.'

'Doesn't that get old? Mike meeting all your girlfriends?'

David laughs. 'He'd only want to meet you because it's the first relationship that's lasted longer than a few weeks. Trust me, it's a big deal.' He turns back to his dinner.

I look at my watch. A few people have had interviews so far. 'Mike should be on soon. They always do the shorter roles first and leave the leading roles to the end of the night, right before the premiere starts.' I blow on a forkful of pasta.

'He still feels bad about walking in on us in the dorm. And it means he leaves me alone.' David swallows a mouthful of food. 'If he thinks I'm heartbroken and mad at him, he won't get on my case about not getting L-A-I-D every weekend.'

My heart skips a beat. 'Don't need to spell it out for me.'

David nods at Max and glares at me.

I laugh out loud and cover my mouth. 'Sorry. And thanks,' I tell him. 'Does it bother you?'

'What?'

'Not getting L-A-I-D every weekend?'

His face falls. 'No. Why the H-E-L-L would you think that?'

I grin and look at him through my lashes. 'You were worried I didn't trust you. Well, I've trusted you for a while. I've just been waiting for you to forgive me.'

'Did you say sorry, Mommy?' Max asks.

David and I snap our heads to Max.

'If you want someone to forgive you, you need to say sorry first, remember?'

I bite my lip to stop grinning. 'I guess three-year-olds hear more than they should.'

'Three and three quarters,' Max tells us.

David leans in close and pretends to whisper. 'Hey, dude, tell me you can't spell yet.'

I laugh, and Max looks at David. 'You need to teach me how to spell. But I can do the alphabet song really good. Want to hear? A, B, C . . . '

David listens to Max recite the alphabet almost perfectly, while I take the empty plates to the kitchen. At least the expensive child care Mike is forking out from his Starbucks wage is preparing him for kindergarten.

'Mike's on,' David calls over the back of the couch.

I run around the kitchen island and plop on the couch. I wrap my arm tightly around Max. 'Oh god, I never realised how nervous I was,' I shriek.

David leans back and puts his arm on the back of the seat, enveloping Max and me.

The interviewer asks Mike about his time on set and his move from England to the States. Within thirty seconds Mike has turned the conversation to how little actors get paid and the rising costs of rents in LA. This can go either way. He can come off looking like he's trying to stick up for himself and the humble lifestyle he's living for the sake of the arts, or on the flip side, come off looking like a spoiled brat, wanting to be rolling in the money like his peers. I cover my mouth in horror.

'What's he doing?' I spit at the TV and David sits forward at my reaction.

> 'So you want to petition for a change in the
> working rights of actors?' the reporter asks.
> 'Well, I don't know about taking it that

far.' Mike shrugs. 'But I bet there are other
struggling actors out there who need that
extra help too.'
'Help up the ladder, you mean?' the reporter
asks.
'Hey, we all need a little help now and then,
right?' He grins.

'We're totally screwed,' I shout at Mike through the TV. 'That was the most damaging two minutes of our very short careers.'

David moves to the edge of the couch. 'I'm sure you can salvage things.'

I glare at him.

'Tomorrow, I'll take Max and Pamela to the movies, then go to lunch. It'll give you and Mike time to talk.' He speaks to Max, 'And we can look for one of those places to eat that have a jungle gym in the corner for you to play on, right?'

'Please, Mommy?' Max begs.

I nod. 'Thanks, David.'

'One condition, ' David tells Max. 'You have to go straight to bed tonight and make sure you brush your teeth without arguing with your mom, right?'

'Okay.' Max jumps from the couch and runs to the bathroom.

'I didn't mean right now.' David chuckles.

I follow Max to the bathroom, then back through the living space where David is loading the dishwasher, to our bedroom, and his feet disappear under the covers in record time.

I collect a small pile of books and lay them on the bed. 'Pick three, and I'll be back in a second.' I take my pyjamas to the bathroom and throw water on my face. I need to send Mike on a media course. These oversights could cost us dearly.

I turn the knob on the bathroom door and hear David through the apartment, already reading to Max. He's getting really into it. I snicker as his voice deepens, and Max giggles. I tiptoe across the hall to keep quiet.

Leaning on the doorjamb, I listen to the story. I could get lost in David's voice all night. The firmness and confidence of it, along with the exotic accent, was the thing that soothed me when I was in labour and distracted me from the nightmare I thought I was stuck in.

'Come on, Mommy.' Max pushes the covers back.

I climb over Max to get in my usual spot at the far side of the bed. 'After three books, your legs are going to get numb on the floor. You should come up here with us.'

David's jaw slacks. 'Three?' He tickles Max on his way up. 'You told me seven.'

Max giggles and peeks through his lashes to see if he's in trouble.

'Don't worry,' I tell David. 'He tries that with everyone.' I giggle then stop abruptly. 'Not that there's been anyone else here reading to him. I mean, there's my mom. And my friend, Sarah, used to visit sometimes.'

David smiles. 'It's fine, really.' He turns to Max. 'I would have read seven.'

CHAPTER
Fourteen

After Max falls asleep, David and I sneak out of the room. David pulls me into his arms as he flops on the couch. 'How do you sleep with Max kicking like that every night?'

'I start him in his own bed, but if he wakes in the middle of the night crying, I let him sleep with me. That way he sleeps all night. I normally stuff a pillow between us to avoid the bruises.' I grunt.

'How bad was Mike's fuck up tonight?' he asks.

I run my hand over his chest and linger around his waist. 'Honestly? I'm not sure. If he was more established, it wouldn't have been as bad. It might even have got more exposure, but he's so new, it could go either way. It really depends on the media and whether they want to destroy him over it. They could spin it either way.'

'Yikes.'

I blow out a breath. 'I might be overreacting. I hope I am, anyway. It was pure luck he was in a minor role and arrived so early, 'cause not many people would have been watching at that time. There are a few people I can call tomorrow, who can maybe put a stopper in the dam before it gets too much air time. The media is one thing, but if producers see him bitching, people might decide they don't want to work with him.'

'You should still give him hell when he gets home, for stressing you out.'

'I might just do that.' I yawn and close my eyes for a second.

'Hey, you want to play a game?'

I open my eyes. 'As long as it's an appropriate game.' I laugh.

'Of course it's appropriate. It means we can get to know each other better.'

'We've lived together for six months. We know each other pretty well.'

'We have to ask each other thirty-six questions and answer them as quickly and as honestly as we can.'

'Thirty-six? You've played this before. I won't even remember the questions to ask you back.'

He scoffs. 'Trust me. I've never played this before. I read about it in a psychology journal. I never found anyone I wanted to play it with.'

'But you memorised thirty-six questions in case you did?'

'Yeah.' He clears his throat. 'I can answer right after you, okay? We're supposed to do this in forty-five minutes and take it from there.'

'Take what from there?'

'You'll see.' He smiles. 'The first one's easy. Given the choice of anyone in the world, whom would you want as a dinner guest?'

I lean back, not wanting to look him in the eye when I counter his question. 'Dead or alive?'

'Why do you ask?'

''Cause I kind of think I'm owed one last dinner with my dad, you know?' I tilt my head to see him nod once. 'And you?'

'Me?'

I laugh. 'David, I have dinner with you most nights. I mean what's your answer?'

He cringes and covers his face. 'Okay.' He slides his hand down his face. 'James Crawford.'

'Who's that?'

'He's a magician I saw in London when I was a kid. I kind of have a fan-girl thing going on, and I have a lot of questions for him.'

I chuckle. 'I didn't expect the serious scientist in you to believe in magic.'

'I don't, but I'd love to know how the secrets behind the illusions work. To bend perceptions in such a way that anything is possible? Magic takes all scientific theories out of their boxes and widens the possibilities. Plus, it's pretty damn entertaining.'

I grin.

'Okay, number two. This one is fitting for you. Would you like to be famous?'

'No. I've seen so many lives destroyed by chasing fame and money. It's not all pretty when you're on the inside.' He looks scared. 'Oh, god. Don't tell me you want to be famous?'

'Well, I have been told I have a face for TV.'

'Seriously?'

'I wouldn't mind. But not everyone should be famous. There are things that can make a person or kill them. It's a fine line. "Be careful what you wish for" kind of thing. If I were famous, it would need to be for something important, like my work.'

'Your contribution to the entertainment industry?' I mock.

He flicks me on the forehead. 'No, smart ass. My research. To know I've made a difference in the world, or someone's life. To be remembered in history, or be known for figuring out how to manipulate something in the universe that mankind uses to their advantage. That would be pretty cool.'

'Like time travel?' *Saving a girl's life?*

He shrugs. 'Plus, if it got me a TV show with extra funding and a paycheck? That wouldn't suck either.'

'It's not a bad idea, actually. I can already assure you that you'd be the hottest scientist hosting a documentary show. It might even get your field more mainstream interest.'

'All I heard was hot.' He stares at me.

'Come on, you said forty-five minutes on this.'

Questions and answers are thrown back and forth between us for a few minutes.

David shifts beneath me. 'Oh, this is a good one. If you were able to live to the age of ninety and retain either the mind or the body of a thirty-year-old for the last sixty years of your life, which would you want?'

'Mind. '

'Interesting. Mine would be body.'

'I didn't realise you were so vain.'

'I'm not, but your brain grows with age. Sure, it might deteriorate, but it could get a whole lot better before then. The body typically fails. Staying in the body of a thirty-year-old means you can still exercise, which helps grow the brain. Not as much danger of falling and breaking bones. You're still young and fit enough to go to work every day. But the mind . . . I'd love to have another sixty years' worth of research in my head.'

I make a sound, totally dissing him.

'You disagree?'

'Sometimes the mind deteriorates in other ways, and it can be devastating.'

'You've seen it happen?'

'My dad killed himself.' I kick my feet up on the coffee table. 'I understand it was depression that took hold of his mind and became this black grasp that he couldn't get out of. But his decision had consequences for all of us. The guilt and blame that those left behind suffer is devastating, even now.'

'I'm sorry.' He threads his fingers through mine. 'I didn't know.'

'Didn't Mike tell you?'

He shakes his head and keeps his gaze on mine.

'What's next?'

'It's kind of morbid.'

'More than the last?'

'Do you have a secret hunch about how you will die?' His tone is flat, but I know his nonchalance is forced.

'Probably.' The answer comes with more acceptance than I expect, but the dread stills runs through me. I thought the days of fearing Nathan killing me were gone.

He senses my discomfort and readjusts his arms around me.

So I give him a different fear. 'I'm terrified I'll kill myself too.' He opens his mouth, but I cut him off. 'Don't say the obvious, that if I don't want to kill myself, I won't. But there was a time in their lives when people who committed suicide didn't think about killing themselves. Depression takes over, perhaps slowly at first, or maybe all at once. I'm terrified I'm already following in my dad's footsteps. Chasing the same career, having the same fears about money and success for my child. The same worries.'

He squeezes my hand. 'I was going to say that you have a head start. You can recognise the changes, so you can look for help before it ever gets to that stage.'

'I hope so. How about you?' I hold my breath, waiting for his answer.

'Not a hunch, really.' He sighs. 'But lately I'm thinking my work might kill me.'

I freeze. I have more future knowledge about the dangerous things David is going to encounter in his life than he does. What if the time travel is the way he dies? When DD vanished, he didn't know for sure he was heading home.

'Too much time in the lab, death by workaholic,' he adds.

We continue with a quick fire round, describing things we have in common and what we're grateful for. This round of honesty and similarities has my attraction for him stirring, and before I know it, I skate my hand around his neck and tilt his head towards mine. I push him down on the couch and he grabs me around the waist. I sprawl on top of him and slip my tongue inside his mouth, kissing him slowly, caressing his face. His hands tighten around me, and I give his hair a tug. He lets a growl roll from the back of his throat.

His hands grip the backs of my thighs, and longing stirs in my belly. He pulls me tight against him, and his erection presses against me. I need air. I need to stop this. I really don't want to have sex on the couch with my son in the next room. I break away from him and try to sit up, but he grabs my hands and holds them to his chest.

'Stay like this, please. I don't mean for things to go further, but you feel amazing so close to me.'

I lie back down at his side. He hooks his hand on the back of my knee and holds on to me. I settle my head in the crook of his arm, wrapping my arm around his waist, and I feel like I'm somewhere I could stay forever.

'If you could change anything about the way you were raised, what would it be?' he asks.

'My dad's drive. No matter what he achieved, he couldn't stop wanting more. I wish he would have been happy with what he had and not felt like a failure. He was always comparing himself to other people. He would become more successful and move into a different level of his career, different circle of friends, and he always felt like he was at the bottom. Then he would surpass his own expectations, and climb onto the next level, bigger house, more expensive cars, and start climbing another ladder all over again. I was raised to believe you should always be better than everyone else, that you shouldn't stop until you're on top, and that's a shitty way to live.'

'I think I would have liked less too.' David agrees. 'We always had dinner parties and family holidays, but Mike has some great stories about being raised in the middle of a family business. Even his younger sister, Caitlyn, was expected to help in the busy seasons of the B&B. I think it brought their family closer. Sometimes it's the struggles in life that bind you together. My parents always had everything and handed it to me.'

'That's awful,' I deadpan.

'I know. My childhood will scar me forever,' he retorts. 'So for this question, we're supposed to tell each other our life stories in four minutes.'

I flinch, and he tightens his grip.

'Will you tell me about him one day?'

'Who?'

'Max's dad.'

'He's gone. Nothing more to know.'

'He's the father of your child, and he shaped your life more than you want to admit.' He kisses the small white scar that runs from my hairline to the centre of my forehead. The one I can normally hide with make-up. He's never asked about the scar, but each time he places his lips there, he simultaneously traces the neat white scar that's the only evidence left of the split mouth I was given. I'm now thankful for the ER doctor calling the plastics resident who took an agonising twenty minutes to make sure my lip was properly aligned before he started on the sutures.

David closes his eyes like he doesn't want me to know he knows exactly how I got it. 'I hope one day, you'll trust me enough to tell me everything.'

I relax, because one day I just might.

'So the next one's kind of cool,' he tells me. 'If you could wake up tomorrow, having gained any one quality or ability, what would it be?'

'I'm not sure,' I lie. 'Why don't you go first?'

'Right now, I'd want to wake up with the ability to prove my research. We have some pretty interesting things going on right now, but it's far-fetched. I know there are a couple of people relying on the outcome—well, one person really, but it might save her life if I can figure it out. It would be pretty cool to know what I'm doing.'

My heart beats faster. God, does he know more about me than he's letting on? Why wouldn't he tell me if I'm in danger again? 'That's a good one.' I try to keep it casual. 'I guess mine would be some variation of knowing I could keep Max safe. Have some sort of ability to be able to protect him . . . from everything.'

'That's like a supermom power.'

I nudge him in the ribs. 'Or Mighty Mouse power.'

He chuckles. 'Yeah, it is.'

David delivers the next set of questions rapid fire, and I'm amazed that I'm able to answer honestly, knowing he'd never make fun of me or use the information against me.

'What's your most treasured memory?'

My heart sinks when I know it's a memory I can't share with him.

'You need to answer quickly, remember?'

'When I gave birth to Max, I was scared. I met someone in the hospital who helped me. It sort of restored my faith in humanity.'

'That's a good memory.'

I search his eyes for any recognition, or understanding of what I told him, but he moves on.

'Flip side. What is your most terrible memory?'

I answer without hesitation. 'I was the one who found my dad.'

He closes his eyes and swallows hard.

The pain of the memory pushes tight against the inside of my throat, my nose, my eyes, trying its hardest to escape, but I won't crumble. I purse my lips together and push the tears down. 'You?'

He shakes his head. 'I haven't had any tragedies in my life.'

'That wasn't the question. It doesn't matter what you've experienced. It's your most terrible memory.'

112

He takes a deep breath and leans closer, lowering his head. 'My parents are both intelligent. They made most of their money from developing software and microchips for an English company. The rest of their money came from investing in future developments and start-up projects that took off. One night they were having a dinner party with a potential buyer, and the conversation turned to their children. I'd snuck downstairs to get something from the kitchen—I can't remember what, but I heard my name. They were all light-heartedly discussing what careers they thought their children would have. My mum joked if I didn't turn out as smart as them, she'd have to get a DNA test to see who my real father was.'

'Oh, David.'

He puts his hand up. 'It was a tongue-in-cheek comment, I know, but when I was ten, I was terrified that if I wasn't smart like my dad, he might not want me as his kid anymore, and I'd get sent away to live with whomever they found out was my real dad.'

'You know, it sounds like, despite knowing the questions, you never practiced your answers.'

'I didn't.' He kisses my hair. After another round about ourselves and our families, David stumbles into a sort of epiphany that hits us both. 'We're both partially resentful of our parents' success and the impact it had on our relationships, although still following in their footsteps and trying our hardest to be as successful as they were.'

I place my hands over my face and moan. 'God, when you say it like that, it puts it all in perspective, doesn't it?'

'They wanted to create a good life for their kids, just like you do, just like I will when I have kids.'

He kisses me softly on the lips. I think he's done, but at the last minute he comes back for more and nibbles my lip on retreat. 'Next question. If you were going to become a close friend with me, what would be important for me to know?'

I drop my eyes. 'I still feel a little broken.' My voice wavers. 'I'd need you to prove to me, every day, for the rest of my life, that there really are good guys out there.'

'I'm trying.'

'I know you are. I just find it hard to trust people, and I think I'm falling for you, and that scares me.'

'Why does it scare you?'

''Cause if it turned out I was wrong to trust you, I'm not sure I could come back from that one. I'm terrified what that would do to Max, having a mom who's that broken.'

He places my hand over his heart and squeezes it tight. 'I promise I won't lie to you, and you can trust me. I won't break your heart.'

'Sometimes it's not intentional.'

'That's scary for everyone. It's important that you know I invest a lot of time in my work, because it's not a job to me. It's part of my life. I'll put you and Max first— little league games and parent-teacher conferences and date nights—but there are days I don't clock out at five. I've never been in love before, so it was never an issue for me. After a few weeks of trying to make a relationship work, I chose university work or studying instead. I don't want to put my work first anymore. I've already chosen you. But it's still new to me, so let me know if I get it wrong. Tell me if something upsets you. Let's not allow the little things to brew into big things.'

I launch myself at him. It's as honest as I could have hoped him to be. I move to the side of his neck to tease him

114

while he continues to ask me questions. 'Tell me what you like about me. Be honest, say things you might not normally say.'

'On top of being a great guy I might be in love with, you're totally hot and sometimes I really want you to fuck me, but I like that you're waiting.'

'Holy shit,' David breathes. 'That's a good one.' He kisses me chastely on the lips and sits back, keeping hold of my hands. 'Tell me an embarrassing moment in your life.'

'Oh, god. There are a few.' I think back, mostly to the teenage years. Getting fired from The Gap on purpose was more embarrassing than I thought it would be. Telling my parents I was pregnant and realising they knew I wasn't a virgin was pretty embarrassing. Knowing my mom knew I was a battered girlfriend was embarrassing, but not in a funny way. But I have to tell him the one that beats them all. 'Showing up to the hospital to give birth on my own was a pretty embarrassing moment. When I checked in at reception, and the woman looked over my shoulder and asked if my birthing partner was with me, I couldn't tell her I was already a single mom, and my own mother was MIA, most likely in a bar.'

'Stella,' David soothes.

'It's okay. I'm over the stigma now. Well, mostly. I know it's more my issue than anyone else's. I'm working on it.'

'I got locked out of a hotel room naked,' he blurts. 'When did you last—'

'Oh, no,' I cut him off. 'You are going to have to give me details. I just bared my shameful soul to you. I need humorous embarrassment to cheer me up.'

He hides his face behind one hand. 'It's bad,' he warns me. 'I was with a girl in college, and we had only been together a couple weeks.'

I nod at him to continue.

'We went to London for a concert and stayed overnight. In the middle of, you know . . .'

'Sex?' I mock whisper. 'Are you telling me you're not a virgin?'

He rolls his eyes and gains his confidence back. 'In the middle of sex, I accidently called her the wrong name.'

'Oh . . . my god. How the hell did you forget her name if you'd been dating for a couple of weeks?'

He blows out a long breath. 'I didn't forget as much as perhaps I was imagining someone else.'

I gasp. 'David. That's awful.'

'In my defence, she was with me purely for sex too.'

'How the hell do you know?'

''Cause our dates didn't consist of much. I tried to get to know her, and she never wanted to talk. We always met in places that revolved around drinking and ending up in bed. The night away was my last attempt at getting to know each other, but we didn't spend much time talking.'

'So it would seem. How did that lead to getting locked out naked?'

'She didn't take it well and ended up screaming and throwing punches at me. I kept backing up to stop her from decking me and ended up at the door. She opened it and shoved me outside the room. Want to know the punch line?'

'It gets worse?'

'It was her flatmate's name.'

I pick up a cushion and hit his arm three times in support of all scorned women.

'Hey, stop. I don't want to end up in the hallway naked again.' He chuckles.

I shake my head.

'You know how I knew she was just with me for the sex?'

'How?' I ask, not sure I want the answer.

''Cause two nights later, I got a booty call. She only finally dumped me after she got jealous when she saw me talking to said flatmate at a party in our house.'

'Did you sleep with her friend?'

'No. But I did like her at the time. She talked to me all the time when I was at their place, and she never hit on me. I think that's why I liked her. She wasn't looking to hook up and do the dirt on her roommate. I know it's a dick move, but I did kind of wish I was dating her instead of Amy.'

'Where's the roommate now?' I'm panicked. What if that was the girl he was supposed to marry.

'Jessica? I may have been selfish when I was getting laid in college, but I'm not a dickhead. I didn't chase after her that night. Mike ended up dating her for a while. They kind of hit it off at his birthday party, the same one Amy dumped me at.'

I take a deep breath and regain myself. 'Just how embarrassing was the nakedness?'

He chews on his lip, and I want to bite it along with him, but I refrain to hear his story.

'I had to take the elevator to the lobby, hands covering my junk, and catch the attention of the front desk. It was late and the old guy on the desk was reading a book. I walked round and asked him to let me back in my room to get clothes. Actually, I asked him for a robe, but he was not amused and said no. He did ride the elevator back upstairs with me and let me into the room. He also waited outside while I grabbed my clothes, one shoe of which Amy threw at me on the way out. He offered me a ten-percent discount for a second room.'

I laugh. 'That was generous of him.'

'Hey, I took it and left early the next morning for the train station. Next question: when did you last cry in front of another person and also by yourself?'

'Sometimes I cry in front of Max, but I lie and tell him I have sore eyes. By myself?' I sigh. 'I'm not sure. A lot of things freak me out, and I tend to over think things, especially at night when I'm alone and Max is sleeping. I worry about the future and what will happen to us. Probably last week I was crying.'

'Last week? We live together, Stella. If you need to cry, I'd much rather you came to me. I don't even need to know what's going on. I'd just want to be able to hold you in my arms while you let it all out.'

I force a smile. I might burst into tears at the comfort those words give me.

We only make it one more question before the doorknob rattles.

'Shit, is Mike home already?' I pick up my phone and stand. 'I haven't even thought about what to say to him.'

The door doesn't open, so David gets up and glances through the peephole.

'He's not alone.' David sniggers. 'Come on.' He grabs my hand. 'I don't want to get stuck out here with small talk. It'll be totally awkward.' He pulls me to my room as the front door opens, and Mike and his date tumble in.

I move Max over to the far side of the bed and pull the covers down to get in next to him. 'We done?' I ask through a yawn.

David takes a second to think. 'No, we have a few more rough ones left.'

I let out a long moan and pat the bed next to me. 'There's not much room, but if you lie down I can lean on you.'

He kicks off his shoes and joins us in the bed, moaning as he stretches his back.

'Get going with the questions. I want to be asleep before midnight.'

'If you were to die this evening with no opportunity to communicate with anyone, what would you most regret not having told someone and why haven't you told them yet?'

I tense, trying to think how to frame this without giving too much away. I want to be honest with him. I've fallen too hard for him to start lying now. I drum my fingers on his chest, stalling. 'I know some things about Max's dad, and I'd regret not doing the right thing with it. I never told anyone because I was scared.'

'What things?' he asks against my hair.

'Can't tell you, but it was a big deal for me to tell you there is something. I'm not being dramatic, and it's not something you can help with.'

He nods and runs his hand up and down my arms, like it could keep me safer. 'If I died this evening, I'd regret not telling you I love you. I want to wait until I know you believe me, and I know it won't scare you off. You don't have to say it back, you don't even have to feel it. I just want to wait until you're ready to accept that. But we're in this game deep, and if I really died tonight, that would be my biggest regret.'

A few questions later, I'm holding tight onto the tears trying to break through.

'Of all the people in your family, whose death would you find most disturbing and why?'

'I need two. The first one is Max. It's not something I like to think about, but ask any parent, and they'll tell you the "what if" has crossed their minds. Even stories of soldiers going to war scare me. What if Max grows up and chooses a dangerous profession? I'll spend the rest of my life terrified I'd get that call. But the other death that scares me just as much is my own. I'd be terrified about what would happen to Max.'

Tears run down both my cheeks, and I have to wipe them away. 'I know my mom and Cici would take him, but then I worry, what if *they're* already dead? And I worry about what it would do to him emotionally. Would he be frightened? Would he think I left him? Most of all, I worry that if I die, his dad would take him and raise him to be like himself. 'Cause I don't want my little boy to be anything like him. He'd destroy Max to spite me.'

I sob into David's chest and clutch at his shirt, trying hard not to wake Max as my tremors shake the bed. I allow myself to cry for a while, because it's the first time I've ever said those things out loud.

David isn't judging me. He isn't telling me to stop worrying or to stop over thinking life. He's just holding me, like he said he would.

My tears reduce and I sit up and reach for the box of tissues on the nightstand. I dry my eyes and finally look David in the eye.

'I think we can change the *when was the last time you cried in front of someone* answer,' he says.

'Um, yeah. What number was that?'

'I forget. Don't worry, we can start again.'

I nudge his side and laugh. 'That's not funny. I have a headache now.'

'Last one,' he tells me.

I stay sitting, starting down at him. 'Hit me with it.'

'Share a personal problem and ask my advice on how I might handle it. Then, I've to reflect back to you, how you seem to be feeling about the problem. Then we'll switch.'

We talk about how Max is asking questions about why he doesn't have a daddy, and David gives me advice on how much details to share. He promises to get some books from the university library on family counselling and help me with the stages Max is going to grow through.

'Thank you.' I squeeze his hand. 'Now you go.'

'I have some information that's critical to my work. It's a source of data that no one has ever had before, but I can't expose it to anyone else at the university. It needs to be guarded, but I worry I'm too busy trying to protect it that I might actually be endangering it.'

'Jeez, David, you know science isn't really my thing. But if you take the science out of the problem, are your fears justified? Or has it more to do with who works on the project and gets the funding and the glory?'

'The fears are real. The issue of protecting the data, and it not being destroyed while it's being figured out, is real.'

Is he talking about his own experiences in time travel? Is he in danger if he exposes himself? 'Then my maternal instincts say protect it. Keep it safe the best you can. If your intentions are pure, it's not a bad thing. Your information or source or whatever it is, *might* be in danger if you can't help it—but it's *definitely* in danger if you pass it on to the wrong people. Think about lying on your death bed. Which scenario would you regret the most? Or toss a coin. Often the decision will hit you when the coin is in mid-air. You start wishing or hoping that it goes one way.'

'Thanks. That actually makes me feel peaceful about the decision we made in the beginning.'

'We?'

'Me and Mike. He knows about the specifics of my work. It's the other reason we came together—for me to work more in-depth on this, and for him to make us rich and famous.' He grins.

'You never did tell me who you know in England that told you guys about me.'

'It was someone Mike met.' He sits up. 'You need to tell me what you think I feel about my problem, then, I'll let you sleep.'

'I think you're confident you've already made the right decision, but you want others to believe it too. That perhaps if the shoe was on the other foot, you'd be outraged anyone could withhold that kind of information source. You're worried your morals took over the decision-making process in something that's normally so scientifically black and white to you. Maybe your experiences here have changed you, and you're not sure if you're happy with those changes.'

He plants a soft kiss on my temple. 'Good night, Stella. It was good getting to know you that little bit more. I'll be on the couch if you need anything.' He tiptoes out of the room.

'Good night,' I say as he closes the door.

At 6:00 a.m. I start the coffee and look for David on the couch. He appears from his room, almost like he can hear me searching for him. He's in lounge pants and nothing else. 'Didn't think threesomes were your thing,' I joke then wince in panic.

'Sophie snuck out in the middle of the night.'

'Ouch, poor Mike. Is he that bad?' I smile, glad the attention is off my previous comment.

'I think Sophie is the kind of girl who's used to sneaking out of rooms.'

I stare at the coffee dripping into the pot as David comes up behind me. His bare feet pad against the tiles before he wraps his arms around my waist and squeezes me gently. He nuzzles my hair and wiggles his bare toes against the back of my heels. I inhale him in and try not to let myself sink into his naked chest too much. Max will be awake any second.

'Morning,' he moans into my hair. 'Just so you know, when we finally spend the whole night together, neither one of us is going to be sneaking out. I want to breathe you in all night and wake up with the heat of you pressed against me. I want to be able to run my hands all over your body and feel your heart beating against my chest, all before we wake up to put on the coffee, okay?' He grins at the side of my cheek.

Pamela speaks from the doorway behind us. 'You might want to book me to babysit that night, otherwise Max will be kicking both of you guys in the face while he sleeps.'

David lets me go and spins around, and I turn, praying Max isn't standing next to her.

She must see the fear in my face. 'Don't worry, he isn't awake yet.' She tilts her head to David. 'But you might want to go get dressed before he sees your half naked body rubbing up and down his mother.'

I chuckle. Giving a guy hell is the most motherly thing she's done for me in a while. David looks lost between doing as he's told and explaining himself.

I place my hand on his bare arm. 'She's joking.'

'Am not,' Mom says and takes the first mug of coffee.

'Just go get dressed.' I nudge him away.

He stops in front of the table. 'Normally I'd want to be dressed when I speak to you like this, but I want to get this out before Max wakes up.'

Mom places her cup on the table and looks up at him, like nothing he could possibly say would stop her from being a concerned mother. It's so foreign to see her this confident. My smile stays on my face as I sit next to her and look expectantly at David.

'I'm not an asshole, and I'm in love with your daughter.'

I choke on nothing but air, and they both ignore me as I take a drink of mom's coffee to stop me from coughing.

'She doesn't fully believe me yet.' He nods his head towards me. 'But when she does, I'll make sure to book you for that babysitting. 'Cause this is the real deal for me, and when she's ready to tell Max about us, I'd really like it if you were on board too.'

A small thump from down the hall, followed by rushing tiny footsteps, lets us know Max is on his way.

David smiles at me and heads back to his room.

CHAPTER

When David and I left the apartment this morning, I switched our lunches so I'd have an excuse to visit him. Cici lent me her car, and I make it to campus in ten minutes.

I knock on David's door. He doesn't answer. He probably went out for lunch when he realised he got my wholegrain bagel. Couldn't have planned it better. I tiptoe across the hall and knock on Liam's door.

David's door swings open behind me and I yelp.

It's not David, though. It's Liam. I catch my breath, which turns into an exaggerated sigh. 'What the hell are you doing in there?'

'Working. You know I'm David's assistant.'

'I know, but I knocked.'

'Sorry, was busy. David went out for lunch.'

I hold up the brown bag. 'I switched it this morning.'

Liam pulls out a similar brown bag from behind the door. 'Then this rabbit food is yours?'

I swipe it out of his hand and step inside. Might as well eat while I'm here. Since I've last been here, an additional desk has been added that looks to be in chaos. Guessing the perfectly stacked, organised one is David's, I move the one pile of notes aside and sit on the desk.

Liam grimaces. 'He's doesn't like anyone touching his stuff.'

'Oh please, I only moved them.'

He shrugs. 'Just as well you're pretty. He might forgive you.'

'Ha-ha.'

The back wall appears to have been knocked out to conjoin three more rooms of its size since the last time I was here. The walls are covered in whiteboards, which in turn are covered with written formulas in different coloured markers.

'You guys making progress?' I ask.

'Why are you here, Stella?'

I take my time chewing my bagel before I answer him. 'You don't want me here?'

'I didn't say that, but you've avoided me since our first meeting. You hardly made eye contact the time David introduced us at the mall. I know you're avoiding me, but I won't betray your confidence. I'm not going to tell him we both know more than we let on. The effects alone could be—'

'Catastrophic. Yeah, I get it.'

'Then why are you here?'

'I needed to speak to you.'

'I'm all ears.' He opens David's brown bag and pulls out a sandwich.

'I know some things about his future and I feel like I'm lying to him.' I swallow a piece of bagel, trying to act natural.

'When David appeared to you, he never told you he was going to be your friend in the future. Do you feel like he lied to you?'

'No.' I jump to his defence. 'He didn't tell me, because how could he? It wasn't the right time for me to know those things about my life. There were more important things going on, and I had to concentrate on becoming a mother. And hell, what if knowing that was the reason I started dating him?'

'You're dating him?'

'That's why I'm here. What if I can change his future or past or whatever? He had a crappy marriage and what if he dates me instead? Can I keep him from that heartache? Can't I tell him what I know and let him make the decision on the path he wants his life to go?

'What if it was you who was the crappy wife?' He shrugs. 'This is why you can't tell him what you know. We might think we're doing good or changing something, but accidently end up pushing people in the wrong direction. Especially since you don't have all the information. David knows the universal effects of knowing too much. He'll understand why you kept things from him.'

The door opens, and David returns. His face lights up like it always does when he's not expecting to see me. Like when I bumped into him at the grocery store. Like he's genuinely happy to see me.

'Hello.' He crosses the room and kisses me chastely on the lips.

'Got lunches mixed up.' I nod towards his brown bag— open and scavenged on Liam's desk.

David scrunches his nose at the dropped sandwich. 'Just as well that's not my desk.'

'I was protecting your desk with my ass.' I grin.

'And what a nice ass it is.' He pulls me closer, and Liam stands.

127

'I'm out of here,' he announces. 'Too much ass talk.'

Once we're alone, David pulls me to the edge of the desk and hitches my legs around his hips. 'Do you know how goddamn sexy it is to find you sitting on my desk, waiting for me?' He covers my mouth with his, kissing me deeply, tugging my hair as he runs his hand through it.

I gasp and when he moves his mouth to my neck, I answer, 'In fairness, I was sitting here eating, but I think we need to schedule more lunches like this.'

'How about dinner tomorrow night? It's Valentine's. We can make good on Pamela's offer to babysit. You started birth control like we talked about, right?'

'Yes,' I breathe. 'We're all set.'

'Good, because I couldn't stand having something between us.'

'Guess that's the plus side of planning a night like this.'

'Health checks and birth control.' He laughs. 'Never thought I'd be in a relationship with someone I wanted to ditch the condoms for.'

Despite the tingling running through me, I'm disappointed. 'We can hardly put Max in Pamela's room while we have sex for the first time. It's weird. Everyone will know what we're doing, and they'll be in the next room.' My libido cools like a bucket of ice water has been thrown over me, and David notices the shift.

'Hey, whenever you're ready. I didn't mean to push. I thought we were at the same place.'

I shake my head. 'You misunderstood. The only problem I have is knowing that Max will be next door. It takes a hell of a lot of trust to bring someone this close and know they'll behave themselves, especially since I share a room with my son.'

'Do you think Cici would take Max for the night?'

'Yeah, and Pamela might like another night with her old friend too. It's been a while since they had an excuse to spend time together. But not tomorrow. I want to check with Max first.

'Of course.'

'He's never had a sleepover before. I don't want him to think I'm pushing him away when I finally have a night off.'

David kisses the top of my head. 'I love that you care so much about what he's thinking. Not many people get to see what their partner's like as a parent before you have kids with them. I've kind of got a good deal. I know how awesome you are as a mom. That's really important. I hope I can live up to your standards.'

I clear my throat. 'You will.' But he won't ever get to be a parent, and I might be the reason why. Either I'm keeping him from another woman, or I'm the one who ends up aborting his child and keeping him from being a father.

'We're going to spend the night together'—he nudges my lips open with his—'with no one next door.'

'No one but Mike,' I correct.

'He's at the other end of the apartment. He's working late all week. And we can keep quiet.'

I shrug. 'I guess that's the best plan we have.'

'God, Stella. Don't sound too enthusiastic about it.'

I smirk at him. 'I was just kind of hoping you'd make me scream,' I whisper.

David growls. 'Oh, I'll make you scream, all right, and I'll clasp my hand over your mouth to keep you from waking the neighbours.' He jerks me against his hips and kisses me hard, stroking his tongue slow and steady over mine. He doesn't give up. He doesn't pull away. He devours my mouth until my lips start to chap, and I have to pull away for air.

CHAPTER Sixteen

I close the trunk of Cici's car, securing Max's overnight bag. When I return to the rolled down window at the back seat, his attention is already on the new colouring book Cici bought him. 'Hey, bud, you going to miss me?' I ask, leaning through the window.

'Nope,' he says, not lifting his gaze.

'What do you mean, no?' I shriek and poke my fingers into the tickly spot in his side.

He laughs and leans away. 'I'm going to have too much fun to miss you. Cici said I can have candy and popcorn, and you're not there to stop me.' He laughs and flashes me a smile.

'Have fun, Mini Me.' I kiss him on the cheek.

'See you later, Gator,' he replies. 'Let's go, Cici. Gran and I want popcorn.'

Pamela smiles from the front seat as Cici puts the car into drive. 'You have fun too.' She grins.

'Mom,' I scold.

'What? Like we don't know what you guys are doing? Poor Mike is the one you need to feel sorry for.'

'He's working late, for your information.' I glance at my watch. It's only four o'clock. We have about eight hours before Mike is due home. Even then, his room is at the other side of the apartment. My stomach flips, and the butterflies turn into tingles. Cici pulls onto the road. I wonder what David can do to me in eight hours.

When I open the apartment door, the curtains have been drawn and the lights are out.

'Are you naked already?' I ask sarcastically. Oh please, don't let him be naked already. I really wanted to be the one to rip open his jeans.

'You in a rush?' he asks from the corner of the living room. He lights candles and rounds the coffee table. 'Thought I could make it appear like night time. You know—dinner, candles, music.'

I cross the room, grab his face, and kiss him deeply, pressing myself against him as I stretch on my tiptoes.

He wraps his arms around me. 'You want to skip dinner and music and go straight to the foreplay?'

'Was thinking we could come back to dinner later, when we're both exhausted. I want to see if you're full of crap.'

He pulls back. 'Excuse me?'

'You once told me you could make a girl come three times before you did.' I bite my lip to hold back a smile. 'You really up for the challenge?'

'Oh, baby,' he scoffs. 'The way you look at me sometimes, this will be an absolute dream.' He bends and throws me over his shoulder.

'David,' I scream. 'This isn't very romantic.' I laugh.

'*Pshew*, you just asked for three orgasms. You're getting dirty, not romantic.'

My breath catches in my throat, and my belly tightens.

In the bedroom, he sets me on my feet and embraces me. 'Just so you know'—he slowly backs me to the bed, and the candles already set up in here flicker in the background—'this is going to be one hell of a first time together.' He loses his grin and nibbles down my neck.

'Because you're so awesome?' I jibe.

He shakes his head. 'Because I love you.'

Shivers run through me. He swings me around, changing direction and leading me to the dresser. He pushes everything off the countertop and sets me near the edge. I suck in a breath when he raises my legs and folds my feet around to rest on his backside. He's trapped himself between my legs, and I don't want him to ever move out. He takes slow, steady breaths.

'You okay?' I ask.

'Just preparing myself.' He chews on the inside of his mouth. 'It's going to be really difficult to watch you come over and over again, before I bury myself inside you and come together.'

The words get stuck in my throat. 'I was teasing, David. You don't have to prove anything.'

He leans into my neck and whispers, 'Believe me, it will be my pleasure.'

I lift his shirt over his head, trail my hands down his chest, and run my fingers over his taut stomach, reaching for his belt. I pull the leather back and unclip the buckle. Pulling the buttons apart, I lower his jeans and they fall with a thud to the floor. He places my hands over my head, pulling my shirt off. He leans back and takes hold of my feet. 'As much as I hate to break this little circle here, I need these pants off.' He removes my jeans and his breathing stalls when he faces my black lace panties. 'I'm going to buy you new ones.'

'You don't like them?' I ask, knowing his strained erection in his Calvin Kleins means he does.

'I'm going to rip these off you later.' He leans down and softly blows over my centre.

Goosebumps cover my body and harden my nipples.

He nudges my legs apart and moves forward, biting on the material that covers my clit, and I nearly have the first of those promised orgasms. He notices me buck my hips and holds onto my ass, keeping me in place. He pushes my legs over his shoulders. 'Don't move.'

I swallow hard as he trails his fingers over the wet centre of my panties. He teases one side of the fabric, like he's deciding whether or not to pull them back and plunge his fingers inside. His slow teasing back and forth has me pushing my hips forward, seeking some friction to help sate the pressure building inside me.

He finally gives in, rips the lace apart and darts his tongue over my clit, then sucks on the bud.

My heart thumps, I let out a moan, and clench my thighs, wanting more.

He teases it back and forth, sucking and licking and I'm shamelessly coming before he's managed to get started. I cling to the edge of the dresser, knuckles turning white as I hold my breath and control the gasps bursting through me.

'Christ, Stella. You don't make it easy, do you?'

I wait for my breathing to return to normal before I reply. 'I thought that was pretty damn easy.'

'Maybe for you, but I was enjoying that.' He rips the other side of my panties and tugs them off, making me jerk with leftover pleasure. He dives back into me and laps his tongue up and down, soaking up the aftermath of his last success. Heat runs through me, and I drop my head back against the wall. Without warning, he thrusts a finger inside me, and the pressure and pleasure has me shooting forward, gasping. 'Didn't want you falling asleep on me.'

'Fuck, keep doing that.'

I've never had a man make me wet this way. David keeps his tongue on my clit while moving his fingers inside me, like he's fucking me already. I move my feet on his back, climbing for purchase while the ache builds inside me again. He straightens, sweeps me off the dresser, and kisses me the whole way as he places me on the centre of the bed. He climbs over me, underwear taut against his cock, rubbing along the side of my leg. I clutch to his shoulders, relishing the heat of his body over mine, wanting to feel every part of him.

He returns two fingers inside me and thrusts while using his other hand to press down on my pelvis. He twists his fingers inside me, and when he finds my G-spot, I whimper. He quickens his pace, fucking me with his fingers, not holding back, as I arch off the bed. He leans over and runs his tongue over my clit and then slaps it with his free hand while twisting his fingers inside me. When I come, he stills his fingers and I pulse around them. He closes his eyes and his breath is as harsh as mine as I try to control the shudders that won't give up.

'Just enjoy it, Stella.' He runs his free hand over my stomach, slips his fingers under my bra. He twists my hardened nipple, prolonging another jerk, and a scream escapes me. My insides contract around his fingers, the pulsing continuing longer than I thought possible.

When I've nothing left, he slips his fingers out of me. I feel empty without him. He lowers over me, kissing my neck and stroking my face. 'If it's alright with you, I vote that number three takes place when I'm inside you, and I promise to make sure you come before me.'

I laugh and close my eyes. 'I don't think I can anymore.'

'Trust me, baby. I can get you wound up again before you know it.' He tilts my face towards his and places a kiss on my lips. 'You want some water?'

I force my eyes open and nod.

'I got some wine for dinner,' he tells me as he moves off the bed. I roll onto my side and shiver. David pulls the covers over and tucks me in. 'Don't go to sleep.' He chuckles as I close my eyes for a second.

When I wake, the room is darker. Night has snuck up on us. A glass of water sits on the nightstand, an empty bottle of beer next to it. Shit. I stretch and bump into David, who sits crossed-legged on the bed, reading a book.

'Oh. My. God,' I say, my voice a touch too loud. 'I'm so sorry.' I sit up and hide my head in shame. 'I fell asleep on you.'

David closes his book and chuckles. 'It looked like you needed it.' He pulls me into a hug and lies back against the headboard, tucking me into his side.

'Our night of hot passion was so boring, you read a book,' I retort.

He grins. 'It wasn't all boring.'

'I'm sorry, David.' I squeeze him. 'I know what it's like to be on the receiving end of selfish sex. And now I've turned the tables.'

'Hey.' His voice is serious, and he ducks his head to meet my eyes. 'We're not going to be that couple who counts who owes who what, okay? I don't play the tit-for-tat game. That kind of shit starts in the bedroom and works its way into every part of the relationship. Having the woman I love fall asleep

136

when she's exhausted isn't something I begrudge. When do you ever get a night off from being a mom to sleep early?'

I force a smile and trail my fingers along his stomach, following the trail of dark hair lower. 'I'm awake and full of energy now.'

'I'd hope so. Five hours of snoring will do that to you.'

I slap him lightly on the abs. 'I was not asleep for five hours.' I glace at the clock. It's almost eleven. My heart falls. I've slept away most of our first night together.

'What's wrong?' He drops his hand to my ass and gives it a light squeeze.

'I wanted this night to be perfect. We're not going to get much time for the two of us in this relationship and I wanted to make sure we took advantage of it.'

'We will.' He strokes my face and runs his fingertips over my lips. 'I cooked dinner. We can eat whenever you're ready.'

I straddle him and his cock jumps as soon as I'm rested on top of him. 'Think I have some business here first.'

'So do I.' He grabs my hips and pulls me forward to sit over his groin. 'I promised you at least one more big one.' He pulls me down for a kiss, and I shuffle back to pull off the last of his clothes, then I take his erection in my hand. My fingers don't fully grasp his girth. He's warm and smooth and rock hard and I can imagine what he's going to feel like inside me. I stroke up and down, and around, covering as much of him as I can. I reach back and unhook my bra, so we're finally naked in bed together.

I part my legs farther and he rolls us so he's on top of me. He runs his hand over me and I'm already wet, waiting for him. His hips are between my legs and he pushes his cock against me but stalls, waiting for permission before going any

137

further. I take a moment, relishing an offering that's never been made to me before. My stomach flips, and I bite back a grin before I tilt my hips, opening myself to him. He slides slowly inside, gentler than I thought he'd be, especially the way he was finger fucking me a few hours ago. The sheer size of him has pleasure spiking. 'David.' I sigh.

'You okay?' He stills inside of me.

'Yes, don't stop.'

He returns to the slow strokes, taking time to match the pace with the trail of kisses he's leaving over my body. Around my lips and the scar leading off to my cheek, down my neck and collarbone. I wrap my arms around his shoulders and rest my head against his when I realise he's making love to me. My heart stops, and I have to swallow the emotion stuck in my throat. He tightens his grip on my hands.

'Stella, I don't want to stop doing this. It's the most perfect thing I've ever done in my life.' He continues the slow thrusts inside me. 'I've been wound so tight for hours, I'm about to come, but I made a promise to you so I'm going to have to fuck you for a little bit.' He sits up and drags my legs with him. Still inside me, he twists me to the side.

The new angle has me gasping. The sheer size of him thrusting in this direction hits right off my G-spot. I moan in anticipation when he rears back. He doesn't disappoint. He slams into me, and the build-up to my third orgasm begins. Jesus, he's fucking me sideways. Our bodies sweat and despite the slap of skin on skin, I can see he's holding himself back, and his sheer determination to make me come again before he does is impressive. He runs his fingers over my clit and lightly twists it. The moment I start to tense around him, he quickens his thrusts and eventually stills, the both of us pulsing around each other.

He leans back on his heels and runs his hands over his face. 'Christ.' He falls halfway over me. An age passes before our breathing returns to normal and his heartbeat, pounding against my chest, slows. 'Let's eat in bed. There's no way I want you dressed or out of this room.'

I find his hand under a pillow and hold onto him. 'Fine by me.'

CHAPTER
Seventeen

Two weeks later
Sunday, March 1, 1998

The sun shines on me outside Cici's Boutique, but it's Nathan standing in front of the store that has me sweating. My throat closes. Why the hell isn't David here? He's supposed to be my knight in fucking shining armour.

'You're not supposed to be back.' No wavering voice, no tears or weakness.

'Just thought I'd stop by, see if you and *my child* want to go on vacation. Spend some time together, you know?' He swaggers as he closes the distance.

I remember how attractive he was the first time I saw him. I literally used the word *swoon* to my friend Sarah when he walked over to us in a bar. His swagger filled me with anticipation of what that body could offer. But now, right here, I see the monster that's hidden behind a pretty face and a pumped up body that's only used to make women swoon or fear him. I'm done with both. Now, I see the threat in that swagger.

His muscles come from steroid use, and someone once told me there's no real power behind them. They're just for show. I felt righteous knowing people could see through the facade—Nathan was weak. The only sad thing was it hurt like hell being on the receiving end of those fake steroid muscles.

'If you're too busy, we can always go without you.'

Ice runs through me. Where did Pamela say she was taking Max today? Nathan couldn't have seen him, or he'd be *there*, watching and waiting for word to get back to me. In fact, he can't know where we live, or he would have confronted me at the apartment.

'I don't have anything to give you, Nathan.'

He grabs me by the wrist and squeezes tight. I don't panic as much as I should, but my heart beats faster in my chest and I look around the quiet street. In another half hour, the place will be crawling with tourists and shoppers. I only need to stay safe and out in the open until then.

I try to pull away, but he jerks me towards him. 'Oh, Stella, you have a lot left to give me.'

A man down the street calls my name. Nathan looks over my shoulder, releases me, and takes a step back.

I swing around, and Tony from the Chanel store and two other guards run towards me.

I caress my wrist that's already aching and step away from Nathan. But I don't run away. I don't want him to see me flee. I don't want him to know that maybe there's a little fear in me. But fear is good. An appropriate amount of fear keeps people alive.

'You okay, Stella?' Tony asks, gripping his walkie-talkie.

Nathan stares at me but backs up and crosses the street.

'I'm okay,' I croak.

He nods. 'I'll come into the store with you and wait until your boss gets here.'

'Thank you,' I whisper. An appropriate amount of fear *and* an escape plan keeps people alive.

Cici wants to close the store and collect Pamela and Max at the playground. There's no way I'm going to risk Nathan following Cici, so I tell her to stay put.

I call Tony, who tells me he pulled Nathan's image from their security feed and distributed it around the guards in the other stores. No one has reported seeing him. It's been an hour since Nathan scarpered away from someone his own size, and this is the window of opportunity I have before he gets confidence to return. I check the security cameras before I sneak out the service door, hop a bus, and wait for a busy junction to switch lines. I take off my jacket and leave it on the seat and slip a silk scarf around my hair that I swiped from the boutique on the way out. I left the price tag on so Cici can still sell it once I'm gone. Once off the second bus, I dart inside a coffee shop, watching the door from the ladies' room. I wait ten minutes, and when neither Nathan nor anyone he might have sent to follow me appears, I cross the street and walk for a block, using the reflection from the store windows as a mirror to see behind me. I seek temporary refuge in a department store, where I browse the make-up sections. A little bit of my bitchy shopper days comes back to haunt me. I complain loudly about the lack of vintage colours in stock and tell the sales assistant to call me a cab to collect me at the back door. First I pull the scarf tight around my face, then slide my fake Ray-Bans from Chinatown over my eyes, muttering about photographers.

Back at the apartment, I throw the scarf and glasses on the couch and run to the boys' room, shouting. 'Michael, David? Are you here?'

Mike opens the bedroom door. 'What happened?' He grabs ahold of my arms, trying to stop me from shaking.

'Max's dad is back.' I'm about to launch into an explanation, when someone moving in the room behind Mike catches my attention.

Mike sees me staring and closes the bedroom door behind him. 'What's going on? Where is he?'

I explain about this morning, leaving out the details of how Tony and the guards probably saved me from being dragged down the street and bundled into the back of some crappy stolen car.

Mike leads me to the living room. 'We're going to sort this out.'

'We're not going with him. I don't care what happens,' I whisper. 'I'd rather die.'

'Stella, listen to me.' Mike gently takes my hands. 'We're a team, remember? Trust me that we'll sort this out for you. We'll get him to leave.'

I lean back. How much can I tell Mike without exposing the crazy notion and possible time travelling David, who shows up older to make the father of my child disappear? 'He left the last time when he realised I wasn't getting an inheritance. He must have heard I was working in the industry again. I've been spreading my name around, trying to get you working.'

'He assumed you had money because you're working as my agent?'

I was trying to make a better life for Max, and I only ended up attracting Nathan back to me. 'I need to pack. I need to be ready to leave.'

'Leave?'

'My mom will come with me. We'll be okay, Mike. But if we stay, we won't be.'

'Stella. You can't run. Let us help you.'

'Do you have any idea what happens to boys who grow up around violence? They go from hiding in the corner of the room, crying, to the one who hits their mother, their girlfriend, their wife. I won't let that happen to Max.'

'You're safe here. David and I are here, and we're not going to let him hustle his way back into your life. In case you haven't noticed, I kind of owe you one.'

'But he'll expect to be able to drag me, kicking and screaming, somewhere else.'

'We won't let him.'

'If he gets his hands on Max, I'd go with him. Of course I'll go.'

'He won't get Max, I promise you. We'll keep him out. Let's wait for David to come home. We'll talk it through. But, Stella, I think it's time you are honest with us and tell us everything about him.'

I don't want to leave without seeing David again, but if he's not home soon, I won't wait. I'm not going to take a chance when it comes to Max, just because I want to see the face of the guy I love before I move on. 'I'm going to start packing,' I cut Mike off before he can speak. 'I'll wait for David. He said he'd be back before lunch, but if I have to leave, I want to be ready.'

Mike's face is stoic. I sigh. I don't want him pissed at me.

'Who's the chick?' I gesture towards the bedroom.

'She's a friend. She just got here. Actually, I think she might be able to help us.' He scampers off to the bedroom. 'Stella?' he says before he's out of sight.

'Yeah?'

'Don't ever think you're alone.'

My heart sinks into my stomach, like it's lying at the bottom of a valley. I didn't think I was alone until today. I expected DD to show up in a ball of white light outside the store, but he never did.

Mom and Max arrive home half an hour later, and Mike emerges from his room alone. Great, now this chick is staying the whole day.

'Hey, bud.' Mike gives Max a high-five.

'Can you take him to my room to watch a movie?' I ask Pamela.

'Of course. Come on, Max. Mommy has some packing to do and then we might go on vacation somewhere.'

Mike waits until my bedroom door is closed. 'I told you we'll help you. You just have to sit tight. I'm going to get David, and we'll come straight back here, okay?'

'I'm packing. Then I'll take it from there.'

Once Mike is gone, I gather backpacks and lay them on the couch. Do I pack for good, or for a few days? I cross the room to the kitchen and open the cupboards. What do we have that's packaged light? What about Max's toys? He'll need something. I abandon the kitchen and look in the green toy box under the living room TV. I lay everything out and see what will fit. I should make an emergency bag so if we get stuck, it can be the main bag with total essentials. I grab underwear, one change of clothes each, and GeGe, and stuff it all in the small bag. I fill another backpack with food and Max's snacks. He'll want his SpongeBob, too. I think I washed it yesterday. I drop the two full bags by the door on my way to the laundry room. I'm wasting time going back and forth. I need to do one room at a time.

Speeding up, I bang into the armchair and don't stop to straighten it. In the laundry room, I gather Max's clothes and a pair of sneakers. On the way out, I pick up empty water bottles.

Mike returns with David and I freeze behind the laundry room door, making sure no one follows them in.

'Looks like Audrey's not the only one who's scared,' David says as they walk in.

Who the hell is Audrey? Does he go around saving all sorts of damsels in distress?

David continues speaking to Mike. 'What the hell do you know about Max's dad anyway? Are we dealing with a total psycho-who-might-kill-us-if-we-get-in-the-way kind of ex, or plain old green-eyed monster jealous?'

'Are either of those a good option?' Mike replies.

Fuckers are talking about me like I'm not even here. Shit, they don't know I'm here. I don't need to hide from them. I stride out of the laundry room.

'Stella, what the fuck?' David yells at me. 'Is there a room you haven't turned upside down? You have to tell me what's going on. Right now.'

I look around the living room and kitchen and see the mess I've made. If I'd been paying attention, I would have realised the place looks totalled.

Mike sneaks off to his room, a grocery store bag in hand. He doesn't need to keep his girl hidden in his room. She could come out to the kitchen, you know. Well maybe not right now.

David leads me to the couch. He rubs his thumb over mine after we sit down facing each other. He sends tingles through me with his gentleness, like he did a few nights ago. He doesn't speak but he holds my gaze, searching. I flinch when his fingers graze my wrists. He holds his breath when he sees the red marks already turning a shade of purple.

'It's not as bad as it looks,' I tell him.

'You're not with him anymore. You don't need to lie about how bad it is.'

'I . . . I wasn't. It's . . . just.' I drop my gaze to the floor, unable to look at him.

He caresses my wrists, and I close my eyes, wishing Nathan out of my life for good.

Mike comes back and sits on the coffee table in front of us. I rehash some details of the day for David, and Pamela and Max join us. We fill Mike and David in on our past experiences with Nathan and how we paid him off before. I leave out the time DD helped at the hospital—Pamela doesn't even know about that one.

Mike is quiet until he drops a bombshell. 'We pay him again.'

'It's no good,' I tell him. 'He came back, and he'll keep coming back. He'll take Max from me eventually, I know he will.'

'We pay him a lot and get a lawyer to help us. We draw up some kind of contract, and he can't come back into the country,' Mike says.

Anger's been boiling in me all day at the thoughts of having to run away from these people who are willing to help me. But what if I really could get Nathan to leave me alone for good? Leave the country? It won't work. Nathan keeps coming back, and apparently, I keep dying every time he shows up.

'How the hell does a contract keep a man like that from coming back?' Even David is getting mad with the ridiculousness of it. Nathan isn't just going to sign an agreement not to hunt me down again.

'I don't know.' Mike turns to me. 'You must have something on him.'

Why? Because he beat me and is an asshole, you figured out he must have a load of secrets, some of which I might know?

'Something we can use as a bargaining tool, to keep him away,' Mike adds.

Nerves turn to nausea in the pit of my stomach. I can't tell anyone. I'll end up losing Max if I tell.

Mike continues, not noticing my unease. 'Audrey said Nathan can't come back into the US, and with the money we give him he stays away for good.'

'Who's Audrey?' I ask confused. Who the hell have they been discussing this with? 'How can you be sure he won't come back?'

'I don't know. What I do know is it works. Stella, you need to stay here, talk to David, and work out what you can use on Max's dad. I have to go find us a lawyer.'

Mike gets off the coffee table, and I stare at his back as he walks out the door without another word.

'What the hell was that all about?' Pamela says.

Max gasps. 'Mommy, Granny said hell.'

Mom pokes Max in the belly, tickling his side and making him laugh and cheer at the same time.

Mike is gone for hours, leaving his secret girl in his room. I'm not as nervous as I was this morning. If Nathan knew where I lived, he would've been here by now. Even if he saw I wasn't alone, he would have made his presence known. Having David here is calming, even though he's been in his room for the last hour, with the girl who's spent the night with Mike. When Mike arrives home, he goes straight to his room. I busy myself in the kitchen, waiting for them to come speak to me.

I've cleaned the counters three times when I hear David shouting. I can't decipher the words. He's mad. What would he be angry about? Maybe they're arguing about the girl. Oh Christ, my heart drops into my stomach. What if she's the one he's supposed to marry?

David quiets down, and I tiptoe to the edge of the kitchen, waiting for one of them to storm out. Mike appears first. He looks frazzled. 'Don't worry, I have one more place to go, and then I think we have this all figured out.'

Mike returns early evening and goes straight to his room. David comes out with a handful of papers he folds over and slides in his back pocket.

'We have the money sorted,' he tells me.

'How much do you have this time?' I sigh. David has been handing over everything he has to me at all points through time.

'More than you paid him the last time. We have half a million for Nathan, plus the lawyer's fees and some leftover to keep us going. But it's not enough. We need something on him that will keep him out of the country. Mike has it worked out with a lawyer. A good one. He says if we can get something

149

to bribe him with, we can pay him to stay away. And there's more. We need to prove to Nathan that he's lost the control he had over you. If you're with someone else, he'll finally see you're no longer his. He needs to see you as someone else's.'

'What, like yours?' I scoff.

David flinches. 'I don't think of you as property. You know that. But that's how he sees women. If I stand by and be the good guy, letting you choose how to live your life and who to be with, he'll think I'm weak. He'll think he can get past me and order you around. I know it's vulgar, Stella, but if he thinks I'm controlling you, like he used to, it might be enough to get rid of him. You said it yourself. He keeps coming back. We can dangle enough money in front of him, it will make him look weak if he squanders it all this time.

'We have a good thing, Stella, and I don't want to hide. I know you didn't want Max to find out yet, but I think that's bullshit. I think you didn't want another relationship yet. But I'm not him. I treat you exactly how you deserve to be treated. If Nathan's as bad as you let me think he is—you must have something on him. What about the cop friend he used to threaten you with?'

'I can't tell you. I'll put you all in danger.'

'Fuck that, Stella. Hell, he probably already thinks you told us, so we're probably in danger anyway, if it's even that big a deal.'

'Fuck you, too, David,' I scream.

'Tell us. It's the final thing we need to get rid of him.'

'Tell me how you got the money first, 'cause I know you don't have money like that lying around. What do you mean you got money to pay him off? How did you get that kind of money, David?'

'What's all the yelling about?' Mike asks from the hallway.

David faces him, pointing back at me. 'She has something we can use on him, but won't tell us.'

I stare Mike down. 'Where did you get the money, Mike?'

'I got it from a friend. It's a loan, that's all,' he answers.

'And is your friend going to come looking for their money back with a baseball bat?'

'I have a contact at the studio.'

Liar, if he had a contact, he would have used it already to get himself a job.

'You've already done so much work for me,' Mike continues, 'and we've not even made any money yet. Consider this your retainer. But we need to know what you have on him.'

I sink into the couch. I can't keep this from David much longer. He's right. If Nathan finds out I'm in another relationship, he'll assume I've already spoke about it. I curl up into a ball, wanting this whole thing to go away. 'Can't we just leave it alone? If we have the money, we don't need anything else.'

'He'll come back, Stella, just like this time. We have to fix this properly,' David tells me.

I'm beginning to realise that even with DD helping me, and David in my life now, Nathan will continue to show up, threaten me and Max every time he needs money. It should have been him who died that night. If I could go back in time and change one thing, it would be that. I was already pregnant. I would still have Max, but that fucker would be the one dead instead.

The tears flow as I argue back and forth with myself. I can't keep this inside much longer. Nathan keeps coming back and I know full well what he's capable of. David wouldn't betray me by telling the police I was involved. He wouldn't risk me losing Max, and Mike is too invested in me helping with his career. I need to trust them—they've earned it.

I raise my head. My gaze settles on David's brown comforting eyes. 'He killed someone.'

CHAPTER

Eighteen

Four years earlier
Friday, September 24, 1993
Hollywood, California

'Sit at the bar and look pretty,' Nathan tells me. 'I want you as a distraction. I want the guys to be jealous of what I have.' He grabs my chin and squeezes too tight. 'But don't distract them enough that they actually think they can fuck you.'

'I wouldn't do that.' I keep my voice soft as he walks the three feet away to the table his buddies are waiting at. He's already been drinking. Cards will piss him off tonight. He always loses. Sitting in a bar pregnant is going to look pretty nasty in a couple more months, when I really start to show. Maybe Nathan will let me stay at home.

I order a soda and perch on a stool. No time to grieve for your father a week after he died when your boyfriend might just send you to meet him.

I close my eyes when the image of my father swinging from the back of his home office door flashes into my mind. The things I've learned in this short week is that no matter how good your life looks to others, there are always things you have to hide. Like, who knew you could look like a millionaire while wallowing in debt? No matter how hard my father and I worked at the business, he still lost it all. Now, I know how hard it is to cut a rope and the helplessness of calling an ambulance for someone who was already dead. I knew right when I used my shoulder to push the door all the way open, that he was already dead on the other side.

Nathan couldn't hide his delight when he found out my dad was dead. Not that he despised Dad, but I saw the dollar signs in his eyes. I'm the only child to a Hollywood legend. It scares me to think what's going to happen when he realises I won't inherit as much as he thinks I will.

I should have figured out working with Dad each and every day, that no matter how much he was succeeding in bringing his business back to life, inside he was already done. The rise and fall, the first divorce, then the second divorce on the table. I saw his life crumbling again. I just never envisioned him tying a boat rope around a door handle, tossing it over the top and tying it into a noose.

I run my hand over my stomach and wonder if Nathan will have a miraculous turn around when he becomes a father. If he'll love his child, like my father loved me. It's not that he's violent all the time, but the worst part is the fear, wondering if this is the time he'll lose control and not get it back until it's too late. But he has me, knocked up and friendless with a dead father and a broke mother who couldn't get her shit together if it killed her—or maybe me. My back stiffens from waiting around and the soda runs through me as fast as the glass is continuously refilled. I swear I've taken three trips to the bathroom in the last ten minutes. When I hop off the barstool, Nathan darts his eyes to me. How the hell is me peeing pissing him off?

I lower my head so I don't make eye contact with anyone. The guy sitting at the table near the restroom gets up as I pass, nearly bumping into me as he steps back.

It was my fault. My eyes are on the floor, and I don't dare lift them to start a conversation. Bathroom Guy doesn't turn around as he mutters an apology but lets me through the archway to the restrooms ahead of him.

Great, now Nathan will think he's my secret lover. I pee quickly and open the stall door, adjusting my skirt at the same time. I don't even wash my hands so I can be back on my assigned seat before Nathan can possibly assume anything happened in the bathroom. I walk to the card game and touch his shoulder so he knows I'm back. 'You need anything from the bar?' I finger the Ralph Lauren shirt he's wearing. Despite being excited when I found a shirt in his size at TJ Maxx a few months ago, I hate that he thinks I still like it when he wears the clothes I bought for him.

He swats my hand off his shoulder. 'No.'

He watches Bathroom Guy return to his table. With his back to us, Bathroom Guy downs the rest of his drink. When he starts to turn around, I spin to my stool to face the bar. If Nathan thinks I'm looking at him, we'll both be in trouble.

'You got room for one more player?' he asks, approaching Nathan's table.

Nathan nods to the empty chair. A new player means at least another hour. I order more soda with three cherries and take my time sucking as much liquid from the cherries as I can.

I stare out the passenger window to the parking lot. The only view is the darkened door to the bar, and my heartbeat doubles. Nathan's waiting for a fight.

'You need to calm down. You didn't get screwed over. You lost,' I tell him.

'I don't lose.' He shoves a finger in my face.

'Can we go? I want to lie down. My legs are killing me in these heels.'

'We'll go when I'm good and ready.'

After a few minutes, three of the guys from the card game come out. Two of them are Nathan's regulars, who shake hands with Bathroom Guy and head off in different directions.

'See, I fucking told you. They screwed me. They know each other.'

'Maybe they were being polite. That's what normal people do when they've spent an evening together.'

His lips curl up at one side. 'Is that what you did? Spend an evening with him? I saw how many times you disappeared to the restroom. No one else pissed that much.'

'No one else is pregnant, Nathan.' It doesn't really matter whether I antagonise him. He's a dick whether I'm nice to him or not.

He starts the engine and swings the car around, following Bathroom Guy out of the parking lot.

I swallow hard and buckle my seat belt. Nerves prickle my skin and chill me down to my legs. I turn the heat up as we follow the car around the hills in complete darkness. Neither car is travelling fast. Bathroom Guy must know he's being followed. It's not like Nathan is subtle about anything.

Nathan flashes his lights. The car up front pulls over, and the driver's door opens.

Nathan puts the high beams on, blinding the man, and steps out.

I glance at the clock. I want this fight over. I don't really care what happens to Nathan. Maybe I'll get lucky and Bathroom Guy will finally teach him a lesson. I hear Nathan's yelling. It's like a Rottweiler snarl you can pick out a mile away. The other guy doesn't look like he's putting up much argument, but he must say something that pisses Nathan off, because he jabs one quick punch to the man's stomach, and the poor guy falls to his knees.

Shit.

I lean forward and turn the full beam off, but it's no good. Nathan still has his arm bent like it's stuck inside the guy. He didn't even put his full force into the punch, that much I could tell. I've seen Nathan punch before; I've been on the receiving end of it once or twice.

Nathan slowly retracts his fist from the guy's midsection. He wipes something on his jeans and turns around, slipping whatever he had into his back pocket. He stabbed him. Fuck. Fuck. What the hell do I do? I feel sick, but I can't even breathe properly. Nathan takes measured steps back to the car, the other man behind him, still on his knees. By the time Nathan gets out of my line of sight, the guy is sprawled on the dirt.

'What happened?' I breathe when he gets into the car.

Nathan grabs my phone out of my hand and tosses it back inside my purse. 'Taught him a lesson, was all.'

'Jesus, Nathan. What did you do?'

'Guy's a pussy. Wouldn't be surprised if someone comes along after us and finishes him off.' Nathan pulls onto the road. 'We went straight home, got it?'

I nod and try to keep the tears back, but a few escape and I rush to swipe them away.

'Hey, don't worry, baby,' Nathan croons and pulls me towards him. 'Nothing is going to happen to me. No one is ever going to know we were here.'

I keep my eyes open when he hugs me. No need to get caught off guard. His designer jeans that he can't afford are covered in blood. I smell the bar on his shirt. 'Remember, I have friends who can help me out of a legal mess.' He pulls my face up to look me in the eye. 'Don't I?'

'You sure do.' I clench my hands when he touches the scar on my lip. The doctor told me not to touch it. To let it heal as much as it can to minimise the scarring. Don't pick the scab or cover it with make-up just yet. But Nathan touches it every chance he gets. Like he wants me to have a permanent reminder of him.

'If you ever tell anyone about tonight'—he glances at my belly—'I'll make you an accomplice. Hell, you are one; being there, agreeing to keep it quiet, leaving the scene of a crime. You were the one who set up the honey trap. Everyone in the bar saw you whoring with him in the restroom. Who's going to believe you weren't involved?

'My friends will help me out. They'll make sure you go to jail. What kind of mother would you be, giving birth in prison? And me, shit, I can get out early. I'd get the baby before you were out of jail and make sure to raise it right.' He sneers before softening his tone. 'Let's forget about this and concentrate on the reading of your dad's will tomorrow. It's going to be a big day for us.'

The reading of a will is supposed to be an emotional time for me, and it genuinely is, but fear dwarfs all other emotions.

I loved my dad, and I wish to god he hadn't done what he did. But I'm nervous. Rumours of his financial burden have started to surface. I know for a fact his financial mess is more than a rumour.

Nathan parks and I get out of the car and follow him around the back of my dad's house to my pool house. When Mom had to move in with Cici and Isaac, Dad let me move in here when I turned eighteen, despite the new wife objecting. I wonder what will happen now that he's gone—how long I'll have before the heartless bitch throws me out?

I toss my purse on the entertainment stand and turn on the TV to the news station. Nathan is already gone to the bedroom. I can wait out here until he's sleeping. We were on a main road. It won't take long for someone to find a guy lying next to a car with the door open and lights on. It's too late for me to call an ambulance. It won't help the guy, not now. And the police will trace the call, know that we were there and left him.

Nathan's playing on his phone in the bedroom. Someone keeps texting him. He's trying to hide it 'cause he switched his phone to silent, but the idiot doesn't know how to turn the vibration off. I pull the movie blanket off the back of the couch and curl under it. Resting my eyes with the TV volume on low, I settle down for the night.

When I wake at seven in the morning, Diana Koricke is covering the story about a body found on the main hills road. She's no longer my favourite anchor woman.

Thank god it wasn't me. I choke on my cry. What the fuck? Some guy is dead, and all I can think of is myself. I wrap the blanket around my shoulders, bury my face in a cushion, and let it all out. I must have cried for an hour. My face is blotchy when I get up and toss the blanket into the wash.

Nathan never wakes before ten, so I text my mom.

I'm in trouble.

Her immediate reply surprises me.

Is it Nathan? What did he do?

How much should I tell her? How much can she actually help?

She texts again.

Delete these messages so Nathan doesn't see them & meet me at Cici's house. I'm sending u another message, don't delete it.

I rock from foot to foot, scrolling through my messages, deleting the last ones I sent and received from my mom. Another one appears in my inbox.

Hi honey. We need to talk about what outfits we're going2 wear 2the will reading this afternoon. Meet me at Cici's house 9am. She has a few things for us to match. Mom x

Holy shit. Mom is stealthy.

CHAPTER
Nineteen

Today
Sunday, March 1, 1998

After the initial shock from my confession wears off, Mike and David resume hatching their plan on how to pay Nathan off. I'm emotionally exhausted and don't listen to their arguments about how this should play out. I'm merely resigned to the fact Nathan might be someone who's destined to be in my universe forever. Even in the alternative future that Liam visited, Nathan had already killed me.

I hug my knees and rock back and forth, like when I rock Max to sleep sometimes.

David catches my eye. 'I need to make some calls.'

Mike returns to his room, and I leave David in the kitchen alone.

I get into bed with Max. I hug him tight, and after an hour, I relax and drift off to sleep.

I jerk awake when I hear a knock at the front door, followed by a scrape along the kitchen tiles as a stool is pushed out. David greets someone and steps out of the apartment. I don't fully relax until David returns half an hour later and cracks my bedroom door open.

'Are you awake, Mighty?'

'Yes,' I croak.

He crosses the room, toeing off his shoes.

'What are you doing?'

'Remember when I said you didn't need to cry alone anymore?'

I purse my lips and nod into my pillow.

He gets into bed behind me and holds me, like he said he would.

I turn into his chest. 'Who was at the door?'

He digs into his pocket and pulls out a diamanté brooch. 'Security company,' he says. 'They specialise in immediate threats. You need to keep this on you. There's a tracker in the back and a panic button right here in the middle.' He runs my finger over the top. 'I have one for Pamela too, since she's normally with Max when you're not.'

'I'm not letting Max out of my sight,' I snap.

'I know,' he soothes. 'But she should have one too.'

I nod, calming down. He wasn't insinuating I should go about my day as usual.

'They've set up surveillance of the apartment and are stationed outside. They're going to keep a close eye on you until Nathan is gone. You're safe, Stella.'

'Jesus, David. How much does something like that cost?'

'I'll worry about it later.'

'They're going to do a job for a college kid on a promise of payment later?'

'I used my credit card. My parents upped the limit for emergencies when I moved here. This qualifies. We can pay the bill when Mike gets the cash. You need to sleep. I'm here, and I won't let anything hurt you.'

'You don't know who he has helping him. He always said he had help, and the body went missing from the morgue the next day.'

'Sh,' David tries to calm my rising panic. 'We have some help here too. Rest. Let me work this out for you.'

The next morning, Monday, Mike assures me that seven hundred and fifty thousand dollars will be wired to him today. My stomach sinks. He's more broke than I am. Borrowing money like that is like borrowing from psycho Peter to pay psycho Paul.

'We'll have enough to pay Luca, the lawyer, and then we can discuss the paper work.'

'How can we word a contract that he won't come back, or be able to take Max from me?'

'Try not to worry, Mighty. That's what we're hiring Luca to do.' David's confidence relaxes me somewhat.

He and Mike talk shit in the living room about how to intimidate Nathan when they finally meet him, and I cut toast into rectangle soldiers for Max's breakfast.

'He won't be happy I'm choosing to stay away,' I tell them. 'He's not going to listen if we go in all nice and ask him to leave us alone.' I'm repeating myself, but I can't seem to stop replaying every possible scenario.

'Bullies respond to bullies,' David says. 'They only respect people they fear. We need to be someone he fears.'

An Irish accent from the hallway startles me. 'You're right,' she says. 'You need to be forceful, and it needs to be David.'

Damn, Audrey is still here. If David hadn't spent the night holding me, I'd be throwing shit right about now. I ease the eggs into the boiling water, throw the spatula on the counter, and circle the kitchen island to get a better look. She's pretty, despite the lack of make-up and tired eyes. Her long red hair is rumpled and tucked behind her ears, but shines like it's used to being styled by a professional.

'Why David?' Mike asks her.

'Because David is going to adopt Max,' she answers.

What the fuck is she talking about? I turn to see David's reaction, and he's not the least bit fazed by her idea.

'It's part of the contract that Luca works out,' Audrey continues. 'Max's dad will sign away his rights and after you two get married, he doesn't come back.'

'What the hell is going on?' I scream.

'Stella, listen,' David says, raising his hand like he's trying to tame a wild animal.

'I'm not going to let the first guy that comes along adopt my child, David.' I'm affronted he'd even suggest it.

'Luca can fix it,' Audrey says. 'He can set up Max's adoption and put in clauses that take any legal and medical rights away from David as well. Basically, you use David's name to take him away from his father, but you don't pass on any legal or parental rights to him. You can sort it out that—'

'Who the hell is this girl?' I stare from Mike to David.

She moves closer. 'You need to do whatever it takes to protect your son. So take the damn help.'

'Okay, enough of the bullshit.' I'll make sure I get all those details ironed out with Luca before I sign anything. 'What I don't understand is, if you have someone who can lend you that much money, what the hell do you need me for? Why don't you just get a real agent? Why the hell are you living here?'

'Hey, I like our new place.' Mike pouts.

This is so not the point.

Audrey slides down to the floor next to the coffee table and looks through a grocery bag for leftovers of the food Mike dumped there this morning.

I turn my attention to David and Mike. 'You've got yourself in some serious shit. People who lend that kind of money want it back, with interest, and they will kill you for it.'

'It was me,' Audrey says, eating chips. 'I gave them the money. I told them to find you. You are going to be important in all of this, but don't think you're getting a free ride. You're going to have to work your ass off to pay them back and get Michael to where he needs to be.'

A free fucking ride? Is she kidding me? 'Who the hell are you?'

Audrey stops eating and pauses for a second. 'I'm from the future.'

This is so fucked up. She can't be serious. The exhaustion from the last twenty-four hours takes over, and laughter spills from my mouth. I try to hold it in, but fuck. This crazy girl has shown up and promised us nearly a million dollars. Why the hell did Mike and David believe her? I'm screwed. I let the laughter consume me, because the next thing will be uncontrollable tears. And I need to stay in control. I need to get myself together. I need to run with Max. I sink into a chair. Where will we go? What the hell was my plan yesterday? When David held me last night, I felt safe. I wasn't thinking about where I should be running to. I was thinking about a future full of David.

David sits down next to me with his arm around the back of the chair. Like he's trying to hug me, while maintaining the space I've asked him for.

David, who is way more naive than DD would have been. Where's DD? If I'm really this screwed, he should be here. Why hasn't he shown up in a ball of light to rescue me?

The three of them continue their conversation, making plans, like I'm not here. I shouldn't be here. I should be running, but I can't move. What if Audrey's not crazy, and DD sent her here to help me? What if she really is from the future and not pranking the hot new time-studies fellow on campus?

Audrey's words draw my attention '. . . You and Stella were already engaged by this time, and me being here has slowed this down. Mike already had a few movies in the pipeline by now, and you get the screenplay signed for pre-production soon. You need to get on that now, and I mean twenty-four seven.'

The light is here. I can see it at the other side of the coffee table. DD is coming back. He's going to rescue me from all this. He's going to explain everything to the younger version of himself.

The light rapidly grows strong, and that horrible piercing noise makes me grind my teeth together.

'Audrey,' Mike screams and jumps towards her.

I want to tell him it's okay, it won't hurt her, it's just DD coming for me, but she beats me to it.

'It's ok, Michael.' Audrey holds Mike's hand. She keeps talking to him, but the noise is too loud to hear them, even from the other side of the coffee table.

The light implodes like it did when David left me at the hospital, but this time it takes Audrey with it.

I stand. Waiting. DD's not coming to save me this time. Despite the ridiculousness of it, I thought I was connected to him. That no matter what, he'd be there for me. But I guess there's a version of him already here, who's been here for me all along.

'Stella?' David says cautiously.

'I know this is confusing,' Mike says.

I run to my room to check on Max. I want to hold him, to make sure he's still okay. I sit on the bed, while he continues to watch cartoons. How the hell he was oblivious to what happened in the next room is beyond me.

'He's okay, Stella. You don't need to worry about him,' David says. 'Audrey has come to us a few times. She's here to help us.'

'Who is she?'

'A friend,' Mike answers. 'She sent us to you. You help us get out of this mundane life, and she says we did it. In the future, you are this remarkable agent, and you make a fortune. So do I, and David too. She has told us how to do it. Now, we just need to make sure we do.'

Liam needs to know there's someone else travelling too. His theories and recordings about time travel need to be updated to include Audrey's involvement, whoever she turns out to be.

'I don't ever want another day like this.' I stroke Max's cheek.

'I know it's scary, but you get used to seeing her come and go,' Mike says.

'Not that.' I approach the doorway to speak to them. 'Max's dad. I don't ever want to feel that . . . helpless again. If I didn't have you two to help me, he would have taken us. We would be dead soon.'

And that's exactly the kind of butterfly effect that Liam spoke about. If we give David too much information, it might affect his ability to harness time travel in the future. What if he and Audrey never time travel? Liam needs to know that keeping David in the dark might save me and Max again.

David takes my hand. 'Audrey told us to find Luca and to make the deal with Max's dad. She even gave us her wedding rings to pawn and pay him off.'

'Why?'

'Because you're our friend, and I didn't want to lose you too,' Mike says. 'In the future, you're never helpless again.'

'Who else did you lose?' I ask.

'No one.' His smile doesn't reach his eyes. I wonder if he's infatuated with time travelling Audrey, like I was with DD. 'Do you think her plan is going to work?' I ask.

'It'll work,' David assures me.

'What do we need to do?' My voice chokes.

'You guys get working on your careers. Let me deal with the rest,' David says.

Mike nods and turns to me. 'How are you at writing?'

CHAPTER
Twenty

'**Are you sure he's** going to show up?' Mike asks while I pace the waiting room of Luca's office.

It's an expensive office with plush carpet and designer furniture, and I know the fees generated here are more than a lot of people make in a year. Hell, some contracts my dad's lawyers worked on racked up more money than someone might make in ten years. 'He'll show. I told him we had the money.' I pull my collar. 'I need to wait outside. I feel trapped in here.'

'Stay close to the door. Nathan's due in twenty minutes, come back in before then,' David says.

I step outside and pace the thick carpet in the reception area while Mike and David finalise payments with Luca. The least amount of time I need to be here the better.

'Tough day?' The raspy voice behind me reminds me of David waking early morning, when he kisses me before sneaking back to his room, but it's DD.

Slowly turning around, I smile before my emotional firewall breaks down and I'm a crumbling sobbing mess reaching my arms out for him. I missed him, but this must be one of the times I *died* for him to be here.

Looking the same as when he came to me in the hospital—older, tired, and worn out—DD wraps his arms tight around my back and presses his face to my hair. I melt into him. This time, we both know we've been more than friends.

'It's okay,' he croons. 'I told you I was here until you were okay, didn't I?'

'I can't believe this is real. When I met you and Mike outside Cici's store, you were so young. I thought I was losing my mind. I just ignored it, until you started talking about your work on the theory of time travel and I let myself think that maybe it was true. Then I met Liam, and that girl, Audrey, disappeared, and you and Mike know all about it.'

DD holds me at arm's length. 'We know about Audrey, but I never travelled before. Not until now, when I'm forty. You can't tell me, okay? Remember that.'

'I never said a word, even before Liam told me not to. He told me about you travelling to him when he was a boy.'

'I haven't been there yet, but if he said I did, then it must happen.'

'It was years ago. How can you not have been there yet?'

'I'm not travelling in chronological order, like Audrey. Each time I leave a place, I travel farther into the past. How many times have I come to you?'

'This is the second. The first was when I had Max.'

'It's too soon for me to know anything about my own travels. My focus needs to be on helping Audrey, and that will lead to this. One day I'll have the time to explain what I know, but right now we have to get rid of Nathan. There's something you need to know.' He runs his thumb down my cheek.

'What?' My heart skips a beat.

'We got rid of him for good. This is the last time you'll see him.'

A booming voice from the hall startles us apart. 'What the hell is this?'

DD looks up, and we stare down at Nathan.

'You again? Well, I wasn't expecting that. Always showing up without a scratch on you.'

I narrow my eyes at Nathan. He was the one who came off worse in their brief scuffle at the hospital. 'If I remember correctly, you were the one who was pinned against a wall the last time you two met.'

'You know what, Nathan. We had a deal. You were supposed to stay away. But now I know better than to bargain with the likes of you. It's time to raise the stakes, bring in the real deal.' The light has already started to form around DD, and I see his jaw twitch. He knows he's leaving.

'You are about to witness how important this woman is to us. On the other side of that door are two really pissed people who are willing to give up everything to protect her. This is your chance to retreat with some dignity and your life intact.'

'My life? You think you can threaten me, old man? You're the one who ended up in a pile of dirt.'

'What the hell is that supposed to mean?' My attitude to Nathan hasn't subsided with his absence.

The light grows, and the noise intensifies. Nathan raises a hand in front of the light and I take a step back.

'I'll always come back.' DD speaks as the light engulfs him. 'Every damn time you do, I'll be here, waiting. I've sent a file to the FBI with evidence tying you to the murder. It's on a time delay. They will get the information in ten hours.

That gives you enough time to take the money and leave the country.' DD manages his final parting words before the light retreats, and he's gone.

'What the fuck was that? He supposed to be some sort of ghost?' The fear on Nathan's face warms my insides.

Luca's office door opens, and David steps out, looking younger and, if possible stronger, flanked by Mike and Luca.

'You must be Nathan. We've been waiting on you,' David says.

Nathan looks from David to me and back again. 'Are you kidding me? What the hell is going on here?'

Luca steps forward. 'Let's continue this inside, shall we?'

Nathan's shorter than the three men, but walks like he's about to pounce on everyone. His stance says he's ready for a fight. Despite David and Mike working out and being blessed in the muscle department, Nathan's the psycho willing to take the cheap shots and not care about the consequences.

'Really, what is he? Like some baby brother version of your sugar daddy?' He sneers as he passes David.

Fuck, he really needs to keep his mouth shut. DD wouldn't have revealed himself to Nathan if he didn't know what he was doing—I hope.

'He's a friend. David had his lawyer arrange the transfer,' I say meekly. God, I'm going to have to find the courage to stand up to this guy. I've spent so much time helping Mike learn how to act, you'd think I could implement some of my own advice for half an hour.

Luca gestures for us to sit around his desk, the chairs spread farther apart than they were when I was in here a few minutes ago.

A few minutes. DD was with me for days the last time. Being cheated out of my time with DD trumps my fear of

Nathan. I stand taller, smugger at the realisation. He's losing the grip he had on me.

Everyone stands, aside from Luca, who sits at the other side of his desk. David stands in front of me, blocking my view of Nathan. My heart clenches. I shouldn't feel robbed. David's right here, protecting me as always. Knowing this is the last time I'll see Nathan, gives me the strength to step forward and face him head-on. I place my hand on David's lower back as I step to the side, coming into full view. David tenses when Nathan's within reaching distance of me. But that was never Nathan's style. He got more satisfaction from the fear he inflicted and the control he had when I was alone with him. Why punch a girl in the face when there are people to help her?

'I understand Ms. Lewis wishes to transfer some funds to you under certain contractual obligations.' Luca leans back in his chair, like he deals with things like this every day. Maybe he does.

'What obligations would those be?' Nathan eyes me, and my natural instinct is to look at the ground. I hold his gaze, and he grins, knowing how hard this is for me.

'Stella would like you to sign parental rights of your son, Max, over to her. You would rescind all legal and medical rights over your child, stay out of her life, and out of the country. I understand you have family in Europe and are keen to return there.'

'You want to kick me out of the fucking country?' Nathan's question is directed at me, but it's Luca who answers.

'Not kick. Simply push. Stella has signed a sworn affidavit, detailing her witness statement to the events of September 24, 1993 and the murder you committed.'

'She's a lying bitch. The body went missing from the morgue. You got nothing on me.'

'We have the body,' I lie. 'I needed insurance over you. I saw a great opportunity and took it.'

Nathan's eyes dart to me, hesitant. There's no way he'd believe me if he hadn't just seen what happened in the hallway, but it's enough to make him nervous.

'You have a way out. Take the cash and leave. Half a million and no jail is pretty good, if you ask me. I told her I could get you for less, but'—Luca waves his hand at me—'she really wants to be rid of you.'

'Half a million? You said your daddy left you nothing. See? I told you she's a lying bitch.'

David takes a step forward, and Mike grabs his arm to hold him back. Nathan tenses, but instead of throwing the first punch, like he normally would, he holds a nervous stance.

David picks up a pen and holds it out to Nathan. 'Sign the damn papers.'

'Who the hell *are* you?' Nathan asks.

'I'm the guy who's raising your son. Stella's mine now.'

Nathan sneers at him. 'I'll gladly take the money, but I'm not leaving the country until it's in the bank. I never did get as much for that watch as I thought I would.' He leans over and signs the papers without even looking at them. Tossing the pen on the table, he finishes. 'Never cared for her anyway.'

'Luca, finish this up and bill me.' David tugs me out of the room.

'Yes, sir,' Luca says.

Mike follows us out to the elevator. Once inside, we collectively let out a breath.

'Do you think it worked?' Mike asks.

'Yes.' DD wouldn't have left if he wasn't sure of that. He was here to show Nathan I had a supernatural guardian angel looking after me.

'Stella, please tell me you didn't steal a body from the morgue?' Mike asks.

'Of course not.' A chill runs through me. 'It was stolen from the morgue the next night. To be honest, I always thought Nathan was behind it. But I only realised when I stepped out of the office earlier that he doesn't have the ability to pull something like that off. I took a chance.'

'A chance? Christ, the whole thing could have fallen apart.' David runs his hand through his hair.

'But it didn't. And I knew this is the time he leaves for good.'

'So who the hell took it?'

'Does it matter?' My hand twinges at my side, and I stretch my fingers towards David's. He flinches when I make contact, before weaving his fingers with mine and squeezing my hand tight with a reassuring smile.

My heart skips a beat and finally, I feel like I have a home. Liam might be wrong. I might not be able to warn David about the time travel he's going to experience, but perhaps I can save him from the heartache of marrying the wrong girl and losing his baby. I can love him better than she ever did. And if I'm her, at least I have the knowledge I need to avoid pregnancy, because I know an abortion would never be an option for me. That's why I can't figure out if I really am his future wife, why I would have ever done it.

CHAPTER
Twenty-One

'**What's you plans for** tomorrow?' David asks me from the kitchen. 'I want to take you on a date.'

I throw *Break The Piece* on the coffee table and take a seat at the kitchen island opposite him.

'You want to take me on a date?'

'I thought it was overdue. We spoke about telling everyone about us. Now seems like a good time, don't you think?'

'Why, because some time travelling Irish girl showed up and told you to save me from my crazy ex and marry me and adopt my child?'

David lets out a breath and leans over the island, getting closer to me. 'She said you were my wife in the future. She didn't tell me to marry you right away. Besides, don't you think if we kept dating and getting on as well as we do, that things would get serious between us? Heck, I already think seriously about you.' He places a kiss on the tip of my nose.

'I do, but I don't want anything to influence your decisions.'

'What about *your* decisions? Are you so impenetrable to time travel influences you're only worried about me?'

'I'm worried about you derailing your life for some young single mom you pity.'

David rounds the counter and snakes his arms around my waist. 'Stella, when I look at you, pity is certainly not something that comes to mind. Dropping to my knees begging to be yours, maybe.' He kisses my neck. 'We're dating already. Your mom knows about us. It's just the going out sort of dates that need to start happening. Let's keep dating until you're ready to take the next step. But I want to take you out in public where we can hold hands and eat ice-cream and kiss in the middle of the street.'

'Where do you want to go?'

'This is your town. Where do you want to go?'

'What have you still to see?'

'Most things. I've seen the university and Rodeo Drive. I've done the Hollywood tour—'

'Wait, you've done the Hollywood tour?' I lean back to look him in the eye. 'Are you fricking kidding me?'

David smirks. 'Got the tour bus around Beverly Hills, the Hollywood sign and everything.'

'Ugh, that is so ridiculous.'

'Only 'cause you're a local. For anyone who doesn't live near the mansions and high-rises, this country is an amazing place to visit.'

'Really, just what is it you find so amazing?'

'Well, except for the local hotties'—he tugs at my lips with his teeth and pulls me into the crook of his arm, guiding me back to the stove where he stirs the marinara sauce—'the culture diversity is pretty cool. I mean, I'm from London, but still, over here it's on a whole other level. Normally we'd need to get on a plane to actually feel like you're visiting another

177

country. And I travelled a lot with my parents, so I know what I'm talking about. You guys have so many integrated pockets of different cultures all over the city. Japanese, Chinese, Korean, and Thai. You only need to spend an hour there, and you feel like you're in the country.'

'You want to go to Chinatown and eat Chinese food?'

'Already did that. It was completely different to the Chinese food we have back home, which is kind of weird.'

'It was real Chinese food, that's why.'

'So where do you want to take me?' He asks.

I think for a minute. 'Ever been to Japan?'

He shakes his head. 'It's on my list of countries to visit when I'm rich and famous.' He smiles.

'No need, when you're in a city that has Little Tokyo.' I stretch up and kiss him on the lips.

'We leave at ten tomorrow morning. Bring your wallet, 'cause you have a ton load of Japanese food to buy me.'

David's turning in the street, looking at the red and white lanterns that run from light pole to light pole. 'This place is insane.'

'It's great, right? We should have actually come down at night, 'cause City Hall looks great lit up in the background, but I want to be home for Max before it gets dark.' I grab his hand and walk through the small square towards my favourite restaurant. The sunlight shines through the trees, highlighting the old buildings nestled in between the new. 'This place right here'—I point—'does the best ice-cream. We need to line up.'

'It's eleven in the morning. You want to eat ice-cream?'

'Hell, yeah.' I hold our hands in the air. 'You told me you'd hold my hand and eat ice-cream, so that's what we're doing.

Then we need to walk over to the New Otani Hotel and see their Japanese rooftop garden. It's a miniature version of the one in Tokyo, and you can see the trees from the street below. We can go the long way around. There's a load of sculptures and museums to look at on the way over.'

'You're into art?'

'Not really. I mean, I don't know anything about art, but I like to look.'

'What's that?' He points to the Watchtower peaking over the top of a building.

'We can get closer to the sites once we've got the ice-cream.' I kiss him and tug him in the direction of the restaurant.

We stroll around the souvenir shops and I point out places I've eaten at with my dad. I tell him where there are the best fortune cookies or the nicest ramen noodles. I swear he looks like he's cataloguing everything I'm telling him.

'I have to ask.'

He twists to look at me, as we continue walking the street. 'Sounds ominous.'

'Do you ever think Audrey has screwed with your life? Like if she hadn't shown up yesterday, would we even be out on this date today?'

'Yes and no.'

'Wow, that's honest.'

He nudges me and turns back around.

'Honestly, I think the first time she appeared to Mike two years ago has influenced things. Mike and I even moving to the US was something she started.'

'So we shouldn't even be together then?' I gulp.

'I wouldn't say that. I mean, there are a million scenarios that might have brought me here. Audrey was just one of them. And I know for a fact, no matter where or when I met you, it would end with me scrambling to get your attention.' He puts his arm around my shoulder and nestles me into his side as we walk. 'I don't care what brought us together, or why. Just that it feels right, you know?'

Outside Weller Court shopping mall, he pulls me to a stop and leans back against a sculpture.

'I want to be with you, and I want to be all in. Not just dating and roommates. I want what Audrey told me. And I've wanted it for a while. You're the one I want to be with, no bullshit, no games. I want a relationship, and for us that means involving your son and also your mother. Hell, even Mike is so involved in both our lives.' He laughs. 'I want to be a part of your life. So, if that means we have family movie night instead of trips to the theatre, that's what I want. If dinner out is Chucky Cheese instead of a candle lit romantic meal for two'—he smiles and leans in for a kiss—'baby, I don't care, as long as we get to do it together.'

'Are you serious?' I take a brave step forward, into his space, and push against him. ''Cause I kind of need that. I need the steady relationship. I need to know you won't split at the first fight. If we're going to do this, date and live together and involve Max, then I need to know it's for real.'

'It is for real.' He slides his hand over my throat and around the back of my neck.

'Okay.'

'What does that mean?'

'Let's tell everyone. Let's move in together and let's make those careers Audrey said we have.'

He chuckles. 'We already live together. You want me to pack up my shit and move into your bed?'

'Yes.'

'Fuck,' he breathes into me. 'I was hoping you'd say that.'

'This is moving fast, David.'

'We've been friends a long time. Not many couples get a time travelling buddy to show up and tell them they're doing it right.'

I swallow hard, stand straight, and pull him back on the path to the hotel. When we're far enough back, I chuckle. 'Do you know what the sculpture is?' I point to the place we were leaning.

He throws an arm over my shoulder. 'Something nautical? It's like two big ropes tied together.' He tilts his head. 'No, not tied. Wrapped around each other.'

'It's a friendship knot. See how the two pieces wrap around each other before heading back in their original direction?'

'Yeah.'

'My dad always told me it was like life. Those people who were truly your friends would always be intertwined with your life. That no matter what, they'd be there for you. Wrapped around you, holding on and taking care of each other, so that no matter what direction you went in, they were supporting you and moving along with their own lives next to yours.'

'That's nice. You know, it's sort of like Audrey and her travels. I always thought of it like the infinity loop. Never ending and always coming back on itself. I never thought it is certain people in our lives who hold the key to the *never ending* part.' He's biting his lip.

'What?'

181

'You know, we basically sealed our fate, in this weird time travel influenced loop, under the statue of an infinite friendship symbol.'

I chuckle and wrap my arm around his waist. 'Yes, we did.'

CHAPTER
Twenty-Two

'Where do we start?' I ask Mike, leaning over his shoulder to look at his notes on the couch.

'I don't know how any of this works.' Mike turns back to the book Audrey left for him.

'That's why Audrey sent you to me, remember? I'm a hot piece of agent ass in the future.' I smirk and sit next to him. 'Tell me everything about her—when she came to you and what's happening, what you've found out about her.'

Mike pinches the bridge of his nose. 'Two years ago, she appeared out of the light and then disappeared again. I was working at a video rental shop, and I took David back to look at the store security cameras. It wasn't until he saw the footage that he believed me. We spent the next year trying to get her to come back to us and researching ghosts and paranormal activity.'

'She's dead?' Maybe DD's dead too. My heart constricts for a second, followed by intense thudding when it tries to make up for the lost beat.

'No. She's real and alive, but at first we thought she might be.'

'So people can travel back from the future and still be okay? They're not in danger?'

'I hope so,' he breathes. 'David is working on the physics of it. She's come to me three times now, always around my birthday. She's told us much about our futures and that you were my agent. We do it, you know.' His smile reaches all the way to his eyes, causing them to twinkle. 'We make the Hollywood A-list and finally get our families in a place they don't have to worry about the price of milk.' He squeezes my hand.

God, Mike needs this to work out as much as I do. His family are struggling too, I can't forget that. DD is safe. David is going to be safe when he travels. And if Audrey has come back multiple times, and David is working on how to control it, maybe in the future, DD knows exactly what he's doing. We can finally put the worry of bills and school fees behind us. We just need to do what Audrey tells us. And what DD told me.

'Audrey said we write the adaptation for this book. First of all, we need to buy the film rights from the author, then get a copy of the manuscript and condense it into one hundred and twenty pages. Both of us can start by reading it and exchanging notes on the scenes we want to keep and why they're important. We'll switch copies and read it again with each other's notes in the margins.'

'I'm going to buy you guys some office furniture tomorrow. We can set up a desk and chair in Mike's room now that I'm moving out,' David says, carrying a pile of clothes from his room to mine. Ours.

'That's a good idea. I'll make you a list of things we need,' I call.

'I've got to say, you're handling this well,' Mike says. 'When we first met Audrey, she scared the shit out of us, until we really got to know her the second year.'

'She helped me. You guys helped me. And she told us things are going to get better. Sometimes you just need the confidence to keep going.'

'So we write the screenplay?'

'I need you to get a head start on this. You know the basics of script layout, since you've read so many of them. My dad left some screenwriting books in Cici's garage. I'm going to collect them later, but the best part is the inside knowledge you have.'

'I don't have any inside knowledge.'

'It's your passion for this book, Mike. That's why it's going to work.' I hold up the novel *Break the Piece* that he used during his original audition with me. 'The story and the character meant so much to you. We're going to take those feelings you had and amplify them on screen. We need to make some cinematography and budget schedules—'

'And a girl. Audrey says we need to add a love interest.'

'And add a girl. I'm going to make an offer to the author tomorrow to option the rights. I'll check the sales rank and see what we'll have to offer her. Then we can budget it and pitch it to the studios.'

'Audrey said Sunshine Studios.'

'In order to get Sunshine Studios interested, we need to get other studios interested too.'

'Okay.'

'Start writing. I can help you in a few days. Let's set a deadline for the end of the month and work our butts off day and night. We already know we did it, right?'

'Almost done,' David chirps, crossing the hallway back to his room. We've been home for three hours, and he's almost finished switching furniture and moving his clothes. 'It's getting tight in there. I'll need to leave some stuff in Mike's room.'

'No problem.' Mike watches David until he's inside our bedroom. 'Is this all happening a little fast, Stella?'

I smile at his concern. 'Don't worry about me, Mike, I've had David wrapped around my finger for a while now.' I wink.

He arches his brow.

I stand at the back of the couch and wait for David to pass through the room again. When he sees me, he opens his arms to me.

'There's no reason to wait around anymore,' David says. 'Mike's guardian angel told us it's going to happen.'

I freeze and David squeezes my side at my reaction.

'If Audrey said we get married in the future, does that mean that's the way it's always been?'

'From what we've seen, the big things in life always work out the same. There's no changing those.'

If that's true, then I was always his wife in the future, just like Liam suggested. Maybe that's why DD came to me, to help change *his* destiny as well. Maybe avoiding pregnancy isn't the answer. Maybe stopping myself from making such a catastrophic decision was all I needed? But how can I stop something I could never fathom myself doing?

'He's home.' David nudges me when Pamela and Max come through the front door.

The panic about my future is put on hold while I rush around the couch and scoop Max into a bear hug. I smile at Pamela. 'Thanks for collecting him. We got through a lot this afternoon.'

'Mommy, put me down.' He squirms when I try to give him a hundred kisses on his cheeks.

'Hey, David and I wanted to talk to you,' I say.

Mike gets up from the couch, but I put my hand on his arm to keep him in place. 'You know how we all live here, like a family and best friends,' I tell Max as we sink into the seat. David remains standing while Pamela perches on the arm of the chair opposite us. 'Well, David and I are going to be dating.'

'What does that mean?'

'Like boyfriend and girlfriend,' I tell him.

'Ew, are you going to kiss?' he asks.

I laugh. 'Yes, we are going to kiss and go out on dates, and David is going to move into my room.'

'We should probably move Max's bed into my room for a while,' Mom adds.

'Why?' Max asks.

David sucks in a breath and shifts his weight from one foot to the next.

It's Pamela who answers. 'Don't worry, you're still going to get to do all the things you do with your mom now. It means that David might be there a little more than he is now.'

'Like how he always comes to the park with us?'

'If that's okay?' David asks.

'Suppose so,' Max says. 'You push the swings way faster than Mommy does.' He jumps from the seat. 'Can I go now?'

I nod, and he takes off to our room, where I hear the crash of his toy box before he drags it through the hall and into Pamela's room, spilling toys as he goes.

'Congratulations,' Mike says to Pamela. 'Your new roommate's a slob.'

David is noticeably tense.

'He's a great kid,' Mike says, slapping David on the arm 'We've been living here long enough that he won't notice much of a difference.'

'Who wants homemade burgers and fries?' Mom asks us.

A collective response of yes's from all of us has her beaming as she enters the kitchen.

'As long as you're making that relish thing,' Mike shouts.

David crosses the room, wraps me in his arms, and pulls me down to the couch. 'Does this mean we can keep going on dates? The full works? Dinner, movie, snogging on the doorstep?'

'As long as I get to pick the movie. Your taste in films sucks.' I slap him on the leg when I stand. 'I'm going to play with Max. See if he has any questions. Mike, get started on what we discussed. David, can you see what office supplies you can bring home for us? And, Mom?'

Pamela turns from the stove. 'Yes?'

'Make coffee and find your reading glasses. It's going to be a long night.'

I leave the room to a chorus of 'Yes, boss' and a salute from David.

This is finally it.

'Shit,' Mom screams. 'Fire!'

I run back to the kitchen where David is pulling my mom backwards from the flames at the stove.

'Fuck!' I run to the cabinet and pull out the fire blanket. I have no idea what to do with this thing. David pulls it out of my hands and frees the blanket from the package in one swoop and throws it on top of the stove, killing the flames that were licking the ceiling.

Max is at my legs, clinging to me before I've even realised. Mike and Pamela are standing to my left.

Pamela stutters, 'I'm sorry. I only turned around for a second, and the oil must have got too hot.'

'It's okay.' David pulls the blanket off the stove and we all assess the burned pan. The black marks from the flames run the entire height of the wall, and when I tilt my head up, the damage can be seen stretching halfway across the ceiling.

'Doesn't look like there's structural damage. It's going to need cleaned and maintenance will have to inspect it. But we might be lucky and only need to pay for a paint job.'

'Just as well we have some spare cash, right?'

Pamela looks pale and dejected. It doesn't take a lot to make her sink low, and the guilt from this near miss will have her plummeting.

'Don't worry about it.' I squeeze her hand. 'It was my fault. I called you away.'

Mike steps up. 'But the relish is still good, right?'

When Cici is checking in a delivery, I phone Liam. 'He came to me again, a few days ago.'

There's rustling on his end, and I hear the click of his Dictaphone over the receiver. 'Tell me everything.'

Halfway through my story of what transpired, including the bombshell of a second time traveller, he cuts in. 'DD told you not to tell the younger version of himself about the time travel?'

'Yes. Like you said about not giving him too much information, he mentioned that his focus needs to be on Audrey.'

'Good. It means we're all on the same page. You met Audrey? Do you think you'd recognise her if you saw her again?'

'Like a time travelling line up?' I quip. 'Of course I'd recognise her.'

'Three of us, travelling through time, one to the future, some to the past, but all knotted together somewhere along the line. This is good. Thank you for bringing it to me.'

'At least your work might benefit from it, even if I can't tell David directly. But, Liam, I need something in return.'

'What do you mean?'

'If this is one big loop of things always turning out the same way, there's going to be information in that letter DD left behind, that might have to do with David and my relationship. Things I need to know.'

'Stella—'

'You want me to bring you more information?' My tone hardens. 'Then get me that damn letter.'

'I'll try my best, but I need something from you first. Come in and watch a video for me. Tell me what you see. But, Stella—'

'I know, I know. Top secret.'

Three weeks later

Sitting in the waiting room of Sunshine Studios, I'm poised and Mike bounces his leg off the glass coffee table, nearly knocking over the two-hundred-dollar fresh flower centrepiece.

'Stop it.' I slide the vase back into place.

'How can you be so calm?'

'I'm not calm,' I tell him. 'I'm *acting* like I'm calm. You should try it sometime.'

'Ha bloody ha.'

'Seriously, Mike. I'm twitching, but we've got to get in there and own that room. We're offering them a budget that will be hard for them to reject. We're going to make them see dollar signs and box-office records. If we walk in there and they sense fear or our hunger, they'll screw us over.'

I place my hands over his. He stops bouncing his leg. 'Right from this moment, I want you to play a part.'

'What part?'

'That of a successful writer, director, and producer you're going to be one day.'

He screws up his mouth. He doesn't want to object, but he's letting me know he doesn't think he has it in him.

'You're a good actor, Mike. This is another performance. We walk in there and sell what we have. It works. Audrey already told us this will work. We only need to secure enough funding that the movie won't be under-budgeted, but we can still be involved with production. And still have enough cash flow leftover to live on while it's being made.'

I send myself a text message reminder to keep Mike working on some short contracts while this screenplay is tied up in legal. My eyes twitch when I try to focus on the tiny screen.

'You look tired.'

'I'm okay, but I need to wrap this up. I want to be home to make dinner for Max tonight. We can pick work back up when he's asleep.'

'And the boutique, are you going to give that up soon?'

I put my phone away and look at him. 'Once some cash is coming in, yes. Until then, I can't.'

'David told me you're not sleeping.'

'Of course I'm sleeping. I'm exhausted. I fall asleep as soon as I'm in bed.'

'But you get up in the middle of the night to write yourself notes, and at five-thirty every morning to get paperwork done before you go to the boutique. We have a small cash flow to survive on right now, Stella. You can give something up and make your life easier. That's what we're trying to do here.'

Panic crawls through my lungs, and I know it's the fatigue that has a hold of my emotions. 'I can't.' I choke.

He takes my hand in his. 'We're a team. We'll support each other until we're all where we need to be.'

'I have to be the one who provides for Max. I need a job I know is going to pay at the end of the week.' I swallow a lump in my throat. 'I just need to know he'll always have a home and food on the table. If this doesn't work out, you guys can pack your bags and go back home. Let me have this piece of assurance to keep me sane, okay?'

'Okay, but, Stella, the first pay check we get is all yours.'

'You don't need to do that, Mike.'

He shakes his head. 'You've worked too long on this for free, and there were months I never had enough to chip in for my share of the bills, and neither you nor David brought it up. You're right. I can trot home with my tail between my legs if this doesn't work out. So let me do this. You've earned it.'

'You've earned it too. Don't you want to send some of that money to your family in England?'

Mike pinches the bridge of his nose. 'David told you my parents were filing for bankruptcy?'

I nod. 'It came up. I knew things were bad, but you never mentioned how far things had progressed. You need this money as much as I do.'

He pats my hand. 'We'll figure it out.'

'How about we both take the cut we're supposed to?' I take a deep breath and get my head back to where it needs to be. 'Let's get in here and kill this.'

'We've got it.' He winks.

CHAPTER
Twenty-Three

David's lab number appears on my phone screen. 'Hello, sexy baby,' I answer.

'Ehem.' He clears his throat. 'I'm not really the baby type of man, but I'll roll with it if you want,' Liam replies.

I cringe. 'Sorry. Thought you were David.'

'You break my heart so easily, Stella.'

I smile at his playfulness. 'What can I do for you?'

'I need you to help me speak to my dad.'

My throat dries. 'Why?'

'He's being stubborn about the damn letter. I explained about your experiences, but he starting shouting. He never shouts. Normally, I'd agree we shouldn't read it. Hell, I've been agreeing with him for years, but his reaction's made me realise something.'

'What?'

He lets out a breath, like he's calming himself before he speaks.

'Spit it out, Liam.'

'I think he's already read it.'

My heart beats faster. I stand and pace, using up the adrenaline that's cursing through me. 'What the hell does that mean?'

'Once I mentioned your name, he got defensive. I think he knows some things about you and David from that letter. Whatever David wrote, it was important enough to send Ethan Bennett into a rage.'

Ethan's not what I expect. I saw a picture of him inside the book he wrote years ago with Liam, but that was a stereotype image you would expect of a physics professor. The suit and tie, the glasses, and the serious look of intelligence you associate with someone in the job. Here in his office, surrounded by day old coffee cups and an overflowing trash can, he looks like he's on the brink of being the washed up, possibly unhinged professor, rather than the well-respected UCLA scientist.

'Excuse the mess,' Ethan says as I eye the place. 'Been kind of busy making sure the universe doesn't fall down around us.'

I nod. 'So I heard.'

'What else you hear?' he all but snarls.

'Dad, Stella is here to help us. Be nice.' Liam clears a stack of papers from the chair in front of the desk and motions for me to sit.

'She's here about the damn letter.' Ethan tilts his chair back.

'The one you already read,' I add.

His mouth drops open, and his desk chair snaps forward. 'How the hell did you know that?'

'Jesus, Dad. When?'

195

Ethan growls under his breath. 'A couple of years after we got it.'

Liam plants a hip on the edge of the desk. 'When you decided it should go into a security vault?'

'I didn't want you making the same mistake I did.'

'Which was?' I ask.

'Having too much information. Sometimes you can know the wrong things.'

'Or the wrong people can know too much about their lives,' I say.

'She catches on quick.' Ethan raises his eyebrow at Liam.

Liam clears his throat. 'I need you to watch a video.'

'Now?' My voice is high-pitched. 'What the hell is so important about it?'

'You'll understand when you see it.' Liam wheels over a TV and VCR unit while Ethan opens a vault safe and pulls out a video.

I squirm in my seat. Nothing good can be on a tape stored in a safe.

Liam loads the tape into the slot and the wind up of the machine fills the silence around us.

'If you don't know what this is,' Ethan growls, 'you still need to keep your mouth shut.'

I raise my eyebrows. 'If it's that important, why the hell are you showing it to me?'

Liam sits on the edge of the desk again. 'We need you to identify the people in the tape. We got it last year and have guessed at who it might be. You're the first person we feel comfortable asking.' He gives his father a warning look.

'Suppose she's the least risky person to confirm it.' Ethan adjusts his glasses.

'Gee, thanks.'

Liam hits play, and the screen is filled with black and white footage that looks to be from a store security camera. The store has display shelves of VHS tapes on both sides, and waist-high stands in the centre aisles. A video rental store, maybe. The angle of the footage is from a height, encasing the entire shop in the one shot. Near the top of the screen is a young couple, the only people in the store. The girl's back is to the camera, but the guy talking to her can be seen clearly. I lean forward and speak before I mean to. 'That's Mike.'

Ethan rubs his forehead. 'Yes, we've met Mike through David a few times. But who's the girl?'

I move closer to the screen, and Liam hits pause. There's a slight distortion to the tape as the pause pulls on screen.

'The footage only lasts a minute,' Liam tells me.

'How much can you really tell from the back of a person's head?' I scoff.

The picture's black and white, like the security feed, and her hair could be red if the picture was in colour. I grit my teeth, reluctant to answer in case I'm wrong. 'She's wearing the same clothes, but I'm not sure.'

'Wearing the same clothes as whom?' Liam asks.

'She said her name was Audrey. She was wearing a cardigan with white trim, the same cut as that.' I trail my fingers across the screen. 'Black Capri pants, ballet pumps. Her hair is the right length.' I turn to face them. 'Is this all you have?'

'No,' Ethan tells me. 'You might as well show her, Liam.'

Liam removes the tape and places it back in the safe. He opens a folder and hands me an A4 still of the woman, taken from the footage.

'Jesus.' I take the picture of Audrey's face from him. It's blurred and looks enhanced somehow, but it's definitely her. 'Where did you get this?'

'From the security tape. There's a reflection in the store window. We were able to zoom in, and reversed the angle on the footage. From there we could see her speak.'

'What did she say?'

'"Michael",' Ethan answers from his chair.

'What?'

'That's what she said, but whoever cut the tape did a shitty job and left a quarter of a second of glowing white light.'

'You have her disappearing on tape?'

'Not enough to be conclusive, but David does.' Liam takes a step forward. 'David sent me the tape last year, with a ridiculous story about why he needed to see what the girl was saying. Is it her?'

I stare at the photo and nod. It's one hundred percent Audrey. 'Based on what she seems to know about time travel, it looks like you guys go on to feed her all sorts of information.'

Liam nods. 'Just in time for her to travel back here and fill us in on all the progress we're going to make in the next ten or so years. The world of time travel is expanding. She's someone new.'

'What do you mean new?'

'She wasn't at the dinner party I witnessed when I travelled to the future. Audrey's a new player.'

'Is that what David put in his letter? Information about Audrey? Or about the progress he's going to make on his research?' I ask.

'Audrey and David's experiences are different,' Ethan tells me. 'Even though they left at the same time, the David from the future—'

'DD. That's what I called him, when I met him. It's easier to keep them straight in your head.'

'Why DD?' Liam squints.

'No reason.' Heat travels to my cheeks. 'We spent some time giving each other nicknames. Labour takes a while. We got bored, is all.'

'Very well.' Ethan clears his throat. 'DD's travelling hasn't been chronological like Audrey's. He went backwards, so each time he gained more information about what was happening and why, he arrived at a time earlier in our timeline. He didn't have anyone to discuss things with. That must have led to him having to make some decisions while he travelled. Some mistakes even. Mistakes that I now have to harbour.'

'You don't have to harbour anything, Dad. We can help with this. We can bring David in on it, give him the information he needs without giving away many details.'

'No, it's too soon. The letter was specific on what was to be done, and the date on which we should open it. Which means he knows full well that interference at an earlier stage will have negative effects on the order of things.'

'What order?' I ask.

Ethan stands and puts his hands in his pockets. 'All you need to know is that man loves you more than anything. Just go live your life. Don't ask DD anything when he returns and visits you again. It could fuck up everything. I'll see you in seventeen years.'

'Seventeen years?' I stand and meet him as close to eye level as my height will allow. 'We're supposed to open the damn letter when we're forty? We have more than enough time to make changes if it's that bad.'

Ethan chuckles. 'Time is the goddamn problem here.'

'You could be dead in seventeen years. How the hell are we going to get the letter then?' I spit. It's harsh, and the bitch side of me hasn't surfaced in a while, but it's the truth.

'I'm glad to see you're not taking chances with your life.'

'Chances?' I ask.

Liam runs his hands over his face. 'Just because we've met someone from the future who knows us there doesn't mean we are guaranteed to survive 'till that time. You can get too cocky,' Liam says. 'You meet a time traveller who knows you in the future and realise you're still alive in 2016, so you think nothing can get you. You might start taking risks you normally wouldn't because you think you'll survive everything. But you still need to look after yourself.'

'So no sky diving just because you think you can't die,' Ethan adds.

'So we can change the future?' I ask.

'In theory, everything can be changed, but so far the big stuff seems to be happening the way it always did,' Liam tells me.

'But don't go betting your life on it. It's still just a theory.' Ethan winks. It's a condescending dismissal and an end to the conversation.

'You're forgetting, my time traveller told me I died many times. I'm doing everything in my power to make changes to the future. And if I survive that long, I'm going to make sure I get my happy ever after.' I storm out of the office, not caring if David can hear me slam Ethan's office door from his lab, and march to the elevator.

Liam chases at my heel. 'I'm sorry. I thought with the two of us, he might give us more information.'

'He did. He just didn't realise it.'

Liam explores my face. 'What did he say?'

'DD's coming back, a version of him who still doesn't know the whole story.'

'That doesn't give us much to work with.'

'It means whatever happened to DD to make him write that letter has already happened in my life—in this time line. DD is moving backwards, so we need to go through everything that has happened, each and every time DD has already shown up to help me, and see if we've missed something. It's not happened for him yet. We might be able to change the past for him.'

'He appeared each time your life was in danger. You think he helped you so much that maybe something bad happened to him while he was in your past?'

'I don't know. But that's not all we have to worry about.'

Liam sucks in a breath. 'He's coming back.'

I nod. 'DD said Nathan left for good. But since DD's coming back, it means something else got me. I'm not out of the woods yet.'

New Otani Hotel, Little Tokyo,
Los Angeles, California

Lying in the hotel bed, in the middle of the day, David runs his hand over my lower belly.

'I can't believe you brought me here,' I tell him.

'I know how much you love this place, and I wanted to do something special to celebrate your first big career break.'

'Thank you.'

He kisses the tip of my nose. 'And somewhere special to propose.' He grins.

'You're crazy.' I bring my hand out in front of me to admire the ring he gave me last night.

He pauses his lazy strokes across my stomach. 'You want more kids, right?'

Panic seizes me more than I was expecting. 'Where did that come from?'

'Technically we're still young, but you already have Max. Did you want to start trying for a baby?' David asks. He's been petting and stroking me for a while and always brings his hand back to play with the ring on my finger. 'You're totally in love with me.'

I try to protest, but he bites his lip, holding back a grin. 'And I'm totally in love with you.'

Hearing it never gets old when it's from the mouth of someone so incredible and sincere. He really does love me, and not in a crazy way. In a healthy, forever, part of the same team, way.

'I just don't want to rush anything that wouldn't normally have happened.'

'It would have happened,' he interrupts me.

I smile. 'It would have eventually, down the line, but not now.'

'You know what? You're right. There's no way I would have proposed to you right now if Audrey hadn't told us we get married. You know why?'

My heart thuds in disappointment, and I try to keep my smile in place. He takes my hand and brings it to his mouth to kiss my knuckles, then down to my new ring. 'I would have been terrified you would have said no. Hell, that you might

202

have even laughed in my face. But I would have wanted to ask you. When you've met the one, Stella, you just know. The only reason I stayed away from you in the beginning was because I wanted you to get to know me and trust me. And I could see how important this job was going to be for you and your son. I didn't want to be the jerk who kept asking you out on dates and interfered with your career for your family. And once we started dating, well.' He smirks. 'You were there. We're great together. All Audrey has done is given me the confidence that you'd say yes.

'I'll take care of you, and I promise to try my bloody hardest to be the best husband and father there is. I'm going to love and treasure you and Max until the day I die.'

I nudge my legs between his and kiss him slow and deep. When I stop, I keep hold of his face. He's smiling. The best guy I've met in my whole life has been smiling the entire time I've been kissing him. I lay my left hand flat on his chest and admire my ring.

His face falls. 'We can get a better ring when we have more money.'

'David.' My tone commands his attention and he meets my eyes. 'It's perfect. I love it.'

'It's not what a girl who grew up in Hollywood should have. It should be platinum, not white gold. And the diamond should be bigger, flawless.'

I harrumph. 'I care more about being in the right relationship rather than having the right ring.'

He smiles. 'We're going to be okay.'

'We are,' I tell him. 'We have other priorities to spend money on. I'd much rather we put Max and a house on the list of goals, than a bigger diamond.'

He runs his hand over my back. 'And don't forget more babies.' He pulls me fully into his embrace and squeezes my side, tickling me as he lets us fall to the ground. 'We are totally having a house full of babies.' He twists me round so I fall on top of him.

'You've really got this whole paternal thing in your head, haven't you?'

'It'll be nice to keep the age gap close for Max. He's four now, and in nine months, he'll be nearly five, assuming we get pregnant right away.'

I swallow hard.

David throws his body on top of mine. 'Let's get practicing, right now.'

I giggle as his mouth tickles kisses along the column of my throat. At least I can keep up birth control until I figure this out.

CHAPTER
Twenty-Four

Sunday, February 28, 1999

'Why is Mike working on a Sunday?' David asks me from the doorway.

I keep typing. 'We're behind. We had to bring in a B-unit for the day, finish up this scene, otherwise the whole next week will be off schedule and we can't afford it. Over budget and late on the first movie is a death sentence.'

'Need any help?' He saunters into Mike's bedroom that doubles as our office, perches on the desk, and nudges my legs open with his feet.

'I don't think that counts as help.'

'No, but Max and Pamela are out, and I'm not going to lie. I thought sharing a bed with my fiancée would result in way more booty time than we're managing.'

'You never thought your fiancée would have a kid who sometimes shares a room with you, is what you mean.'

He narrows his eyes. 'I didn't mean that in a bad way.' He takes his hands out of his pockets and rests them on the edge of the desk. 'What's wrong with you?'

I lean back and blow out a sigh. 'Nothing, just tired. And stressed.'

'I happen to have some inside information—future knowledge, if you will—that this is all going to work out okay.'

I smile. 'Yes, but we still have to work and complete the things you and Audrey have told us we do. We can't get cocky. So don't bet your life on it.' I swallow.

'Me and Audrey?'

Shit.

'Don't tell me you're not involved in this somehow.' I grin, trying to recover. 'There's no way you aren't out there in the future, not filling Audrey's head with details to pass on to us. You and your damn butterfly effect and all.'

David's phone buzzes, and I swing back to the computer to check the daily schedule.

'What do you mean, he fell?' he asks.

My heart flutters, taking a slight reprieve that if it was Max injured it would have been my phone that rang.

David holds his hand up, indicating for me to wait. 'I'll be right over.' He hangs up.

'Mike fell off a ledge at work. He landed on his head. He was unconscious so an ambulance is taking him to the ER.'

'Wait.' I scroll back over the daily log for *Break the Piece*. 'He fell off the ledge?'

'They said it was pretty bad. Why?'

I point to the computer. 'He was scheduled to do a low-key stunt today. He was supposed to be harnessed, so it should've been okay, but it was an eight-foot drop. If he landed on his head from that height, it's bad.' My voice wavers.

'They told me to bring him an overnight bag.' He opens Mike's dresser and tosses some things into a small backpack.

The apartment bell rings, and the last person I expect to see standing there is Liam. He looks dishevelled. His hair is loose and his stubble grows longer each time I see him.

'David's not here,' I tell him.

'I know. He called me on the way to the hospital and filled me in. Wanted me to document it. But I also need to document everything on David's life too.'

'Document it?'

'We're taking notes on Mike's life, especially the things Audrey never told him. Either she knew and kept it from him, or—'

'Or things are changing?' I close the door as Liam crosses the threshold and takes off his coat.

'We're not sure yet. I've been trying to make changes for a long time now and nothing seems to stick. Maybe Audrey didn't know, or she left it out on purpose.'

I chuckle. 'You think Audrey really wants Mike dead?'

He raises an eyebrow. 'Now wouldn't that be a Hollywood plot twist?'

'What can I do you for?'

'I wanted to update you. I figured David wouldn't give you the specifics of what we're working on.'

I smile. 'He's not withholding anything from me. As far as he's concerned, I'm not involved in this. Actually, *I* don't think I'm involved.'

'Of course you are. We've been working on the timing of Audrey coming and going. We have a database, and it looks like she shows up each year on Mike's birthday.' He lays out a photocopy of a spreadsheet. A few days surrounding February twenty-nine each year are marked.

'What's this?' I ask. 'Audrey travelled all the way back to 1992?'

'No, I did. We were on vacation in England that year.'

'On Mike's birthday?'

'Apparently.'

'David said that Audrey was in a car crash in the future, on Mike's birthday. It was the day she started to travel. It's the last thing she remembers. Did the crash bring her here?'

'Amongst other things. It's important, though.' He points towards the year 2016. 'It looks like David might have been in the same crash, and I think that's when he started travelling too.'

'So how do we stop it?'

'I don't think we do. We need to let this play out. We need to wait until 2016 and make sure Audrey and David are in that car.'

'Your dad said we can open the letter before that.'

'It's labelled towards the end of 2015, a couple of months before the crash.'

'DD's giving us a head start to figure things out.'

Liam shoves his hands in his pockets. 'But not enough of a head start to influence any changes. It's like he wants us to know things, but only enough to participate and not change his course.'

I look at the spreadsheet. 'The crash is on the twenty-ninth of February?'

'Right on the expected time of Mike's birthday. Audrey arrives here to us, at Mike's birth time each year. So, in 2016 that will be a minute before eight a.m.'

My mouth dries. 'Surely a car crash that sends people though time is bad enough to kill you?'

'I'm going to see if I can part-time study in nursing. I can enrol in EMT courses over the summer to keep the knowledge refreshed over the years.'

'Why?'

'Because, I'm going to be there.'

'In the crash?'

'In 2016, I'm going to make sure I'm right next to them. I can help them as much as I can if we need it, but also . . .'

My shoulders relax. 'You want to travel by proxy?' It's a realisation, rather than a question.

'I think that's how it worked the last time, being so close.'

'So why haven't I travelled? I've always been next to DD when he left. And Mike? He's been with Audrey when she travels. Why have you been the only one to get sucked along with them?'

'I don't know. But what I do know is David knew they were in the wrong place. He practically made Mike make a wish on his birthday cake, and when he blew out the candles, everything went back to normal for me. Like it reset. It must have been his birth time. In a different time zone it was late afternoon.'

'It was his birthday,' I correct.

He shakes his head. 'No, everyone has an exact anniversary time of birth, and it changes slightly each year due to the hours in the day and what time zone you are in. Especially for Mike since he was born February twenty-nine, a leap year. Somehow everything aligning at the same time made it possible.'

He looks hesitant, like he's holding back what's on his mind.

'What?' I prompt.

'I think I have to save the Cute Punk Girl. There was another guy at the dinner table with Mike and David. I told you how the girl looked at him, with adoration and what I now realise was a bit of lust.' He chuckles. 'He was new to the group because I saw them introduce themselves when he sat down. He looked so cool and collected, I wanted to be him. I started to grow my hair out, and then when I was fifteen, I got some tattoos. Before I knew it, the sleeves were done, the workouts in the gym helped me grow into something—'

'Similar to him? You covered yourself in tattoos, she must have been some kinda cute.'

He looks me in the eye. 'The tattoos became addictive when I was a teenager. But the older I get . . . '

'Oh, god, it was you? You were the guy in David's and Mike's future?'

'The five of us sat at the dinner table, and we didn't belong there. It was like we were all in a different reality. You were dead and Audrey wasn't there.'

'You saw your future?'

'I saw a version of my future. And the man I was then, he wasn't comfortable there. He knew it had to change. But when the light came and took them, he saw that Cute Punk Girl was going somewhere else. He panicked. He was losing her. He looked at her like he was losing the love of his life, and even when I was a kid I wanted to help her. I wanted to save her.'

'From what?'

'I think. . . in the middle of them leaving, or skipping different realities, she was getting lost, or left behind or maybe even dead. I need to go back there and warn her, make sure she doesn't get lost.'

'Who was she?' I whisper.

'I don't remember.'

CHAPTER
Twenty-Five

'**How do you do** it? Watch the woman you love disappear all the time?'

'I don't love Audrey.' Mike's voice has no conviction. 'She's a friend.'

'You just believe her when she said you were friends in the future? You didn't question if she was here for something bad?'

'Why would she lie? She's scared being here, and we're trying to help her get home. She says David knows what he's doing. So while David is trying to figure this out, I make sure she's okay while she's here.'

'Is that how it started?'

He drops his gaze and turns away from me. The purple shade of bruising seeps out from the edges of the gauze on his forehead. 'You wouldn't understand. It was like I always just knew her. From the first time I met her.'

'You never even realised there was a piece of your soul missing, until she was standing in front of you and you felt that empty ache inside your chest where she should be? Like somehow, somewhere, maybe back in the beginning of creation, you guys were part of the same person, and along the way, you were separated into two?'

Mike's voice croaks. 'Yes. But she's married to someone else. And she's trying to get back to him. Every time she leaves, she's not thinking about showing up in my life next year. She's hoping she'll make it back home. Imagine meeting the one you're supposed to be with, in the most absurd circumstances, and knowing that in the future, they aren't going to choose you.'

I slide my hand into Mike's and squeeze it tight, my heart aching for myself as well as him. 'I understand.'

'About having a time traveller as a friend?'

'About falling in love with people who should be with someone else.' I lay my head down on Mike's shoulder. I can never stop wondering about the chicken and egg scenario. Were David and I fated to be together or was it always this time travel loop that threw us together? Did my desires for him and the want to save him from someone else actually keep me in the picture and keep us both on the same doomed path?

'You guys are perfect for each other.'

I nod. 'But Audrey's influences have already put us together. I'm scared I'm derailing David from where he should be. What if you were both supposed to stay in England? Or be with other people. Time travelling has already changed so much. What if he was meant for someone else?'

'There's no one out there better for David than you,' he tells me.

I shrug. 'She doesn't have to be better if it's fate. Sometimes it can be worse, or maybe the same, but different anyway. Sometimes it's the circumstances that you need to experience to make you into the person you need to be. What if I was trying to stop him from having a doomed relationship, but ended up being the cause of it?' I sit up straighter. 'When Audrey spoke of our marriage, he looked happy, like it was something he'd be happy about. And for the life of me, I don't want to tell him, that maybe it's a butterfly effect and we should've never been together at all.'

Mike throws his feet onto the coffee table with a thud. 'If I had the chance to marry Audrey first, I'd probably take it. David's happy. There's no point in worrying about things that might have been when we can't change it.'

'What if I fuck his life up even more?'

'One thing I have to believe is—if this thing with you and David was never meant to be, circumstances will come about to break you guys apart.' He pinches the bridge of his nose. 'But the whole world can't sit around and not date, or take a chance on love, in case they're worried they are screwing with fate. Sometimes you have to lose to make you realise how important it is to grab onto that perfect person when they come along.'

'Then why don't you grab onto Audrey when she comes back?'

'She's already married to her perfect match. I can see it in her eyes every bloody time she speaks about him. She's heartbroken that she's not with him. I don't think the universe wants me to sweep in and break her heart.'

'I'm in love with David, and for me—he's my soulmate. I'm just worried it wasn't the original design. Our experiences define us. What if we were both supposed to have shitty relationships to appreciate each other that little bit more?'

'Fuck, he appreciates you, Stella. Audrey says you guys get married. But, please, don't do this unless you can stay with him forever and stop doubting your relationship. If you guys get married to keep Max safe, there better be some love there too.'

'You're saying that David would enter into a sham marriage to keep me and my son safe? Is that the only reason he'd ever marry me?'

'Of course not.' Mike lets out a low whistle. 'You can't analyse this forever. You're going to have to take a chance. Right now, you guys are in a relationship that both of you want to lead to marriage, despite being a little premature due to the circumstances. But if it's not meant to be, fate will intervene.'

I take a deep breath. 'Do you suppose fate would do something quick and let me know right now, 'cause I'd really like to enjoy being married to David, and not worry about whether some mystery woman is going to show up in his life and he'll leave me.'

Mike chuckles. 'I think that's an issue for a lot of people. You're just going to have to trust him.'

David appears with Max through the front door and tosses Mike a paper bag. 'Got your prescription.'

'Thanks, man.' Mike winces trying to sit up. 'So, why didn't you mention you met Jessica last week?' he asks, peering into the paper bag.

I glance at David, who tenses ever so slightly as he takes Max's coat off. He recovers quickly and shrugs. 'Forgot, I guess. Only spoke to her for a few minutes, so not much to gossip about.' He sits down next to me and places a kiss on my lips. 'Did Mike tell you he has a date? Fucker fell from a window and got a date with a nurse.' He winks.

'I got a date with Jessica, my ex-girlfriend, who just happens to be a nurse.'

'You dated her in college?' I ask.

Max pulls his box of Lego from under the TV and scurries to the kitchen, tipping it onto the tiles.

'Yeah,' Mike says, swallowing back two painkillers. 'David used to date her roommate Amy for a while. Well, in fairness, he dated a lot of people's roommates.'

My heart tenses, and David looks at me.

Mike groans as he bends over and takes forever to stand up. 'I'm going to lie down.'

'Get some rest. We can't afford for you to have any time off,' I tell him. 'When this wraps next month, you're straight into the next two movies back to back.'

Mike salutes me on his way down the hallway, and I peer over the back of the couch to check Max is out of ear shot.

'So Jessica—the girl you imagined fucking—is back and dating Mike?'

David rubs his eyes with his thumbs. 'God, Stella. If I'd known there was ever a chance we would have bumped into her again, I wouldn't have told you that story.'

'How do you feel seeing her again?'

David glares. 'Nothing. She was someone I liked when I was in college and making my way around a whole load of girls.'

'No, you liked her more than the average girl.'

'I did. But I didn't love her.' He places his fingers under my chin and tilts my head up. 'You—I love. Please, don't let someone who isn't anything come between us.'

'You'd tell me if there were any feelings there, right?'

He nods.

'Please, tell me she's not going to come over here all the time?'

'She might. And she's a nice girl, Stella. But Mike is licking his wounds over Audrey. I don't think it ever got too serious with them anyway. He left her in England without a second thought when he moved here.'

'Why does Mike sound like the bad guy? Didn't think he had it in him.'

David scoffs. 'He's not a bad guy. Jessica was passing time with him too. Sometimes, two nice people in a relationship don't always work. Neither of them is mean enough to call it quits when it's overdue. This might go on for a while, but it will fizzle out eventually. Don't get hung up on this. We have a movie to wrap.'

'And don't forget the secrets of time travel to figure out.'

CHAPTER
Twenty-Six

Tuesday, October 31, 1999
Los Angeles Airport, California.

I pick Caitlyn up at the airport and I already love her quirkiness.

'Sorry I missed your wedding.' She tells me. 'The thoughts of being confined to the same aircraft as my parents while they bickered for eight hours was too much.'

'That's okay.' I smile. 'Although Mike was looking forward to you coming. He misses you.' I crank up the air conditioning. 'Aren't your feet hot?' Who flies to LA in denim shorts and Dr. Martin boots?

'Yeah, hence the shorts to cool my legs down.'

I can't help but stare at her legs and know that Mike is going to have a heart attack at his kid sister grown up into a twenty-year-old hottie about to be the centre of male attention.

'You know, Mike's turned into quite the business man.'

She smiles. 'Good for him.'

'I'm glad you came out here. You just graduated, right? Well, it will be nice to have some more family on board helping us. Living in the public eye is tough. The past year especially since Mike's career exploded. To have an assistant that you can trust, especially when you're working out of your home, is a big deal.'

'He always promised me he'd make it big one day and bring me out here with him. I thought that day would never come.' She sighs.

'You don't like England?'

'England is fine. It's a change in people I'm looking for.'

'Oh, any male person in particular?' I ask.

'Huh, I wish.' She digs in her purse and pulls out an arrangement of old cassette tapes and scribbles some notes on one of the blank inserts.

'You know, CDs really are the thing over here. I don't even have a player for you to listen to those.' I point to the car stereo.

'It's okay, I brought my Walkman.'

'So who are you running from if it's not a guy?'

'My parents' divorce,' she tells me while shoving the tapes back where they were.

'Mike never mentioned it.' I slow down to approach a set of lights.

'He doesn't know. That's why I'm here.'

I slam on the brakes and our seatbelts catch us both before we hit the dashboard.

'Jesus, do you even have a licence?' she asks.

'Mike doesn't know?'

'Why would he? He moved out years ago when he went to university. I was the one left listening to the arguments all day and night. Figured if I studied hard, I could enrol in university early. When I finally moved into halls of residents I was thrilled. But I guess graduating high school early actually screwed me, 'cause guess where I ended up? Right back home and in the middle of the dinner table snide comments and shouting matches. Actually, I think it might be a good thing that they're separating.'

I put the car into drive when the lights turn green. 'I'm glad you're here to tell Mike in person. I don't think he has any idea.'

She smiles. 'He told me when he was rich he'd pay me to clean all his rooms. We were younger, he meant it as an insult, but I still can't believe my big brother did it.'

'Well, don't be so thrilled for him. He hasn't told you how many rooms he has.' I grin.

When we pull into my driveway in Calabasas, Caitlyn's jaw drops.

'Is this Mike's house?'

'No, it's mine and David's. Mike is gone a lot of the time, so he hasn't bought a place to live yet. I was joking about how many rooms he has. You can still clean all my rooms if you want.' I laugh. 'You're going to be staying with us. My office is here, so you won't have to travel for work.'

'Thank god. I heard LA traffic is a nightmare. Plus I have transport issues right now.'

'Mike leaves his cars here when he's out of town. I'm sure he'll let you borrow one.'

'Cars, as in plural?'

'He only has two, hasn't gone too mad yet.'

When we walk into the foyer, I point to the left. 'You're in the guest suite down here. Unless you want a room in the pool house with my mother?'

She shakes her head. 'Here is fine. Thank you.'

'Living space and kitchen is down there too. Office, storage, and gym are to the right. Basement access is through the kitchen. All of Mike's stuff is down there. He has it organised, but now and again you might need to pull some things for him. Stay out of the attic. It's David's work space.'

'Got it.'

'I need you to start work tomorrow. We only moved in last month so there's a lot of office things to be unpacked and organised.'

'Will do. I appreciate you helping me out, especially if Mike is out of town a lot.'

I thread my arm through hers. 'Trust me. Once I put you to work, you're going to regret saying that.'

CHAPTER
Twenty-Seven

One year later
Friday, January 5, 2001

I run down the hallway to David's lab, excited about having someone to share this moment with this time around. I should be dreading it, but maybe it's been delayed enough. Right outside the door, Ethan calls my name from the office opposite.

I spin on my heels and face him. 'Yes?'

Ethan stands and makes his way through piles of papers that are stacked on the floor space, over to me. 'I've been looking out for you for a while.'

'I've been avoiding the place. I knew if I saw you again, it would probably make my blood boil.'

He tilts his head. 'It was not my intention to make you feel that way. But you see, information comes at a price.'

'And what price is that?' I ask tartly.

'Knowing what it will do to you when you try and protect everyone from the truth. When you try and allow things to play out the way DD asked me to. When you try and do the right thing, knowing that good people will probably get hurt anyway.'

I step forward. 'Who's going to get hurt?'

'People always get hurt when they're dealing with people they love.'

'I need to go.'

'I'm sorry for making your blood boil. Please believe me, when the time comes, I'm sure you'll understand.'

'Maybe not, if I'm sure that it's something you could have helped avoid.'

'You can't avoid the inevitable, Stella. Of that *I'm* sure.'

I turn on my heel and knock on David's door. The door's recently been upgraded with secure entry, and passes are limited. Waiting, I know Ethan is still standing behind me.

'As a friend of my son, I wanted to let you know that we'll be there for you. If you ever need anything, don't hesitate to come to us. When you're hurting, sometimes those who aren't as close to you can be the ones who offer the best advice.'

'And why would I do that?'

'Because you're going to do the things you always did. It's inevitable.'

Fear runs down my throat. He couldn't possibly know what I'm dealing with today. 'A little less vague, Ethan?'

He smiles tightly. 'Congratulations.'

'Yeah, yeah, you said that at the wedding,' I scoff.

He closes the door when we both hear the electronic beeps indicating the swipe of the pass card on the other end of David's door.

David greets me with his no bullshit, excited to see me grin, and I step into his open arms, my boiling blood temporarily forgotten as I place a kiss on his lips.

'Hi.' He opens his mouth to kiss me back.

'Hi.' I grab his bottom lip in between my teeth and tug on it as he pulls me into the lab. 'Are you alone?' I whisper.

He grins. 'Hell, yeah, I'm alone.' He grabs my ass and presses his hips into mine.

'My period's late.'

His face lights up again. 'You're on the pill.'

'I'm almost two weeks late. With Caitlyn talking about taking off to go travelling, I'm stressing over finding a replacement for Mike. As well as scheduling his new contracts and converting the basement for him to store all his shit in while he's constantly out of town, I thought it could be stress. Then I was sick over the holidays and that can screw up birth control.'

'Did you do a test?'

'No, I was waiting for you.' I pull the test kit out of the pharmacy bag and wave it in the air.

He snakes an arm around my waist, taking his time to trail his fingers over my skin. 'We haven't spoken about this in a while. You know I want kids. We're married. We're raising a child already. There's no need to freak out.'

I take a deep breath. 'I just don't want you disappointed if it's negative.'

'Let's go pee on a stick then.' He swats my ass on the way into the bathroom down the hall. As we walk through the office to the other door, I get a sense for the amount of work that's going on in here. Each time I get here, there are more notes, and more white boards on the walls. There's an extra desk next to Liam's. 'You getting another assistant?'

David scoffs. 'No. Liam has decided to pick up his medical training again.'

'Again?'

'Yeah, he did some pre-med courses before I met him and now he's in the middle of refreshing his EMT.'

'So the desk?'

'His medical notes. I swear the man is like a machine. He switches from one subject to another so easily. As long as he has a separate work space for studying, he said it won't affect his work in the lab. Even thinks the fresh approach might help us out.'

So he's really going through with the idea of being in that crash, for Audrey and for David.

'He even bought a separate laptop.'

I nod, not really listening. All I can focus on is the fact that Liam is preparing for the inevitable. If Liam and Ethan are so sure about what's going to happen in the future, could they possibly know about *my* future? Did DD mention it in the letter Ethan read?

David opens the bathroom door and leads me in with him. I crouch down on the toilet and he unwraps the stick for me.

'You want to hold it as well?' I mock.

'Sure, if you want me to.' He grins.

I swipe the stick from his hand.

'Are you excited?' he asks.

I can't help but smile. His enthusiasm is infectious. 'Yes.'

David stands in front of me, reading the instructions as I place the cap on top of the stick.

'We need to wait at least two minutes,' he tells me.

'No, we don't.' I stare at the blue lines.

'What?'

'I'm pregnant.' I show him the test and vomit rises at the back of my throat.

He grabs the stick out of my hand, staring at the lines.

'When you're pregnant, the lines show up pretty quickly.'

'Oh my god,' he whispers. 'We're having a baby.'

I wish I could get excited along with him. But his future is playing out exactly as it always did.

He picks me up and squeezes me tight. He rubs his face in the crook of my neck and inhales. 'You're having my baby.'

'I'm having your baby.' I hope.

CHAPTER
Twenty-Eight

One month later
Tuesday, February 6, 2001

It's late the next day when I arrive home and I drop my overnight bag by the kitchen door. My mom's cooking dinner, and Max is colouring at the kitchen table.

'Where's David?' I ask, making my way over to hug Max.

'Upstairs,' Mom answers. 'How was the conference? I didn't know you had a trip until David told me you were gone.'

'It was last minute.' I keep my arms around Max until he squirms out of them complaining.

'Everything okay?' she asks.

'I need you to take Max over to the guest house with you, if that's okay?'

She nods with concern in her eyes. 'Dinner's ready. We can eat over there, Max.'

Each step up the attic stairs is heavy and takes the breath from me, knowing that I'm about to destroy the man I love. It's killing me that I won't be able to confide in him. That I have to lie to him.

In all the scenarios I ever imagined, I never imagined *this*. I pause at the top of the stairs. He probably heard me climbing the steps. Do I knock or do I open the door and drop the bomb on his life? I turn the knob and he swivels in his chair to greet me.

'Hello,' he draws out with that unbelievable smile on his face.

I stare at it, trying to commit it to memory in case he never smiles like that for me again.

'What's wrong?' His face slips into concern as he walks towards me.

I didn't realise the tears had already fallen. My life has already crumbled.

I put my hand up to stop him from taking me in his arms. It will be worse when he lets me go.

'You have to know that I'm sorry.'

'For what?' His face pales.

My lips tremble, and I know I have to find the strength to keep the tears under control to speak. I have to tell him before I fall apart. I stare at the floor. I can't look him in the eye or see his face when I end our marriage. When my voice comes out, it doesn't break like I thought it would. 'I had an abortion.'

CHAPTER
Twenty-Nine

Monday, February 26, 2001

Mike paces my office, pinching the bridge of his nose as he barks orders at me and Caitlyn. 'I want a view of the Eiffel Tower, Stella. Not a lean over the edge of the balcony and squint type either. I want to be able to have the doors open and for it to be the first thing I see.'

'It's Paris,' Caitlyn scolds. 'Every fucker with money wants that view. And I can't get you anywhere.'

'Do your job and get me the room,' Mike tells her.

'I don't understand why you go to so much trouble for your birthday. You're going to be on your own.' Caitlyn scoffs. 'It's stupid. I swear you're losing your mind.'

'Stupid was last year and ordering an eight-foot Christmas tree for his cabin and full decorations at the end of February.' David drums his fingers on the arm of his seat. 'And phoning the hotel ten times to check they got the international shipment of sausages. That was celebrity scandal right there.'

Mike rolls his eyes at David. 'Get on the phone, Caitlyn, and work it out.'

'Fine.' Caitlyn drops her stack of papers in Mike's lap, and he flips her off on her way out.

If it were anyone else, I'd tell him to check his "fuckin'" attitude and get the hell out of my office, but I understand Mike. He's setting this up for Audrey, and when you're madly in love with someone from a different world, you'd do anything for them—anything they ask you to do—without questioning the ramifications.

David sits calmly in the chair on the other side of my desk, staring at me. He does that a lot now. He stares, like he's broken, like he can't figure me out. He's run out of words, out of questions, and now he's just trying to understand me inside his own mental torment. I don't think it's working. I'm losing him already.

It's been almost three weeks and although we haven't separated, he's detached from me. He's still in my bed, but he won't talk to me. Not like we used to talk. Everything is strained, and being that close to him at night, knowing we're a million miles away from each other is worse than if he'd stayed in the spare room.

At least then I could hope he might forgive me and one day come back. Instead, we're headed down the path of separation like DD told me. Every night I'm terrified it'll be the last time I get to sleep near him, to smell him on the sheets. I don't think I can survive waiting another fifteen years like I'm supposed to.

I run my hands over my face, pinching my cheeks. Pain will stop the tears. Mike mistakes the frustration for his behaviour and apologises.

'I just want it to be perfect.' He practically drools.

'I know you do, Mike. We're trying our best,' I tell him.

'Did you order the things from the pastry shop we were recommended?'

'I sent it yesterday.' I check my emails for their reply and point to the screen. 'It's here.'

'And they'll be open earlier than usual? You know what? I'm going to call them myself.' He grabs the phone off the console on my desk, and I have to lunge over the desk to pull it from his hands.

'No, you won't. You're completely irrational right now and I don't need some employee leaking a story to the press about how you chewed them out over mis-ordering some goddamn croissants. Now get the hell out and let me handle it.'

Mike relaxes. 'Thank you. I have to go. Dave, I need you to come with me to buy a ring box for Audrey.'

'That doesn't sound like a two-man job,' David says.

'It's freaking me out. I managed to track down and buy back her wedding rings and I don't want to give her the box the guy in the pawn shop had. I want to at least get her my own box. You know, something that she knows is from me and not just her husband's old rings back. I went to Rodeo Drive this morning and there's every colour and shape and material. It's kind of ridiculous.'

'What's ridiculous is that you have a smoking-hot girlfriend who you've sent away for the weekend while you go buy wedding ring boxes for someone else's wife.' David thinks Jessica, his ex-college crush, is totally-smoking-hot? Gee, that helps.

'Shut up, man, you know it's not like that. And that's why you have to come. So I don't accidently pick up some red-velvet heart-shaped thing.'

'Why can't Stella go with you?' David rises out of his seat as he speaks. It hurts him to say my name. Every time he says it, he needs to move, like the action will make the pain less.

'Because you have experience in this,' Mike tells him.

'Do I?' He raises his eyebrows and turns his gaze from Mike to me. His guarded expression has slipped, and he looks like he wants to smile or laugh. He must remember himself too soon, as the playfulness leaves him, and the strain is back. Oh, I get it. He doesn't want to do anything that would signify he's moved on. To move on would mean accepting that it's happened. I want to take his hand and tell him I wasn't okay with it either.

David looks me in the eye when he answers Mike. 'I just took the one the sales guy said came free with the rings.' His voice is flat, like he's trying to slide a knife into my heart. Like he's trying to pretend that our marriage was perhaps a sham from the start.

David crosses the room and opens the office door. Mike smiles timidly at me as he follows him out.

'Call Cici and tell her I'm on the way over to pick up the winter coat and clothes I ordered,' Mike tells Caitlyn in the outer office.

'Mike,' I shout loud enough for everyone to hear.

They stop, and David stares at me as I speak. Just stares right through me.

'Get her a white leather one. It's simple and elegant, and David's right. It's not about the box or even the rings themselves. When the man you love asks you to marry him, it's all about the marriage, not about what he's holding in front of you.'

Mike's great at reading a room and responding appropriately. It's part of what makes him that extra bit more successful than most—his ability to put people at ease. 'That's great advice, only it's another man's rings and another man's wife.'

I chuckle as they leave, and know that as soon as I'm finished here, I'll run across town to help them out. Audrey gave us those rings to help save me and Max. The least I can do is make sure those two don't screw up something as simple as a ring box.

Mike has accustomed to the grander things in life and for Audrey—he's searching for the perfect fucking ring box in a Beverly Hills jewellers. Which suits me fine—I can visit Cici while I'm here. David stands at the corner of the jewellery store, leaning against the window, chatting with Jessica as I drive by and search for a parking spot.

Oh Christ, this is not going to go down well if Jessica realises Mike is buying something for another woman. Despite Audrey and Mike's relationship never stepping over the boundaries of friendship, even I quickly figured out that Mike's heart belonged to someone else. I'm sure Jessica must feel it too. I throw the car into the first spot I find. I'm practically jogging in heels to the corner of the store. I freeze when I hear David's voice talking to Jessica. He sounds relaxed. Happy even. It's been so long since I've heard anything but a stoic tone from him. I stay around the corner out of sight, desperate to hear the old David that used to flirt with me in that voice. Fuck. He's flirting with her.

'You can't say things like that, David.' Jessica keeps laughter in her perfectly cute English accent, but I can hear the flattery there. That little bitch is enjoying this.

Who wouldn't? David and Mike are two of the hottest up-and-coming guys in Hollywood. And here she has a piece of them both snapping at her vagina.

'Hey, don't take that the wrong way, Jess. Mike's practically my brother, but all I'm saying is, remember that I was chatting you up first.'

'Oh, you so were not. You were dating Amy, and I was there to meet Mike. You were just being friendly.'

'If you remember correctly, Amy dumped me that night, 'cause I spent most of the evening chatting very closely to you. And you can't deny it—you were flirting back.'

Jessica stays quiet for the briefest of seconds. 'Maybe, but then I came to my senses.'

'You mean Mike finally showed up for the date.'

'And the rest is history.'

'So it would seem,' he says. 'Do you ever wonder what would have happened if he never interrupted us that night?'

'No, David.' She laughs. 'That's the kind of thing you can't say.'

'My life would be a hell of a lot different, I'll tell you that.'

'David,' she says in warning this time.

Thank god, at least she has some decency in her.

'That's not what I meant. Well not totally.' He laughs, but the humour he had a moment ago is gone. His pain is back. I can feel it. 'Something happened to Mike that night. A friend of his showed up and gave him some . . . news.'

'What do you mean?'

'It's nothing. It's just something that freaked him out at the time. He's over it now, so no need to bring it up. It was just the thing that made him take me away from you in the kitchen, remember?'

'I remember. When he got there, he pulled on your arm and took you downstairs to talk to you.' Jessica chuckled. 'I thought he was mad at you. We were getting a little close at that party.'

'That's what I mean. Mike's not normally that forceful. I honestly think, if he hadn't been freaked out by her visiting that night, when he showed up to the party, he would have seen us, and left us to it. He's not the sort to intervene. And hell, Amy and I were breaking up anyway. I think you and I might have hooked up that night. And without anyone showing up to give Mike a push into acting, we would have stayed in England, and my life wouldn't be currently falling apart here.'

I always knew Audrey had interfered with Mike's life path, but by default, Mike interfered with David's. Mike told me that if people aren't supposed to be together, then the universe will make sure they're ripped apart.

Well, David and I have been well and truly ripped apart. I take the final step around the corner, sealing my fate. There's no way David will want to come back from this. It's his perfect excuse to finally leave. He's admitted that Audrey's very existence in our time line has screwed with his life, beyond what he ever wanted. That it took the girl he wanted away from him—and left him with me instead.

Jessica's face ashes. I feel sorry for her. She has no idea what's happened between me and David these last few weeks, or with Mike and David and Audrey all these years.

'Stella,' she chokes. 'This is so not what it looks like.'

David doesn't even flinch. He doesn't care what I think it is.

'I know, Jessica. I just needed David to know that I heard his regret about our relationship. Now, if you wouldn't mind,

I'd like to keep this between us. The last thing I need right now is to be working out how to handle a leak like this with the press. It could turn to scandal very quickly, and I know that's not something you want for your own relationship either. If you would mind not telling anyone, not even Mike. I'd appreciate it.'

Jessica nods. 'Mike doesn't even know I'm here. I was shopping in Cici's and saw David standing on the street and stopped to say hi,' she says as she backs away.

David doesn't say anything. Why would he? He's done nothing wrong. Only voiced some thoughts and opinions, some time travel theories, perhaps, someone might argue. Someone might argue if they had feelings left inside of them. But I wore him down. He doesn't have any anger, or jealously, or infidelity he needs to cover up.

'I always felt like I'd stolen you,' I tell him.

His eyes snap to mine and for the first time in seventeen days, I see some fire there. Seventeen. I've been counting.

'Stole me from what?'

'From whom? Was always my question. I thought I was so lucky to have met you first.'

'First?'

'Before someone else. Before someone better came along that you might have wanted to marry.'

'Stella, no.'

The tears run down my face before I realise he's fighting for me. Those two words were the most honest-to-god gut reactions he's shown me for a while. Panic at the idea of losing this.

'I never thought the person might have been stolen from *you* before you guys even realised the implications of what Audrey being here might be doing.'

David scoffs and steps toward me. 'No.' He takes a moment for the finality of the word to sink in. 'Stella, I was mouthing off.'

'I can't do this anymore, David. I can't do *us* this broken.'

He places his hand on my arm, his voice raw. 'Then let's try to fix us, okay?'

My heart doubles in speed and gets lodged in my throat. The tears blur and form stars in my sight. He wants to fix us? I'd been so prepared for the inevitable, I never thought there might be another way. 'I want to fix us too.'

Mike walks out of the store, a small jewellery bag in hand, and lets out a breath, mirroring the tension I've been holding inside since the day I lost my baby.

'You guys screwed up,' he says.

We both turn to look at him. He unties the black ribbon holding the bag closed, dips his hand inside, and pulls out a red velvet, heart-shaped box. 'This is all wrong, right?'

CHAPTER

Thirty

The knock on my front door is punctual, 9:00 a.m. sharp. What did I expect from a professor who specialises in time?

I straighten my pencil skirt on the walk from the office and open the double doors to not only Ethan, but Liam too. 'I thought you would have been on your own,' I say in greeting.

'It's not a problem, is it?' Liam asks.

I shake my head.

'I figured it was important enough to bring Liam along,' Ethan replies. 'Why else would you summon me to your home?'

I open the doors to invite them in. 'Summon is a little harsh, don't you think?'

'What would you call it?' Ethan asks as they follow me to the office off the foyer area.

I ignore his question and sit behind my desk. The two of them fall into the chairs opposite.

'I wanted to talk to you in person, to tell you that I was screwing with the inevitable.'

Liam sits forward, but Ethan remains laid back.

'What do you mean?' Liam asks.

'A while back, your father told me that everything was inevitable, and based upon the information David has been providing me on his visits, and our experiences these last few months, I was beginning to believe him. But things have changed. Things are going to change.'

'What's happened these last few months? You and David are having problems, everyone knows that. But what specifically does that mean for the travels? What do you think you're about to change?' Liam asks.

'Nothing,' Ethan interrupts.

'Everything.' I raise an eyebrow, challenging him. 'I thought our path was set, that we'd divorce, like we did the first time round, but David is trying. I'm willing to grab on and fight too. Now that I know everything, I'm choosing to save my marriage. I'm choosing a different path, and with David trying to get there with me, I wanted to let you guys know that I'm changing my future. To hell with the consequences.'

'Stella,' Ethan chides. 'Have you ever thought that this was exactly what always happened?'

'You don't know that,' I shout.

'Except that I do.'

I stiffen in my chair. 'Oh, you're smart, alright. One way to keep everyone in place here is to wave some information in front of them. Tell them it's all laid out in some mysterious letter that only you have read, that no one else can. All of a sudden, you're going to control what people do and don't do. You can control the decisions they make. Just throw around a few cautionary tales and tell them it's in the damn future letter, and then force them to make life-altering decisions that you want.'

Ethan swallows. 'I know how grief can make us behave differently—'

'Grief? Who died?' Liam asks.

I dart my eyes between Liam and Ethan.

'How did you know?' I ask Ethan.

'The same way I know everything.' He shuffles in his seat, uncrossing his legs.

I look him over. 'You knew before I even knew for sure.'

'I worked out the rough dates myself based on the information DD left behind. He explained exactly what drove him to make those dedicated years' worth of research, and wishing and hoping for a chance to save his family. Are you really willing to screw that up because you're scared about being alone for the next decade?'

'He wants to try and work things out.' The croak in my voice betrays the hardened bitch routine I've been perfecting.

'Of course he does. And I'm not advising you otherwise. I'm just trying to prepare you for—'

'The inevitable. I get it.'

'Things this big always happen the way they were supposed to. No matter what you change or how many times you try to change them. You might have another few months together where you guys try to work things out, but I wanted to let you know that it's still going to end the same way. Especially now,' Ethan says.

'What does that mean?'

'The damage to David is already done. We can all see it. And now it's probably going to be worse on him. Because no matter what, you can't tell him the truth. You promised DD, and you're in too deep now. If you two are going to try and work through this, David will see the lies. He'll know that you're still holding back from him, and that will be the final nail in the coffin.'

'And back to the lab where you want him, right?' I whisper.

'It's not that simple, Stella. I'm not in a position to say I know everything, because if I did, I wouldn't be sick to my stomach with the information I have.'

'And what information is that, Ethan?'

'Knowing that lives hang in the balance. Say too much and someone dies. Wait too long, someone dies.' Ethan rises to his feet. 'I just hope I make David proud when the time comes. He trusted me with his whole life in the past, and it's not because I'm particularly good at physics or the research and methods of time travel. Hell, he and Liam are the experts. I think David trusted me as a man and a husband and a father to hold a secret. That no one in their right mind would keep a letter for twenty-three years without becoming curious. He knew that after I read it, I'd be able to comprehend why it was so important to wait until the right time, and to keep his secrets safe, and that I'd be in the right position to pass it on when the time comes.' Ethan lays a sheet of paper in front of me. It's a spider diagram labelled with different years shooting off the central circle. As I grab it up to read, Ethan spares me the need. 'David was never meant to be your husband.'

I hold my breath and scan the diagram to see where it says that.

'One of the times he travelled, he wound up in an alternative future where he was never your husband, and you and Max—'

'We're dead. I know.'

'That's not what's important. What's important was in that reality, where the time travel never happened, where there were no outside influences or changes to the universe as we know it, where Audrey never appeared to Mike, and David's research was never taken down that path—he never even met you.'

My heart falls into the pit of my stomach. 'I understand what you're saying. David never should have married me, so I should let him go.'

'I'm telling you the opposite, Stella.'

I snap my head up.

'For whatever reason, the universe decided to create a paradox and allow time to change. David chose to leave that reality and save your life over and over and over. He loves you, and his love for you and Max was the thing that drove him to figure out time travel, for crying out loud. He sacrifices everything for you. And you will only have the relationship you had in the *past*, if he has his heart broken *now*, so in the *future* he will try his hardest to change things. You two might have the chance of a relationship later, but if you don't let him go now, he won't have as much need to strive in his field. And if he never travels, the universe won't have its paradox to offer you. We'll be stuck with an alternative past, where you two never meet.'

I open my mouth and snap it shut again. 'So I have to let him go. And fight with him. And break his heart and get mine broken in the process, just to keep the past the way it was.'

'And to keep Max alive.' Ethan reminds me.

'I understand.' My head feels heavy as I try to turn away from them. 'Max's life isn't something I'm willing to risk.' I can't be the one to end this relationship. I can't throw David out. It will kill him and ruin any kind of relationship we can salvage for Max. I'll need to wait and let it play out the way it always does. David's going to leave me eventually. I feel like I'm suffocating. I can't fix us, and I can't even tell him why.

CHAPTER
Thirty-One

One year later
2002

I hang up the phone and scribble notes on a pad while punching the intercom to the attic. 'Guys, I need to speak to both of you down here.'

It takes David and Mike ten minutes before I hear them descend the stairs and appear at my office door. Mike offers his apologies for the delay while David loiters in the threshold.

I nod and dismiss his need to justify their tardiness. 'We have a great offer on a half season TV show.'

'I've never done TV before.'

'Not you,' I tell Mike and slide the notes over the desk. 'David.'

David meets my eye and waits for me to explain.

'A documentary is being cancelled and they need six episodes to fill the slot. Your name got passed to them through the physics department, and they found footage of you being interviewed at an event with Mike. They sound excited.' *Smart and hot.* I smile.

'I guess this is it then.' David crosses the room and picks up my page of notes.

'What do you mean?' I ask.

David shrugs. 'Audrey mentioned something about me having my own TV show.'

'Reality TV station, or something, she said,' Mike interrupts.

'Huh. I need to look into that.'

'He needs to be involved with production, if he's going to take things further than presenting,' Mike says.

'Don't you think I know that?' I snap.

'Jeez, relax.' Mike blows out.

David holds the paper up to me. 'Is this all they're offering for six episodes? I know it's a slot filler, but that's a low opening negotiation.'

'That's per episode, honey.' I mock. 'Want me to get a calculator for you to times that by six?' I smile despite my heart being heavy, knowing that I don't get to be proud of what he's achieved and celebrate with him like I ought to.

'Okay then. Get things started and we can talk over the next couple of days.'

'Wait, you want me to make the deal for you? Don't you want your own agent? This is going to be some sort of conflict or something.' I chew over my words.

David tightens his jaw. 'Despite everything, I trust you with this.' He holds up the paper to me. 'And I'd rather pay you ten percent than some stranger.'

'You don't have to give me your pity business, David,' I snap.

'This is your job, Stella. And you're good at it. So do your job and let me get back to my work.' He tilts his head towards the attic. 'Other agents and managers aren't going to understand why my work is important. But you can deal with all the bullshit and let me get on with things.'

'Fine.' My tone is flat and resolved to being David's agent for what is probably going to be a long and successful career, especially if Audrey mentioned it.

David slams the paper on the desk. 'I'm trying to get past this, but you won't help me, Stella. You keep shutting me down. You won't even give me a proper explanation for why you did it.'

Mike stands up and places a hand on David's chest. 'You need to calm down, man.'

'I told you. I did it 'cause I realised I couldn't have another child. I can't be dependent on a man to get me through this again. I'm finally in a place that I can afford to look after Max and give him everything he needs. I didn't want to be stuck in a relationship 'cause I was scared about what would happen financially.'

'Stuck? You felt like you'd be stuck with me?'

Mike walks out the door, but I see him waiting at the other side of the wall. I'm not sure if he's there to calm David down when we're done arguing for the hundredth time or to comfort him. 'That's not what I meant.' I drop my gaze to the table.

'Well, you obviously meant it enough to kill our baby for it.'

'That's not what happened.'

'No? Then what would you call it? Saving yourself? From me? Would it really have been so bad to spend the rest of our lives together?'

'What if it wasn't forever? Don't think I haven't noticed how you look at other women now. More and more, you're wondering if you should have been with someone else instead.'

'Of course I have. When your wife betrays you like this, of course you're going to wonder where in the hell you fucked your life up. I've wondered what my life would have been like if Audrey never showed up and put those changes in Mike.'

'When Audrey told you guys to move here and find me? That's where things got fucked up? When she told you to marry me?'

'She didn't tell me to marry you, Stella. I wanted that.'

'But she planted the idea, didn't she?'

'No, the idea was already there. I just didn't think you would have ever said yes. Maybe *you're* the one she pushed into this marriage. You're certainly the one who's destroying it.'

'That's not my intention.'

'You know what the strangest part is? I never had to think about whether my feelings for you were real or not. When I fell in love with you, it was the most confident thing I've ever felt. There was no bullshit with us. We just went for it. So if you had gotten over whatever you think was going on with Jessica, then you would have seen it didn't matter how many old girlfriends or crushes showed up. I was yours. I never wanted to look back and think about what could have been in my life, because I had it all, right in front of me.'

'Well, now you can get on with your life's work, figure out the damn time travel thing, and go off and make sure you never met me, and finally get your happy ever after.'

'It wouldn't be worth it.'

'What?'

'Giving up on you and Max. Not even the perfect happy little life would be worth missing out on the short time we had together. We were good Stella. And I don't want to give up those times, even when we were just friends, or when Nathan came back, you needed us here.

'It's time I moved out. We've tried for so long, but we can't live like this. I'm not going far. I still want to be part of your life. We were friends before. I'd like to think you were the best friend I've ever had, and I want to keep being a dad to Max. But you broke me. I've tried, I really have. But this last year's been the hardest time of my life. If I stay, things will get to the stage where neither of us will want to salvage any kind of friendship, and it scares me to think I might not have you in my life in the future, even in the smallest form.' He runs his hand around the back of my neck and places a soft kiss on my forehead.

'You've been thinking about this for a while?'

'It's not a decision I'd make quickly,' he tells me. 'Maybe one day, this is the thing I'll be able to fix.'

I stay seated in my chair and do something I never thought I'd be able to do. I let him go.

CHAPTER
Thirty-Two

Four years later
Thursday, March 2, 2006

Mike and I have fallen into a support system of sorts, except he doesn't realise I'm going through the same torture as him, where we wait for the months to tick by and clock up to years. Hoping and praying that the next ten years will pass and when both Audrey and David travel, they'll return safely. That finally I'll have David back with all the knowledge of what he's done for me over the years. We'll finally be able to put things behind us and get on with our lives.

Maybe even our marriage.

Each birthday that comes for Mike, he gets Audrey back for a day, and I envy each and every hour they have together, so much so, I make sure Michael is scheduled off work and left alone with her and I wallow with the reminder that I don't get those stolen days with David or DD. David kept his word and was present in Max's life for birthday parties, and parent teacher conferences, and every weekend, and dinner on Tuesdays and Thursdays. He's here for us, but he's far away.

How did the three of us become Hollywood's trio, household names, and wish away the years? David loves the new aspect his TV career has brought. For each event, he takes a new date, and girls are always photographed leaving his apartment. He hasn't introduced any of the women to Max, which I'm thankful for 'cause the divorce means he can sleep with whomever he wants, whether I'm still in love with him or not.

Max and I wait at the kitchen table for David to join us for lunch.

'How did Mike's Oprah appearance go?' Mom asks, moving around the counter tops making herself a luncheon plate.

'I'm not sure. I haven't spoken to him yet.'

'Didn't they film yesterday?'

'Hmm.'

'And what, Stella? It's not like you not to follow things through.'

'I was with him for the recording. It went well. I haven't had time to speak to him about it.'

'Ah, the old Mike-never-works-on-his-birthday rule. That's kind of getting lame. Was he still giving you hell for scheduling Oprah?'

'Well, I did tell him, you don't say no to Oprah, and it was only three hours of his day. He got back to the important things right after.'

'What was he doing that was so important you couldn't debrief him about Oprah?'

I sigh. 'Something that was important to him. He's coming around later today. If you want to sit in and talk about the recording you can.'

She smiles. 'No thanks, honey.' She kisses me on top of the head. 'I have a decorating appointment to get to.' I'm glad I started involving her more in the business. One day a week admin work for me and interior decorating contracts fill up her days. Even David has hired her to help with a few assistant things he's needed.

The front door slams closed and footsteps echo through the foyer.

'Hello,' David calls out.

'Kitchen,' I shout.

David drops his keys on the granite and takes off his jacket. 'Hello, ladies.'

Pamela kisses him on the cheek on her way out. Traitor.

'What has you in such a good mood?' I eye the clothes he was wearing yesterday and falter. 'Wait, don't answer that.'

His smile wavers as he tries to hold it in place. 'Audrey is what has me happy. Or has Mike happy. So I'm vicariously happy.'

'I can't believe you're going to live across the road from us, Dad,' Max says. 'It's almost as good as when we used to live in the apartment with Gran and Uncle Mike.'

'Don't you like living in our house now?' I ask Max.

'Sure, bud. I used to live in this house too, remember?' David sits between Max and me at the table. 'We still have some memories here.'

'Yeah, but this is where the fighting was.' Max looks down at his plate, and I swallow hard.

I glance at David, and he nudges Max on the arm. 'Hey, you want to know the best thing about living in the house opposite you guys?'

Max shrugs.

David pulls out walkie-talkies from the kitchen drawer. 'I dropped these around yesterday, so when I go home tonight, we can test them and see what kind of range we're going to get.'

'Cool! Mom, look, we can talk to Dad every night.' He jumps into my arm at the table. 'You don't have to be sad when you're alone anymore.'

David stiffens at the table but doesn't look at me.

'That's awesome. Why don't you run upstairs to your room and see if you can talk to us down here.'

'Okay, on it.' He speaks into the walkie-talkie.

'What are you going to do with your things in the attic? You finally have a place big enough for everything.' I hand him the salad bowl and cut into the lasagne.

'If it's alright with you, I'd rather leave them there. The attic's not fully converted across the road and there isn't a room big enough to display all the things how I like it. I'm a little nervous that some things might get mislaid in the move.' He swaps dishes with me and continues to fill his plate.

'Okay.'

'If it's a problem, I'll move it. But I thought it would be nice for Max to know that I'll still be over here most days working when I'm not in the university. Plus, you and Mike are working from your office. When you need me for a meeting about the show, I'll be close by.'

'You bought a house across the street, David. You're pretty close by.'

'You said you were okay with me moving here.' He drops his fork.

I hold my hand up. 'I am, but . . . '

'But what, Stella? You really should have voiced any concerns you had before we crush Max's heart again.'

'The girls,' I blurt out. 'I don't want Max to see girls coming and going from your house all the time. Even if you're dating them, god knows they never last long.'

'Is that the only problem?' He sighs, sounding relieved.

'Yes.'

'Then that's okay.'

I nod.

He picks up his fork and continues eating. 'I'll just make sure and fuck them at their place.'

'Attention, soldier, can you hear me, over,' Max says through the walkie speaker.

David answers him, and I take a moment to think of something to change the subject. Anything to take the attention away from the pain in my throat. Four years of watching the man I love sleep around town makes me question if what we had was real. Each girl is a twist in the gut that I struggle to forgive. Because when David gets back to me in another ten years' time, apparently I'm going to forgive everything he's done, and every girl he's fucked. I'm going to have to swallow my pride and try to push those images out of my mind because I love him, and although it wasn't my fault, I was the one who broke him.

'All went okay with Audrey's last visit?' I ask.

'I think so. I spent some time with her yesterday, and we ironed out some holes in the time travel line. I'm pretty sure this morning is going to be her last appearance for us.'

'Hmm, ten years. How do you go from spending ten years falling in love with someone one day a year, to knowing they're never coming back?'

'By knowing that you're their future husband.'

'What?'

'I told Mike this morning, so I guess it's okay to talk about it now.'

'Audrey's married to Mr Perfect. We all know how much she wanted to get home to her own family.'

'Audrey's married to Mike in the future. That's why she was travelling. She wasn't some random person who works for Mike. She's his wife and that's why she was so invested in making sure that his life played out exactly as it was supposed to.'

'But why didn't she say anything this whole time?'

'Because she was scared that Mike would never fall in love with her all on his own. She didn't want to influence anything.'

'Like she might have influenced us?' He ignores my comment. 'Mike already loves Audrey.'

'I know that, and you know that, and I guess Mike knew that, but he held back out of respect for her marriage. He was always jealous of her husband, knowing how in love she was and how hard it was being away from her family. If you think about it, they really only knew each other for ten days.'

'But he spent each year in between becoming obsessed with her. Missing her, wanting to share his life with her.'

'And now he can.'

'How? She's left and you worked out that the travelling line was going to stop on his thirtieth birthday.'

'Yes, but now he gets to meet the twenty-five-year-old Audrey in this time line.'

'The real one?'

He crunches his face. 'They're both real.'

'I know, but the one who won't disappear on him each time.'

'Exactly.'

'What's he going to do? Is he going to go to Ireland and try and find her? Where the hell is she supposed to be right about now? Did she at least leave you some information?'

'No, she was a little guarded about that. But she did tell me to meet Mike for lunch in Venice Beach this morning after she left. Turns out, she was waitressing there, or is waitressing there.'

'You guys met the real Audrey this morning? Why the hell didn't you lead with that?'

David shrugs. 'Just a little jealous, I guess. Mike's finally going to get everything he ever wanted.'

I clasp my hand over David's, and he carefully retracts it from underneath.

'So.' He slides his empty plate away from him. 'I'm guessing we give them a couple of weeks, then invite them over for dinner. What do you say?'

'You want a dinner date? With me?'

'Not a date.'

My heart lands on the floor.

'Just a meeting of sorts. We need Audrey to know that over the next ten years, we don't regret the time we had together.'

'I don't regret it.'

David stands and leans on the back of the bar stool at the other end of the kitchen. 'Neither do I. But naturally, things are going to be tough between us over the next few years.

We're still bickering, and everyone knows we had a hard separation. We need Audrey to know that despite everything, it's okay that she makes sure we got together.'

'Why? I hurt you.'

He nods. 'But it was the best couple of years of my life.' He shoves his hands in his pocket. 'Plus, I got to be a dad to Max, and I won't give that up no matter what.'

'Thank you for helping us. You saved us from Nathan, so many times. I don't think you realised.'

'Any time, Mighty. And just so you know, you saved me too . . . right before you ripped me apart.' He slides his keys off the counter and saunters out the door.

CHAPTER
Thirty-Three

Nine and a half years later
Friday, September 18, 2015

Mike, David, and I are having a meeting in Mike's living room about a joint television project for David and Mike, but as usual, the talk returns to Audrey.

'I don't understand why you won't start talking about this with her now. So she's prepared for when it happens. She'll have six months to come to terms with it and figure out what might help her, or us, in the past,' I say, when really I want to know what David's opinion on knowing things about your own impending time travel might be.

Mike sighs and pinches the bridge of his nose. 'I've told David a million times. I'd rather he spent his time trying to stop all this, than wasting energy and time on how to correctly tell someone they might be the first person to ever time travel.'

'What does Liam think?' I ask. 'Perhaps having an opinion of someone who's emotionally removed might be worthwhile. Or Ethan. Have you talked this over with him?'

'I haven't told either of them the specifics of how it's not just theory,' David says.

But they know. I nervously tap my pen off the side of my iPad until David snatches it out from under me. How the hell have they all been working for years without explaining to each other that they *each* know this huge secret? God, have they wasted valuable input from one another?

Mike glares at him. 'Maybe this is something you should be discussing. We've known them long enough and they're in a position to help.'

'I agree.' I pitch in. 'You might be surprised. They're not exactly idiots. They may have figured out that you already have experience with the things you're coming up with. I mean, why else would they be taking something so ridiculous and putting so much money and belief in it, unless they think it's possible?'

'They're also in a position to take the information to the wrong person. To take all the research, Audrey included, down a more sinister path,' David argues.

I scrunch my nose at him. 'What the hell does that mean?'

'That means we have managed to keep Audrey alive and out of the hands of people who wouldn't give a fuck if they hurt her to get answers. If we start bringing in other people, we might not be in control anymore.'

'Were we ever in control?' Mike cocks his head to the side.

Mike's front door slams closed and a female voice shouts out, 'Hello, bitches, I'm home.'

'Caitlyn?' Mike asks, bouncing from the couch towards the door.

Thank god, at least this'll be one less worry for Mike. David and I follow him out to the hallway where he's swinging Caitlyn around.

'Back in one piece I see.' Mike holds her out at arm's length. 'I can't believe you've been backpacking for so long. Who knew one continent could keep a really annoying person so busy.'

'Well, I had to come pay you back eventually.'

'Hmm, I was wondering if that was ever going to come up.'

'Jeez, Mike. Her bags are barely even in the door.' David points to the full to the brim, covered in dirt, green and black backpack leaning against the front door. 'Give her five minutes before you launch into the sensible brother routine.'

'No,' Caitlyn practically screams. 'I need a job, and since I owe you a ton of money, I was thinking you'd be more inclined to give me my old job back.'

'You want me to pay you, so you can pay me back? How the hell does that work?'

Caitlyn slides her arm through Mike's and walks towards the kitchen, scooping mine on her way past and giving me a kiss on the cheek. 'Can you grab those?' She tilts her head from David to her bags. 'There's more outside.'

He mock salutes her and walks past us.

'What were you guys all doing home in the middle of the day?' She takes a seat on the couch and curls her feet up. 'I was expecting Audrey and the kids.'

'Audrey is at the charity office,' Mike tells her. 'And the kids are in school. Well, the girls are in school. Andrew's in day care one day a week when Audrey has to go in to the office. Mostly I work from home when I'm not on set.'

'Oh good, that's kind of convenient if I move into the guest house.'

'Caitlyn, you can't just come back and work for me. You were gone for years. I had to replace you.'

Caitlyn stops twirling her purple hair extensions and places her hand over her heart. 'You can't replace your own sister, Michael.'

'Ha-ha,' Mike says humourlessly.

'I'll have a look at things and see if I have some jobs for you,' I tell her. 'And David too. I'm sure between the three of us, we can pull a full-time job together.'

Caitlyn quietly claps her hands. 'Thank you, thank you.'

Mike rolls his eyes at me. 'Okay, but you can start with David. He doesn't have a P.A. and I'm sure once you start doing all his shit for him, he'll realise he needs one. Then he's the one stuck paying you.'

'Great! He always did love me,' she chirps.

'Come on. I'll help you make up the bed in the guest house, and you can tell me all about the asshole.'

She darts her eyes to me. 'What asshole?'

I grab her hand and pull her up. 'The one who had you pack up and come home all of a sudden.'

Caitlyn's shoulders drop as we walk out the kitchen patio doors. The sun shimmers off the pool and Caitlyn stops and takes a deep breath. 'God, I love this house.'

David finally returns from the hallway. 'You didn't tell me you had a cab full of bags, Perra, and no cab fare,' he calls after us.

Caitlyn turns to him and blows him a kiss. 'Thanks, boss, I'll make sure and earn it back.'

'What'd I miss?' David asks Mike as I close the patio doors.

The bed is made and Caitlyn flings her bags on top while I grab a laundry basket for her.

David opens the door and drops a zip lock folder containing a manila file into her hands before she has her bag open.

'I heard I got stuck hiring you. I need you to take these documents over to Liam at UCLA. Do you know where our lab is there?' David asks Caitlyn.

'No, tell me and I'm sure I can find some hot young student to show me the way.'

David rolls his eyes at me.

'Fine, I'll take her.' I slide my shoes back on, holding onto his arm for support.

'The whole point in *me* paying her is so we can get more things done. If you're going over there anyway, I can send her to my office to clean up or find some other shit to do.'

'David,' Caitlyn mocks in a sing-song tone. 'When you hire someone new, you have to train them. And that includes showing them where you fucking work, douchebag.'

David takes the folder from her, rolls it up, and swipes it at her ass like it's a sword. She holds her hands out, palms out, and takes the folder back off him.

'If you were my sister, I would've left you in England,' he calls after us.

Caitlyn chuckles as she shoves her arms into her hoody at the door. 'He's so easy to wind up, isn't he?'

I nod.

'You two need to get back to annoying the hell out of each other. You were so much more fun when you were a couple. This polite thing you've got going down is just weird.'

I sigh and head towards the SAAB that Mike has assigned Caitlyn to use. 'Trust me, it's better than it was.'

'If you say so,' she mutters as she opens the doors.

It takes more than two hours to drive across to UCLA.

'I have to say, I never missed the traffic. I'm not sure I can get used to this,' Caitlyn fumbles with the key fob to lock the car.

'I don't think you'll have to come over here much.'

'That's a shame.' She grins at a group of guys as we walk into the science building and cross the hallway.

'David usually brings confidential papers himself. He doesn't trust couriers. It's saying something that he asked you to do it.' I stop and glare at her, waiting for the elevator.

'I know, I know. Don't fuck it up.'

'Come on, I'll introduce you to Liam and get you set up with ID cards and key entry.'

'Wow, who knew David took security so seriously.'

'Yeah, well, there's a lot at stake here.' My ID card lets me in the first set of doors, and we wait in the make shift glass panel foyer. 'And a lot of money and time invested in his research. If the wrong people were to get their hands on this, some damage could be done.'

'Well, hello,' Caitlyn whispers as she leans to the side. 'Wouldn't mind doing him some damage.'

'That's Liam,' I tell her. 'He's David's lab assistant. Well, to be honest, he's like another David. He knows everything around here, and he's the only person David has ever relinquished control to.'

'Urgh, I'd so relinquish control to him, too.'

'Caitlyn,' I snap. 'Seriously, can you cut the crap?'

Caitlyn straightens. 'Sorry.' She attempts to smile, but I know she didn't mean to piss me off.

Liam swipes his access card to leave the inner office and greets us at the door. 'Hi, Stella.'

'Liam, this is David's new personal assistant.'

Liam grins and offers his hand for Caitlyn. 'Nice to meet you.' His gaze drops to their hands and he takes his time scrolling back up to Caitlyn's face.

For fuck's sake.

'Can you make sure she has access here? David sent her over with files for you. I'm only here to show her around today. She'll be doing most of the drops from now on. David's going to be busy at home for the next few months and he needs someone to run back and forth.'

Liam's eyes widen and he looks at me. 'You're telling me I can send everything I need through Caitlyn, instead of waiting for you or Mike or god forbid having to drive over there myself?'

'Exactly,' Caitlyn says. 'Use me for whatever you need.'

I try to hold in my laughter, but the blush covering Caitlyn's face makes my heart flutter. Oh, she likes him. I turn my attention to Liam, who has his hands in his pockets and is rocking back on his heels, smiling at her but not making fun of her Freudian slip like I expected him to. Hmm, Liam's chin-length dark surfer hair, pulled back in a hair tie, is the kind of guy Caitlyn usually drools over. I never noticed that he has a decent build under his T-shirt, and, oh god, his tattoos. Caitlyn is going to flip when we get out of here.

'So.' I clear my throat. 'I have a lot to do. If you two want to get this over with, we can go.'

'Get what over with?' Caitlyn asks.

I nod to Liam. 'Ask her out.'

'Stella,' Caitlyn gasps.

Liam puts his hand up to stop the argument he can sense coming out of Caitlyn.

'I know you want him to ask you out. And you.' I turn to Liam. 'This is the quietest two minutes I've ever heard you, so I know you want to ask her.'

I look from Liam to Caitlyn, who tries to hide her smile behind her hand. 'I would say yes. Just so you know.'

Liam blows out a gasp. 'Good.'

'Good,' I echo. 'So, if you can get the access sorted and send it over to Mike's house. Better still, drop it off yourself tonight when you're done and you can pick her up for your date. Now, if I've finished match making, I have a job to do.'

'You're Mike's assistant too?' Liam asks.

Caitlyn snorts. 'Not anymore. I quit on him a few years ago. It was a last minute thing and left him hanging. He won't re-hire me, so David's stuck with me.'

Liam tilts his head. 'You quit, but he lets you hang around his house, and David trusts you with trailing his life's work from one end of the city to another. What'd you do? Cast a spell on them?'

'She's Mike's sister,' I tell him.

'Caitlyn Knight?' he asks, his voice a little hoarse. Realisation lights up his face. 'Of course you are.'

'Don't worry,' I tell him. 'Mike won't be mad you asked his sister out.' I pause. 'Will he?' I ask Caitlyn.

She shrugs. 'I don't know. Boys usually go missing after they ask me out. I never get the chance to find out what Mike thinks.'

We both giggle, but Liam's face has turned ashen.

'Don't be such a scaredy cat, she's joking.'

'I'll see you tonight.' He grins at Caitlyn.

We turn to the main door and head outside.

'Wear something warm,' he calls after us. 'I'm going to take you somewhere a little unexpected.'

'God, that smile is lethal.' Caitlyn pants. 'I wonder how many different ways I can get him to smile like that.'

I chuckle. 'You've turned into a piranha.'

She nudges me on the side. 'Only when they ask nicely.'

'I can't believe you brought me straight to your place already,' Caitlyn moans from the other side of my office door.

I drop the page of the contract and hang my head in my hands. 'You know I usually like my assistants to keep quiet and not yell at me while I'm working.'

'I've been home for four hours. I haven't even unpacked or slept. Mike's new accountant keeps calling and asking for a meeting. How do I access your calendar?' Caitlyn thumps on the keyboard like it will make the calendar pop up any quicker.

'Schedule something for next week. I'm busy.'

'He says it's a priority.' She appears at the door. 'You should get some sort of colour coding system set up.'

'I have an assistant, Abigail, who has her own system.' I scoff.

'Then where the hell is she, or the system?'

'She's on vacation. I didn't want to use an agency to fill her for the week. But you're here now, so stop bitching.'

'Liam's picking me up in an hour and I haven't even showered. I haven't shaved my legs in two weeks, so do me a favour and take the accountant's call so I can find a razor and some deodorant.' She grins at me.

'Tell him he has sixty seconds to tell me what's up before I bump him back to next month.'

A few minutes later my office phone rings. At least she remembers how to transfer a call. 'Stella Lewis,' I answer curtly.

'We need a meeting today,' Anthony tells me.

'I know you're new and want to make your mark, Anthony, but I'm busy. This shit isn't going to fly in the long run.'

'There's nearly a million dollars missing from Mike's personal accounts.'

Fuck.

I slide my chair back and close the office door. 'Is someone stealing from him?'

'Honestly, it doesn't look like it. It's two large chunks. One I've managed to trace to a house purchase for seven hundred and fifty thousand dollars. The other payment looks like cash, but I can't be sure.'

'Who'd be so stupid to take it in large amounts?'

'No one. When people are stealing, they start small. Move some things around until it gets lost. But there aren't any other suspicious transactions. This looks like it might be someone who knows it will come out eventually and doesn't really care. The house purchase was last week. The cheque was cashed today. I'm applying to the bank to release the security feed to see who cashed it. But my gut's telling me it's the wife.'

'Audrey wouldn't steal her own money. She and Mike have joint access to all assets. She doesn't need to hide anything.'

'Then why has she bought a three-bedroom home in Lakewood? Look, it's none of my business, and normally when the wife is doing a cloak and dagger run like this it's for good reason. In my personal opinion, she's not taking much, so I'd love to turn a blind eye and let her go before Mike tries to stop her. But I was hired by Mike and not the wife, so I'm obliged to tell you guys when there's suspicious activity on his accounts. I'm going to ask that you investigate this without him.'

'You better watch what you're implying, Anthony.'

'All I'm saying is no one knows what's going on behind closed doors. I've done my legal obligation. You don't have to do anything with the information. Let her go if it's the right thing to do, Stella.'

He hangs up. The beeping tone on the other end speeds up and I remember that I'm supposed to place the phone down. What the hell is Audrey doing? What would be so bad that she's preparing to run? I know the steps. Get your plan together. Stash some cash, if you can. Have somewhere to go. A three-bed house in Lakewood is certainly somewhere you wouldn't expect to look for Audrey Knight and her four kids. *Jesus, Mike. What the hell have you done?*

'Caitlyn, call Audrey at FEED US, ask her to lunch.'

A few minutes later, Caitlyn appears at the door. 'She isn't there. Hasn't been in for a few weeks, reception said.'

I close my mouth and try to act natural. 'Okay.'

'What's wrong?' Caitlyn asks.

I smile. 'Nothing. I'll catch up with her later.'

'Are you covering for her?'

'Covering for what?' I screech. Shit, that was not natural. I know how this plays out, and letting the husband's sister know something is up is not okay.

266

'Is she having an affair?' Caitlyn gasps.

'No, Caitlyn, I just asked her to lunch.'

'But you're acting all weird. It wouldn't be the first time someone's cheated on Mike. Remember the shit you had to hide from the press when Jess screwed that guy in Miami? He called off their wedding. It was heartbreaking to see that happen to him. What if Audrey is going to break his heart too? Oh god, what if this is the reason I had to come home early?'

I rest my head in my hands to tune out her babbling. Just lie—or act, it's the same thing. 'I'm worried about Mike's reaction to you dating his friend. I wanted to ask Audrey what she thought, that's all.'

Caitlyn stands straighter. 'I'm going on a date. Not dating him. Besides, Mike has no idea what I've been getting up to or with whom these past years.'

I tilt my head at her. 'Maybe don't lead with that.' I slip my heels back on under the desk and text Anthony.

Send me the address of the property.

I pick up my purse to leave and freeze. Liam's voice echoes in the hallway and Caitlyn giggles in response. I roll my eyes and prepare to tease them on the way out, but Ethan's voice speaking next has me stalling. 'Can we get on with this?'

'Of course,' Caitlyn stutters. 'She's inside.'

Fuck. She knows not to send people through without checking with me first, but when my office door opens David is with them.

'Well, to what do I owe the pleasure?'

David tilts his head ever so slightly. 'It was you who asked us to meet here.' His eyes widen.

Is he trying to warn me against spilling my time travel knowledge to Ethan and Liam?

I look around the other two men. 'No, I didn't. So, who the hell called this little shindig?'

Ethan pulls out a faded white envelope from his briefcase and my heart stops.

'It's time.' Ethan places the letter on my desk, and I need to throw up. I run to the adjoining bathroom and lift the toilet lid before throwing-up into the bowl.

David follows behind me and holds my hair out of the way. 'Are you okay?'

I raise my hand to push him back, but he passes me toilet paper and stretches over me to flush.

'I'm sorry,' I tell him.

'Don't worry about it. Are you sick?'

'No. I'm sorry about everything. I knew.'

'Knew what?' he asks.

Ethan answers from the other room. 'Stella knew about the letter you left yourself.'

David walks back to the office, and I trail behind him. Liam has taken a seat in the armchair, and my eyes fall on the letter I've waited to read for an eternity.

Ethan remains standing and addresses David. 'In 1994, you appeared in my office, the same age as you are today.'

David looks from me to the letter on my desk.

'You travelled through many years, much like Audrey has, and left yourself this letter, with the instructions that it should be opened today.'

'How?' David asks.

'Mike's fortieth birthday, in the same crash that brought Audrey to you,' Liam says.

'Then why are you telling me this now? It's too early,' David turns from Ethan to Liam.

'Because you need more information than Audrey does. You need to make sure you figure out the science and travel along with her,' Ethan answers.

David picks up the letter and studies his own handwriting. 'You knew about this?' he asks me.

I swallow hard. 'You told me not to say anything. That I could interfere with the future.'

'That was all theory,' he snaps. 'Never would I have thought I'd be travelling.'

I shake my head. 'I . . . I mean the other you . . . '

His eyes widen. 'You met me, when I was travelling? When?'

'You saved me,' I tell him. 'Every time you showed up, I was in danger, and you saved my life.' The tears roll down my cheeks and I deflate in the leather high-back behind my desk.

David rips the letter open and flips through the pages then closes it in half and sits across from me at the desk.

'Before I read this, I need you to tell me the truth. Tell me everything, Stella.'

Ethan leans forward, but David cuts him off before he opens his mouth. 'You're next. Once she's done, you're telling me everything you know, too.' David sits on the edge of my desk, turning his back to the others.

I nod and settle in to tell my account of DD over the years and what David is going to do. My emotions stay in check when I recall the events of my life and I replay them like a displaced narrator. Until I get to the morning in early February 2001.

Maybe now we can finally grieve together. He'll know the reasons why. He doesn't even have to forgive me, because it wasn't my decision either. He'll finally be there for me—because I need someone to hold my hand too.

CHAPTER
Thirty-Four

Fourteen years ago
Monday, February 5, 2001
Calabasas, Los Angeles County

I slam the front door and head to the kitchen to salvage some coffee. Once I get Max ready and dropped off at school each day, I can normally get straight into the home office.

'I thought you're switching to decaf.' David shoves on his shoes, while balancing one arm on the kitchen counter.

'As soon as you make a pot of decaf in the mornings, I will. But until then, I'm going to enjoy the left over, nearly-cold coffee without having to go to the effort of making a new pot.'

David rests his hands on my hips and kisses me slowly on the forehead. 'Did you sleep well?'

I nod. 'I never heard you get up this morning.'

'I had some things I needed to do upstairs.'

I harrumph. 'The attic is becoming like your dungeon. Every time I need to find you, you're up there.'

'I'm keeping all my records on Audrey there. At least it's close by when things make sense in my head.'

'Are you running?' I gesture at his workout clothes.

'Yup, I'll be back in a couple of hours. Going to the gym straight after. I'll bring you back lunch, so text me what you fancy later.'

'Okay. You got another Amazon delivery.' I point to the brown box on the counter.

He rips the tab open and slides the small pile of books out.

I eye the titles, all about babies and toddlers.

'I see you've exhausted the pregnancy and birthing books, finally upgraded to the baby books.'

'Mock me all you want, Mighty. But I want to be fully prepared when the time comes.' He turns his attention to my stomach. 'Cause when this baby comes out, I have a feeling all hell might break loose for a while.' He giggles.

'Don't listen to Pamela. She tends to exaggerate. I was so not that psycho when I had Max.'

'Better safe than sorry.' He scrunches his nose and kisses me.

I part my lips for him, and he groans as he slides his tongue into my mouth. He backs me up against the fridge and hikes my leg around his waist. He pushes the kiss deeper, expelling all space between our bodies, leaving me breathless as he trails kisses down my ear and the side of my neck.

'I have work to do,' I tell him.

His mouth has already found its way across my clavicle and down my chest. He nibbles on the top swell of my breast before placing a chaste kiss on the side of my cheek.

'Just kissing you goodbye is all.'

'Yeah, right, might want to get rid of this before you step out of the house.' I run my hand over the strain in his shorts.

'I know a great way to get rid of it.' He winks.

I slap him on the ass and shoo him out the door.

I lift the coffee pot, when the familiar bright lights grow in the middle of the kitchen. The coffee pot rattles as I try and place it back on the tray. Audrey never comes to me. And it's the beginning of February.

The growing light retreats and DD stands before me. The same clothes, the same unshaven face, the same forty-year-old, broken-looking 'cause-his-wife-had-an-abortion Divorced-Dave.

Oh.

No.

'Stella.' He chokes out the word.

'Don't. Don't say it. I don't want to hear it,' I whisper, clutching my stomach.

'You keep dying, Stella.'

'What?'

'I've been to this day seventeen times. And I can't change it. I've tried so much to change it. Each time I interfere, I get sent to an alternative future. It's my time, 2016, but it's all wrong. I always end up sitting at that damn birthday dinner with Mike, and we all know it's not the place we're supposed to be. I manage to reset things somehow and come back to this day each time and we come up with a new plan. It's like I gravitate towards you when you're in danger. I always come back to you. It's like my universe can't function if you're not safe. My version of reality, of the whole fricken universe will never be okay if you're dead. We try something else to save you each time, but nothing will work. You and the baby always die.'

I drop my cup and it smashes on the tiles. The coffee splashes on my feet, and up DD's legs. Neither of us flinch.

'The first time, I came back so I could change your mind about keeping the baby. And you did. You said you never had any intentions of having an abortion, but when I got back to my time, you and the baby had died in childbirth. There were complications. I came back a second time to warn you, but nothing makes a difference. You've changed hospitals, you've changed doctors. We paid for specialist consultants. We found different complications each time I change things and we've prepared ourselves and the medical teams for them all. We've had planned C-sections, inducements, bed rest, everything. But every single time, you both die. There's nothing I can do to stop it. The only way to keep you alive is not to have this baby. I tried to go back to before we conceived, but I don't know how to get there. I can't go beyond this point. Audrey's moving forward each year she comes, but it's like—'

'You're going back to catch every time I die,' I whisper. 'You told me the first time you came to me.'

'How many times do you remember me coming?'

'Twice. Each time Nathan came back, you were there, helping me.'

'This is what happened in my original timeline. This is why you did it the first time-because I told you to. You survived and Max didn't have to grow up without his mother. You never told me why you had an abortion, and you can't. I need to spend the rest of my life trying to figure out how this time travel works and try my damndest to stop you from making this decision. It will get me here to help you every time you need me. And it will make sure that you do this, Stella. You need to have an abortion. There's no other choice. Believe me, I would have found it if there was.'

'I lose you,' I whisper.

'You can't tell me. I need to let go of you and grieve. I need to place these memories somewhere and let the younger version of myself keep going with Audrey's research, because when the time is right, this will all work out. You need to do this, Stella. Our baby will never survive, no matter what we do. But you can. Max needs you. He's going to grow up to be such a wonderful young man, but it's because of you. You once told me the thing you feared was leaving Max without his mother, so do this for your son. Survive for him.'

'But our relationship doesn't survive this, and our baby—' I whisper through the tears. I'll never forgive myself for making DD look this broken, for not being able to tell him. For being selfish and saving myself and Max.

'Oh, baby, but you're alive. That's all that matters. We can't change the big things. No matter how hard we try. And if I get back home to you, I'll understand now.'

'If you're going in reverse order, tell me. Is this the first place you've travelled back to? Is it the last time I'm going to see you?'

He nods. 'Yes. I'll go back to every time he hurt you and keep you safe. But I need you to save yourself from this first.'

I hang up the phone and look at DD. 'I have a five o'clock appointment for this afternoon. I need someone to drive me.'

'You should book a hotel for recovery. Tell David you have work in New York and need to leave right away.'

I run my hand over my belly. It's not swollen yet. You wouldn't even know there's a baby in there. 'Are you sure?'

'Mighty, you know how much this kills me. I wouldn't be here telling you to do it if I wasn't sure. But this time, I want to do it right. I want to hold your hand and look after you and go through this with you. 'Cause we're about to lose our baby, and we need each other.'

I nod. 'Can't I say I had a miscarriage? I remember the look in your eyes at the hospital, and you were so broken when you told me what happened. Why do we need to put both of us through this?'

'Because with a miscarriage, I'll want to try again, and that's not something we should risk. This way, I'll want to know that I have a chance of maybe changing things one day. I'll throw myself into my work. I'll come up with the answers, something that eventually gives Audrey a chance at survival, and I'll figure out how to come here. I'll get it wrong the first sixteen times.' He chuckles without mirth. 'But eventually, I'll save you, and I'll understand. And then, I think I'll end up at the hospital, ready to save you the first time.'

'Why?'

'Because I love you, Stella. We were the real thing. And we can be again. I'm so sorry for all the tears and pain that I'm going to cause. But I love you and I loved that baby so much. I took all of my grief and anger out on you, and it wasn't even your fault. One day, I hope you'll be able to forgive me. If you don't, I'll understand, and I'm okay with that. Because you'll be alive to hate me for the way I've treated you.'

'I won't hate you, DD.'

He nods. 'I'm not going to hold you to that promise.'

A suite at the Roosevelt Hotel should excite me. An indication that I can afford such luxuries in my home town for a night away. DD drove me back here from the clinic, took his time with my bag as I checked in, and refused the bellhop assistance to the room. I'm only a few steps inside the room and I can't move any farther.

I don't want to sit down, relax, take a nap or a bath, or anything that would be an indicator of moving on from this. I need to stand still. I want to stay here, because taking another step will be like admitting I've accepted this and moved on. I run a hand over my flat belly, stilling when my hand reaches lower, where the baby was this morning. Don't cry. Crying will be doing something. And doing something will be the same as taking another step into this room. Another step in my life, knowing my child will never be born.

It doesn't help knowing that Max will still have me. In fact, it makes it worse, knowing that wherever you go after death, my baby, the one in this reality who never managed to grow bigger than a peanut is there without me. Suddenly, I wish I hadn't listened to DD. If I had waited eight more months, when we died together, the baby wouldn't be alone. The tremors wrack out of my throat in a low scream, tears choking their way through my sounds. I let my baby die alone.

DD wraps his arms around me, and I sink into him, screaming. I let my legs fall. I don't deserve to be able to stand. DD, however, feels the need to keep me in one piece as he grabs my thrashing hands and holds them, and me, tight against his chest. He buries his head next to mine. Only then do I feel his body shake with me.

We cry ourselves into exhaustion, until we both merely cling to one another, slumped in the middle of the carpet near the doorway. Our bodies have no more tears, no more energy to push them out, but it doesn't take the pain away. I untangle myself from DD's arms and slide over to lean on the back of the door. Taking his hand, I pull him with me, and we sit side by side.

'I never gave you the chance to show me how much pain you were in. I always assumed it was a decision you were okay with.' He drops his face into his hands. 'I'm sorry that I'm not going to be there for you.'

'You're here now.' I place my hand over his and squeeze it. 'I spent so much of our relationship scared that I'd taken you away from your wife. And here I was, the whole time, the one who put that haunted look on your face.

'It's coming. I can feel it.'

'I can see it.' I stretch my hand out to the light forming near his head. 'Tell me you know how to get home when you're done here?'

'No matter what I do and say, I don't blame you. Not really. Deep down I always knew that if you did this, there must have been a reason. I was so hurt that you never came to me and let me help you, let me be with you. I'm going to think a million reasons of why you'd do that. I'm going to question everything. Your love for me, and your loyalty, but please know, I never would have doubted you if it weren't for this. And no matter what, you can't tell me. It's going to get bad. Our separation is going to be messy and I throw myself into my work. And my work leads me here, to save your life.'

I never knew that words could physically knock the wind out of you. Our marriage isn't going to survive this. I struggle to breathe and hear the rest of what he says, over the echo of my pulse and the noise that accompanies the light trying to take DD.

'I'm always there for you when you need anything, and I'm always a dad to Max. Even after all these years, he still feels like my son, even though I only had him for a couple of years. He feels like mine. *You* still feel like mine.'

'When you get back to your own time, you'll finally know the truth, and we can work things out, okay?'

'Absolutely, but I don't expect you to wait for that long. We've both had some people come and go in our lives, and you need to know that I'm okay with your decisions, Stella.'

'No,' I sob, 'I don't want anyone else, DD. I only want us.'

He runs his hand down my face, collecting my tears with his thumbs as he goes. 'I know, Mighty, I know. But fifteen years is a long time to wait for me.'

'Wait, you were at a dinner party with Mike and Liam. The one you said didn't feel real.'

'Yes,' he shouts over the noise.

'Who was the girl? She's in trouble too. She doesn't leave with you guys when you reset your reality.'

David opens his mouth to speak, but the light has intensified and imploded in a split second, answers disappearing into blinding oblivion with DD.

CHAPTER
Thirty-Five

Today
Friday, September 18, 2016

I fetch myself a bottle of water from the mini fridge and return behind my desk, emotionally drained as Liam and Ethan wait for David to react. An eternity passes and I couldn't care. To be able to sit and let myself get lost in the emotions of grief, without having anyone judge me, or feel the need to be okay with my decision, I sit. David stretches and takes my hand and passes me a sheet from the letter Ethan has kept closed for two decades.

I unfold the page, surprised it's only one line in the centre.

Ask her for the truth. Then ask for her forgiveness.

I crunch the paper in my hand and the sobs tear out of my throat. David leans forward and catches me as I crumble onto the floor and let the years of heartache consume me.

After my tears subside, Ethan interrupts us. 'I'm sorry, but we need to keep going.' He hands us a box of tissues and when David stands, he tugs me to the couch next to him. 'Maybe Liam should tell you about the time he travelled into the future.'

David's body goes rigid around me. 'This is why you made contact with me in England?'

Liam runs his hands through his loose hair. 'Once we found you, it was imperative that we made contact. After that, you were the one who actually made the progress. You moved here and started your own work off the back of Audrey travelling. Dad and I were simply here, waiting.'

'Tell me about your travels.'

'I went forward in time. A version of what might have been,' Liam tells David.

'How do you know it was a version of the future and not simply *the future*?' David asks.

'I was a boy at the time and I witnessed our future lives from the sidelines. The adult version of me was sitting at dinner with you, Mike, and who I now know is Caitlyn. Although things were different, you guys never left England. Never had the careers you have now. Never had the wives you have now. In that reality, Audrey had never travelled, and Jessica was there instead. She was your wife.'

'You never told me that part,' I say.

'When we spoke of this, I didn't know who Jessica was,' Liam says.

'No, but I guess all sorts of interesting theories appeared in your diary journal once she showed up and you found out she was Mike's ex-girlfriend.'

'Not as interesting until Mike and Jessica started dating again.' Liam tosses back. He takes a deep breath and looks apologetic. 'What good is it to speculate on what might have been?'

'You got me hung up on the fact that David was in a 'might have been future' where I was dead.'

'What?' David spins me around to face him. 'You said I saved you in your past.'

'But there must be a version of reality, or a version of a possible future where you failed one time. And that was the version I visited,' Liam explains. 'The time that none of our lives played out like they did here, and Stella and Max paid the price.'

David chews on his finger. 'So we fix it. We figure out how to make sure I do everything I need to, so that version of the future never comes about. Ethan says the work is on track. We're already on the right path. Audrey has travelled in this version of our lives. Mike and I moved here.'

'And you married me, not Jessica. Maybe that was wrong. I always worried I stole you from a different life. Maybe you should have married her.'

'And let you die?' David spits. 'Is that what you want? For you and Max to be dead?'

'No, I just—'

'Doesn't matter much,' Ethan interrupts. 'David's right. We are in a different version of events. The problem is at one point in David's travels, he does something serious enough to get lost. To cross over into the alternate future. Our job now is to find a way to keep him on the right path.'

'He doesn't have to go. Now that we know everything, we can keep him safe. We can keep him here,' I tap on the table.

'If he doesn't travel in the crash with Audrey, he'll never save you any of those times in your past,' Liam says.

'What if he doesn't come back?' My grip around David's hand tightens. 'When he left me in the hospital, he never knew if he was getting home. What if that's why? Because he knew there was a chance he was going to get lost somewhere?'

'And now that will be the case,' Liam tells us. 'By having this conversation, David will know that when he leaves you in 1994, everyone is nervous about where he might go next. Which means there might never have been any danger. But us worrying about it here, has made a loop of that fear that we'll be stuck in forever.'

I slouch on the couch and rub my head. 'This is ridiculous. You said when everyone disappeared at dinner in that alternate future, they were going somewhere.'

'We need to find out where, and make sure Caitlyn goes with them.' Liam tells us. 'Make sure she's safe, because right now, she's the one I'm worried about the most.'

'You don't have to do this, David.' I run my hand over his arm. 'It's too dangerous.'

'This is my whole life's work. Trying to help Audrey and figure this out. I'm not going to ignore all I've learned and sit back and not try to save you in your past. Remember when we talked about the butterfly effect? When one small thing can change everything? Well, the reverse is also true. *Not* changing one small thing can change everything as well.

'I can't live in a seemingly perfect future, complete with a new wife, knowing that it cost you and Max your lives. I used to think that the universe would change things if it all got too fucked up, it would snap us back to the reality we were supposed to live out. But what if the life we were living, me and you, was the one we were supposed to have? What if sitting in an alternate future, laughing and drinking beer with an old friend was the mistake, the life that needed altering?'

'What if you're wrong? You haven't been there yet.'

'I'm not wrong, because when I look at Jessica, my heart doesn't flutter the way it does when I look at you. We had hard, painful times, but it was real. Every day and every emotion was real with you, because the love was real, and the universe was real when we were together, and even when our relationship ended it still felt real.'

David lets go of my hand and stands. 'Liam and Ethan need to see my notes in the attic and we can finally start working together on this. There's a box in storage marked 2016—it's time to pull it out and work together. See what's connected.'

'Where are you guys even going to start?' I ask.

'We need to travel by proxy.' Liam smiles at me. 'When Audrey travels in the crash, we need to make sure David and I can harness that ability and go along with her.'

'Every time DD left, I was right next to him. The light never took me along. I'm sure Mike is the same with Audrey.'

Liam slides his hands in his pockets and smirks. 'I agree. We need to build a time machine. Lucky for you guys, we've already started.'

'You've spent a lot of time telling Mike you would try and keep Audrey safe.' I tell David. 'Even if that meant putting a stop to her travels.'

'I know. But I never knew who else I'd be risking by not letting it go ahead.' David catches Liam's eye and pushes the door open, but halts in his track.

'I was there?' Caitlyn asks from the doorway.

I jump, forgetting she was working in the outer office. 'What were you doing listening?'

'It took me a long time to find you.' She's looking at Liam. 'All I ever knew was your first name.'

'What do you mean find me?' Liam steps forward.

'You left me a bunch of tapes when I was a kid. You said I was going to save David's life one day. And that I needed to be ready. I needed to figure out how to anchor myself to him or we'd both get lost forever in the switch.'

'The switch?' I ask.

'Between realities.' Caitlyn turns to me, then back to Liam. 'Versions of the future. That our families would be shifting between a few of them, and I had to make sure I went along too.'

'What tapes are you talking about?' Liam asks.

'Information on where to go, what to look for. How to start harnessing the ability to control movements in time.'

'To travel by proxy?' Liam's eyes narrow. 'And you're coming too?'

'You said in the tapes that Mike never travelled with you in the crash, and it was lucky he didn't or there would have been a conflict.'

'What conflict?' I ask.

'That he was in love with someone called Audrey, and that he'd be focused on trying to find and save her. His energy would pull us apart. But I travelled there with you, and once we found ourselves at a dinner party, I had to know what to do, to bring David home.'

'That's where you've been these years?' David asks her. 'Travelling for Liam's research?'

Caitlyn nods. 'I never knew that you were all involved.' She looks at the ground and kicks her feet around. 'Honestly, I never really knew if it was true or if I was chasing someone else's crazy dream. Until Mike married Audrey, and then I knew I had to keep going.'

'Huh. This is interesting,' I say.

'What is?' Ethan asks.

'Them two. They were the only ones together in both versions of a future that David visited.' I smile tightly. 'It's like, out of everyone, they are the ones who were really meant to be together.'

Caitlyn shakes her head. 'We're not together. We've never met properly.' She blushes.

'No, but the moment you did, the two of you were interested in each other. And you were the only ones in the other future that could have had a relationship without the interference of time travel. It's just, I don't know. A little disappointing that the rest of us don't get that guarantee too.'

David's phone beeps and he dumps his coffee cup in the kitchen sink. 'You guys want to order in dinner? Audrey's going to be late at the charity tonight and Mike is sending out SOS signals.'

Caitlyn catches my eye and before she can speak I stand. 'Can't. I was on my way out somewhere important.' I take David's hand. 'I need to go, but can we talk tonight when I get back?'

He stands and kisses me on the forehead. 'Of course. I'll take Liam and Ethan upstairs and we can see what we can start working on.'

We all file out to the hallway, Ethan and Liam heading towards the stairs to the attic office. David follows me to the front door.

'You guys head up. I'll be a second,' David tells them.

Liam calls back to Caitlyn. 'Don't forget your coat. This should only take a few minutes then we can get out of here.'

At the front door, I pause to put my boots on. I straighten up when I feel him standing too close to me, but lose my balance a little as I try to push my heel into the other boot. His arm instinctively reaches out for me and my insides melts at his touch on my back. With the knowledge that we might be able to salvage our relationship, his small touches mean more than they have over the years. There was a time when we were together he would touch me like this, when we were getting ready to leave the house and he wouldn't take his hand off me. He'd start with resting his hand on my back while I was adjusting my hair in the mirror. Then he'd hold my coat out for me and run his hands down my arm. He'd wind his fingers in with mine and hold onto them when we locked the front door.

Sometimes he'd pull me under the crook of his arm and walk me the three feet to the car. I remember turning into him when he'd open my door and he would kiss me before I got into my seat. Sometimes it was a long kiss, a deep kiss. Despite spending the whole day with me already, and despite going wherever we were going together, he would take the extra time to kiss me, to let me know that he missed kissing me. Other times it was a chaste kiss on the lips or the cheek or the tip of my nose. But it always lingered. He always took his time. Like he always wanted me to know how important I was to him. How much he loved me, loved kissing me, loved helping me into the damn car.

It's gone now. His touch, his kisses. He stopped me from falling over, but when he lets go, my heart continues to tumble off the cliff.

'Ready?'

I gulp and smile tightly. My back is already cold. It wasn't cold before, but somehow the absence of his touch has been reawakened.

David beeps my car and opens the door for me. It's silly. It's just a car door, but it's something he hasn't done for me in years. My heart has been battered at the bottom of the valley floor for so long, I never thought about what I'd do if he asked for it back.

'I'm sorry,' he says.

I move forward and touch his arm. 'Don't apologise.'

'There's so much we need to talk about, and I can finally listen to you. I'm not going to have a hundred different scenarios running through my head.'

I nod. 'I understand, I really do.'

'I was horrible to you,' he whispers. 'The other women. The snide comments and passive anger.'

'We can talk about it tonight.'

'I hope you can forgive me. I made a promise to you in the beginning. You told me you needed me to prove every day that there were still good guys out there, and I let you down. We were so good together, Stella.'

'We were.' I wish I could rest my head on his shoulder and inhale his scent, imagine that there haven't been a hundred other women over him in the last ten years since we've been separated. 'But sometimes, love isn't enough.' Once in my car

288

I type the address the accountant sent me into the GPS and take a deep breath.

David's shoulders sag as he walks back in the house, knowing I've ruined our moment. I watch his tense stance at the door, and wish I could wrap my hands around his waist from behind, and squeeze the reassurance into him.

I should remember the good things he's done and not concentrate on the things I had no right to get mad about when we were separated. I should remember how he always took Max for the weekend when he said he would, showing up for golf lessons, and little league practice, and school shoe shopping. Prom photos at the house, and the time I panicked when Max was seventeen and never came home after a night out. How he texts me happy birthday every year. And he thinks I don't realise, but every year on the due date we were given for our baby, he tries to text me, but never sends anything.

I put the car into drive and push the gate fob, remembering the first time I noticed the three dots indicating he was typing, appearing on my phone. I was about to text him about work, but when I saw he was typing, I waited. They kept disappearing and reappearing, like he was deleting and rewriting. I couldn't figure out what would be taking him so long to put together, and then I saw the date at the top of my phone. It was an hour later and the dots were still randomly blinking. I called him. He was in a bar. It was eleven in the morning. I called Mike to collect him, and as his manager I was left with the clean-up of the scandal he left behind with a random girl in a bar in the middle of the day. There were pictures. She looked like me. I hated him for that. I had no right to have feelings about him with other women. That annoyed me the most, because in my heart, he was still my husband. And I knew the day would come when he'd forgive me, and I'd comfort him for feeling bad about everything he ever did to us. But now that day is here, I hate him for every woman he ever touched that wasn't me. Because, in my heart I still felt like his wife, so in my heart, I still feel like he cheated.

CHAPTER
Thirty-Six

It takes me an hour and a half to get through traffic to Lakewood. The GPS has me pull right to the drive of the property that Audrey bought last week. Her Mercedes is parked at the back of the driveway, which is nestled in between the two neighbouring houses. She has the car as far away from the road as she can get, with some packing boxes and building material resting on the bumper. If the neighbours saw it from the road, they wouldn't think twice about it—she's moving in after all. But if you're trying to hide your licence plate, it's a good way to be inconspicuous.

Despite the evidence of renovations about to be undertaken, it looks like she's the only one here. I ring the bell and her footsteps travel to the front door. She doesn't hesitate as she unlocks the bolt. At least she isn't scared that someone is visiting her. Shit, who's she expecting?

Her face falls when she sees me. 'Stella? What the hell are you doing here?'

'We need a chat, don't you think?' I cross the threshold without being invited, and Audrey closes the door behind me.

'It's going to have to be quick. I have some workers arriving and I need everything wrapped up to collect the kids. How the hell did you even find out about this place?' she leads me down the hallway and into the kitchen. 'Shit, does Mike know?' Her face falls and she looks defeated.

'No, I didn't tell him. And I won't. I just need to know what's going on. Why are you leaving?'

Her eyes widen. 'I'm not leaving,' she snaps. She looks around the house. 'Ah, shit. Stella, this is so not what you think it is.'

'Then what the hell is it?' I hiss. 'If you're in trouble, Audrey, you know I'll help you.'

Her face softens. 'Thank you, Stella. But this is a birthday present for Mike. That's why I'm keeping it a secret.'

I try not to turn my nose up, but I guess I'm not as good an actor as I think I am. 'No offence, but I don't think he's going to like it. No matter how many guys you have working on it.'

'Not the house, smart ass. The money.'

'You're going to have to explain in full sentences, Audrey.'

The doorbell rings and Audrey sighs. 'I have to get that. Put the kettle on. I'm going to be a while.'

I stay put while Audrey answers the door and two men shake her hand. She introduces them as the renovation foreman and building supervisor. They assess the hallway and I retreat to the kitchen to find the kettle.

I turn the faucet on slowly so I can hear their conversation. They move onto the living room, discussing best methods for finishing for a resale and their additional month turnaround time.

'You told me it would be finished in January. I have decorators and staging booked and a bloody open house scheduled for then.'

Audrey's flipping a goddamn house. Fuck. I'm relieved and feel stupid and emotionally drained. I sink into a dusty chair at the kitchen table and wait thirty minutes for Audrey to return.

'Why the hell do you want money for Mike's birthday, Audrey? You guys are more than millionaires.'

'He is. But I'm not.'

I flash my eyes to read her face. 'I thought you guys shared everything. No pre nup, no monthly allowances. Just plain old-fashioned *what's yours is mine* sort of thing.'

'We do. But let's not dance around the fact that everything *we* have is what Mike earned. His fortieth birthday is a big deal. He works hard. He comes to bed exhausted most nights. And I wanted to be able to earn some money and buy him something big from me. Something that I worked hard for. Something I put in effort and sweat and worry and deadlines and could come out on the other end and give him. He's given me everything. I just wanted to show him if I had the opportunity to work, I'd give him everything I earned too.'

My heart constricts a little. 'That's really nice, Audrey.'

She smiles. 'I kind of hope the sentiment is something he'll like too, 'cause I've got to say.' She leans forward and whispers, 'I should have come up with this brilliant plan earlier. This is costing more than I thought, even with managing it myself and if I don't sell it, I've spent nearly a million dollars on a sentimental birthday present.' Her stifled laughter turns into a snort and full-out giggles.

'Don't forget that everything you earn on this flip is taxed too, so you're going to have to deduct nearly forty percent for the IRS.'

Audrey pinches the bridge of her nose and screams, 'Fuuck.'

I laugh with her. 'God, Audrey, what the hell did you want to buy him anyway?'

'A watch.'

'All this for a watch?'

'This is so stupid. I should have just had the store hold it for me and then paid for it on credit card the day before his birthday. It would still have been a surprise.'

I take her hand. 'Come on. Let's go shopping. I'll pay for it and when you sell this you can pay me back.'

'You don't need to do that.'

'Kind of do. I thought you were running off and I feel bad.'

She sighs and follows me down the street to my car. 'Thank you for coming to rescue me. Even if it wasn't needed.'

I hug her. 'Any time, chica.'

'I need to wait until these guys finish up. But I'll meet you on Rodeo around six, okay?'

'Perfect.'

I park outside Cici's and head inside for a coffee while I wait for Audrey's text.

She's waiting for me outside Rolex. 'You know you don't have to do this. The store will hold it for me if I ask.'

'Your husband would kill me if I let you put something on lay-away.'

She giggles. 'He wouldn't.'

'I know, but it makes me feel better for splurging.'

'I have it picked out.' She links her arm through mine and skips through the door. 'I saw it a while back and I know he'll love it. Liam was looking at all these watch catalogues over at David's one day, and this one caught my eye. It's really

294

understated and not too flashy, so he could wear every day.' She leads me over to a glass display where the sales assistant is standing.

'Can we see the light blue Oyster, in platinum?' Audrey asks. Turning to me, she continues, 'Seriously, it's the classic watch with the presidents bracelet strap, and it has the day of the week display as well as the date.' Audrey's jumping around like a child in a candy store.

The assistant slides the watch onto the display board on the counter for us to view.

My heart stops when I see David's watch placed on the leather board in front of us. *Beat, damn it. Take a breath and start beating again.*

'I know,' Audrey says. 'Isn't it just perfect?'

My heart hammers in my chest and I breathe in relief. Holding back the tears at the watch that once temporarily saved my life, I answer her, 'It's perfect. Wrap it up,' I tell the assistant.

I hand over my credit card for the fifty-five thousand dollar watch and know I would have paid a million dollars for it to save Max and me from Nathan all those years ago.

'We need two,' I tell the assistant.

Audrey raises her eyebrows at me.

'I missed David's birthday. Someone should have bought him something, too. Forty is a big deal, like you said. Don't worry, I'll wait until you give Mike his, so I don't ruin the surprise.'

She hooks her arm through mine. 'I wish I'd seen you guys together. Even now, you can see how in love you both are.'

I smile at her, gritting my teeth under my lips.

CHAPTER
Thirty-Seven

Five months later
Sunday, February 28, 2016

Before I even open my eyes, I know it's morning and I know David's awake. Neither of us slept much. With Mike's birthday tomorrow, and Audrey and David's impending travels and car crash, rest isn't something my mind was going to allow. Every time I turned in bed, he was moving to accommodate me and settle right back next to me.

'What's your plans today?' he asks.

'I was going to sit here and bite my finger nails all day. Might throw up a little. Haven't decided yet.'

'You don't need to be nervous. This's happened before. It always works out the same, remember?'

Hm. 'Yeah, but no one has seen beyond tomorrow. We know what happens in the past, but what then? We have no idea if Audrey or you make it home safe. That's why Mike is freaking out so much. That's why you should be freaking out too.'

David kisses me on the nose. 'I love you, Stella. That's all you need to know.'

I turn to face him, the panic rising in me. 'That's not exactly a reassurance, David. It sounds more like a goodbye.'

'It's not. You have to trust us. We've been working on this forever.'

'The last time you visited me, you weren't sure if you were getting home. Something happens when you're travelling to make you think that. Maybe you should stay here.' My gut clenches. If he stays, he'll be safe. And Max and I might be okay on our own.

'There's something you need to see.' David tosses the covers back and gets out of bed. He's pulling his underwear and pants on when my bedroom door opens and I pull the covers over me.

'Hey, Ma, you up?' Max opens the door and startles when he sees David one leg in his pants.

'Shit. Sorry.' Max turns around. 'Still getting used to someone being in here.'

'Max,' I scold, and he hovers on the threshold.

David laughs while he buckles his belt and pulls his shirt over his head.

'Sorry, I was looking for my black V-neck. Do you know where it is?'

'Do your own laundry and you'll know where everything is,' I tell him.

'Funny, since you don't do yours.'

David taps the top of Max's head on the way out. 'Don't be cheeky to your mother.' The two of them leave the room together, and I grab my dressing gown and follow them downstairs.

'I need to cancel golf this morning.' David pours coffee and hands me the first mug. 'I need to show your mom something.'

'Urgh, you could have text me half an hour ago and I would have stayed in bed.' Max takes my mug and groans as he lowers himself onto the bar stool.

'Couldn't. I was busy half an hour ago.'

'Dude, that's so not cool.'

I roll my eyes. 'He's lying.' I nudge David in the ribs, and Max takes his coffee and paper to the living room.

'Where are we going?' I ask David.

'Want to go see my really cool time machine?' he asks.

Instead of heading for David's car in my driveway, he tugs me to the end of the road and crosses the street to his house.

'Shouldn't something like a time machine be locked up somewhere secure, like oh, I don't know, in your super-duper lab?'

'They were until recently.' David opens his front door and we step inside the mirror image layout of my house.

'There's more than one? How did you even move something that big without the neighbours noticing?'

David chuckles. 'You'd be surprised what I can sneak in this house.'

'Don't remind me,' I scoff.

David tenses. 'I wasn't meaning to be smart.'

'I know.'

He runs his arm down mine, kisses my cheek and heads towards the stairs.

I follow him to his bedroom and into his closet. 'You don't have to apologise, David. We were separated.'

'Doesn't make it any easier, though, does it?'

'Sometimes it did.' I smile. 'I knew I could call you all sorts of things in my head those times.'

He leans against the island dresser. 'Do you know if we sold both our houses you could afford to buy your dad's old house? It's been on the market for a while.'

My heart hammers in my chest. 'I did think about it last year when it first went up for sale.'

'Why didn't you say anything?'

'Honestly, I was scared to take such a big leap. Max is hardly ever home, and Mom has her own place. There's no need for such a big property. It would be buying something just to prove I could. And I decided a long time ago I was going to choose happiness over proving myself.'

'You're happy here?'

'I'm across the street from you. It worked really well for Max growing up. Even now, when he's home, he doesn't need to choose between us.'

'It could be something we could do together, after this is all over with.'

'You're going to sell your house, so I can buy the one I always wanted?'

His smile reaches his eyes. 'If it's something you still want, then yes. Or, you know, if you ever got the opportunity to buy it as an investment property, you might want to look into it.'

'Ha, yeah, right. I don't have enough cash lying around for an investment that size.'

'But if you did, you should think about it. It would be a way of getting it back, without having to live there.' He smiles and opens his safe in the wardrobe.

'You keep the key to the place you're hiding your time machine in there or something?'

Pulling out a jewellery box, he opens up a watch with a cheap leather strap. 'Kind of underwhelming when you see it.'

'See what?' I look closer at the watch. The face is covered in multiple dials, and interval measurements.

'My really cool time machine.'

My heart skips a beat, and I watch one of the hands tick over a full second before my heart catches up with itself. 'That's a time machine?'

'As close as we could get.' David unfastens the strap and places it around his wrist. 'We realised that we weren't going to be able to build something that would actually facilitate time travel, so we opted to try something that can harness onto time and locations, and hopefully time jumps, like when Audrey leaves.'

We walk out of the closet and sit on his bed.

'Will this make it safer for you? Bring you home?'

'That's the theory. You see—'

'Give me the layman's idea on how it works.'

'It's an atomic watch, so it's the most accurate method of time measurement. The watch itself came with time zones and city locations already functional. It's why there are multiple faces and hands. Liam and I upgraded it to take account of leap second jumps and have included some things Liam was working on with anchoring yourself to the earth's core. So that when the earth's rotation in time—'

'You're losing me.' I hold my hand up.

'When Audrey jumps, we should be able to leave with her. Where we go will be determined by a few things, like where the universe wants us to go. Much like Audrey didn't have a choice each year where she ended up. With this, we should be able to make sure we leave in the first place, and that we influence the time and locations to some extent. This way I can make sure I get to the right places to save you.'

I drop eye contact with him and look at the carpet.

'I still don't like this.'

David stands up. 'Well, I do. I'm not going to risk a past where you need my help and I can't be there for you.'

'You said there was more than one. How many did you build?'

'Three. Liam and Caitlyn have one each.'

'Because they were at the dinner Liam saw in the future?'

'Yes. Liam thinks Caitlyn needs as much guidance and experience she can get with this so she doesn't get lost.'

'There's a possibility you might get lost there?'

'I'm not sure. It's why Liam wanted one last trip around the equator, so Caitlyn can orient herself with the centre of the earth. If she can feel it and gravitate herself to certain locations, she has a chance of controlling where she ends up if things go wrong.' He looks at his watch. 'Including their unscheduled stop over in Blackpool.'

'What are they doing there?'

'Liam wanted to show Caitlyn the pub he saw. In case she ends up there. She'll have a better feeling for her environment.'

'Shouldn't you have gone too?'

'That isn't my concern. Liam's nervous. He's covering all bases, just in case.'

'Including running off to get married after a whirlwind romance? They're scared this might be the end for them,' I tell him.

'They're in love.'

'Doesn't mean they're not scared, though, right?' I walk out of his room and down the stairs towards the kitchen. 'Why don't Audrey and Mike get a cool watch too?'

'Mike never travelled before, so he needs to stay in this timeline, like he always does. And Audrey always got on fine without interference from us on that level.'

'Let's hope so. If she doesn't get home in one piece and Mike finds out about this.' I tap the glass on the face of the watch. 'He might just kill you,' I whisper. 'We should speak to Audrey.'

He looks at me, then turns to the freezer and pulls out ground coffee.

'I tried to yesterday. We were shopping in Cici's and I saw that cardigan she wore. The blue one, with the white trim. Cici just had a delivery. I held it in my hand, staring, knowing this whole situation might unravel without any of our influences and Audrey saw me holding it. She'd already picked out the black Capri pants and she snatched it out of my hand so enthusiastically. When she was in the dressing room, I got the ballet pumps from the shelf I already knew she'd buy, and the black vest to match and my heart sank. I knew I was going to have to give her some sort of warning. That she might hate me, that she might not believe us. But I have to tell her. She needs to leave here tomorrow with some sort of understanding of what's happening to her.'

'I know,' he says. 'I'll do it. I'll do it now.' He grabs his keys. 'Tell Max we'll re-arrange golf next week, okay?'

'Okay,' I whisper.

He catches my chin between his thumb and finger and pulls me in for a kiss before heading out the door.

My fingers linger over my lips as I keep the taste of David with me as long as I can. Since having him back these past few months, I don't take the little things for granted. I turn off the social media apps on my phone and take a book from the living room back to my house. I need a rest from work these next couple of days, and Abigail is on call to cover any emergencies that might occur for Mike or David, in the career context anyway.

I twist my watch around on my wrist and throw the last of the baking crockery into the dishwasher. It's nearly midnight and I haven't heard from David all day. Things either went really well or really bad. Who the hell is going to believe you when you tell them you might start time travelling tomorrow and to mentally prepare yourself. I wonder how much information about him and Mike he managed to pass on. And me and Max. I tap on the favourites icon on my phone and the call buttons for Max or David appear for me to choose from. I hit David and wait with the phone on speaker.

'Shit, Stella. The phone just scared the crap out of me.' David's voice is hoarse.

'Did I wake you? Why the hell didn't you call me before you went home?'

'I'm not home. I'm sleeping on Mike's couch. I thought that was him calling.'

'Why are you sleeping there? Did Audrey take it that badly?'

'Fuck. Oh, Stella, I was sure you had seen it on the news. I was going to call you, but the girls have been stuck to me all day. They were pretty shaken up, so I was trying not to make a big deal out of it. I've been on movie and popcorn duty all day.'

'What was on the news?' I march into the TV room and toss cushions on the floor, searching for the remote.

'Andrew was in an accident in the pool.' David's voice wavers. 'It was bad. Mike pulled him out, but, Stella, his little body was so limp. We revived him, and the paramedics took him to the hospital. Audrey and Mike went with him. They're waiting on him to regain consciousness. I think this is the reason she goes,' he croaks softly through the phone.

'When Nathan came back and Audrey helped us, she said something to me. And there was something in her voice, even then I could hear it, like a mother's prayer. She knew. She knew she was there for something to do with protecting her son.'

'She never told us about this.'

I pick up my coat and keys and close my front door behind me.

'Why wouldn't she try to warn us?'

'Maybe she forgot. She must be in shock right now, and the trauma of time travelling along with a car crash she's about to be in must be pretty intense.'

'We have to make sure that when she travels this time, she remembers exactly what happened to Andrew, so she can warn you guys better.'

'I know,' he tells me.

'I'm on my way over. I'm going to call Max to sit with the girls. Time is running out.'

My heels echo on Mike's foyer while I pace back and forth waiting for Max. I keep glancing at the top of the stairs, hoping I don't wake the girls.

'We have no idea when we'll be able to speak to Audrey alone.' David looks at his new fangled atomic watch. 'It's already two a.m.'

Shit, I need to give him *my* watch. What if I don't get the chance later?

He stretches on the foyer couch. 'Liam and Caitlyn's honeymoon was supposed to be over yesterday.'

'They were delayed getting out of Manchester. They should be landing in another couple of hours.'

'What if they miss it?'

'They won't. They don't. It's always been this way. I'm going to leave Liam a voicemail.' He swipes his phone and brings it to his ear.

I hear a car pull up and I open the door to greet Max on the driveway. The passenger door opens and Abigail gets out.

'Mom.' Max wraps his impossibly big arms around me and kisses my cheek. 'I picked up Abigail on the way in case you need us to run any errands. That way we'll have someone here with the girls overnight.'

I smile at Abigail in her sweats. 'This is going above the call of PA duties.' I pull her into a quick hug. 'Thank you.'

'Don't worry about it.'

It takes David less than a minute to finish his voicemail.

'All set?' David asks.

'Sure.'

Max gives him a hug. 'Tell Mike and Audrey we're thinking of them, okay?'

I look between my two men and hope I can live in a reality that I get to have both of them in my life.

'I'm going to take my own car as well,' I tell David. 'Meet you in the parking lot?'

'Okay.'

When we park at the hospital, I open my door and the fresh air is sobering in the dead of the night. I run my hands over my arms, and we jog into the hospital. David pushes the call button for the elevator. When the doors ping open, he places his hand on my lower back and allows me to enter first. My heart starts beating again at the bottom of the valley. One bruise is healed, our relationship, but I feel like we're starting at the bottom again with the threat of what might await him on his travels. When he lets his fingers linger until he is fully inside the elevator with me, my heart is trying its damn hardest to stand up and claw its way back up the cliff.

'I have something for you.' I pull out his belated birthday present. 'I know now doesn't seem like the right time to give it to you, and now you have your own one, but you need it.'

I slip the watch out and gently slide it over his left hand. He glances out of the corner of his eye when I push the watch over his hand and adjust it around his wrist.

'You bought me a Rolex President?' He stares at the thing like it might change into something else if he takes his eyes off it.

I shrug and step back. 'It's for your birthday. It just took me a while before I felt like I had the right to give it to you. Just so you know, I always felt like your wife.' I lower my voice. 'I mean, I know I'm not.' A laugh escapes me. 'I just need to start adding up all the girls you were fucking since we separated to know that we weren't together. But sometimes, I forgot. And that's what hurt the most. I would have got you something for your fortieth, but we weren't together then, and it made me sad that I couldn't get you something special. I see something in a shop, or a commercial, and the idea barrels into my brain and I think, "Oh, I'll get that for

David, he'll love that." The sentence is formed in my head and my hand is reaching for my purse to pay for it, and I have to remind myself that you weren't mine to buy things for.'

'I didn't fuck nearly as many of them as I let you think.'

My laughter starts in my belly and pushes out of my mouth despite me trying my hardest to keep it in. 'That's the most romantic thing you've said to me in years.' We exit the elevator into the canteen and head towards the back of the room.

'I'm assuming you have a plan? It didn't go too well when I tried to speak to Audrey this morning,' David says.

'We need to wait here as long as we can.' I sit in a seat at the corner of the room with a view of the door, but far enough in the back so we won't be seen. 'Mike will get them coffee eventually, and that's when we speak to Audrey on her own.'

'He'll try to stop her.'

'I know. That's why you drove here. When Mike tries to chase after her, you need to make sure you drive with him. You can slow down the pursuit, give Audrey enough time to get onto the freeway. It happened there, right?'

'Probably. Based on the information Audrey managed to remember over the years. And the force of impact, it's the best location we've been able to come up with.' He taps on the other watch Liam has made for them.

'And she said she was arguing with Mike before the crash? Which means she knew what was happening, and she chose to get in the car.'

'She must believe us when we tell her it could save Andrew.' David looks at the ground. 'Didn't work this time, did it? We never managed to stop it.'

'Maybe we can this time.'

I take David's hand and glance at his new watch. 'It's two-thirty. The crash is around eight a.m., right?'

'Yes.'

'We need to keep an eye on the door and when Mike comes in here, we sneak out and speak to Audrey alone.'

David leans back in his seat, the small action manoeuvring the loose grip I have on his wrist out of my hand.

'Hey, want to pass some time?' I ask him.

'Yeah?' He rests his feet on the blue plastic chair on the opposite side of the table.

'Given the choice of anyone in the world, whom would you want as a dinner guest?'

He smiles. 'You. I've missed too many meals with you. I always did miss you, I was just . . .'

'Broken? You told me that a few times.' My voice cracks.

'Grieving,' he corrects and wraps his arm around my shoulders. 'You know in theory, this should only take forty-five minutes. But knowing us, it will take up most of the night.' He kisses my head and passes me a pile of napkins. 'Just in case you need a tissue. Now tell me, who would your dinner guest be?'

When Mike enters the cafeteria at seven-thirty in the morning, I nudge David from his snooze in the plastic chair. We slowly gather our phones and belongings and quickly exit the side door. David points to the elevators and pushes the button for the fifth floor once we're inside.

'Do you know what room Andrew is in?'

'Yup.' He checks the brown plastic signs stuck to the wall for directions, and I follow the patterns of balloons and stars painted on the wall of the children's ward. I pause outside the room and glance at Audrey through the checker glass. David doesn't notice my hesitation and knocks once while opening the door.

'We have a conversation that needs to be finished,' he says harshly while checking his watch.

I wonder if he would be more sympathetic if time were on our side. Or if Audrey wouldn't have looked as panicked if she realised everyone's lives were just bouncing off of each other. I don't know where the intertwining changes started, or if any of us could ever survive without each other.

CHAPTER
Thirty-Eight

David takes a pen from the end table and pushes back Audrey's sleeve. He writes the word *Andrew* on her forearm after he has given her a bombardment of information on what's about to happen to her.

'You have to make sure you don't forget this time. There's so much about to happen, that your mind will have a hard time adjusting to everything. I think you were suffering from some PTSD. Your son nearly died. You have just found out that you hold the key to the theory of developing time travel and you're about to experience it. You might not make it back home safe, and you're going to be alone out there. We'll be there, but we're younger, and we don't know you. You need to be cautious with what you tell us, but we need to know enough, and when you leave on Michael's thirtieth birthday it's the last time. We need to know to look out for Andrew. We can stop this from happening. It has to be the reason any of this ever happened to you. There has to be a reason.'

I look up from Andrew wired up to machines on the bed, everyone still waiting for him to wake. 'You have to do whatever it takes to protect your son,' I repeat the words she spoke to me many years ago. I dangle my keys in the air, knowing I'm dangling an opportunity for her to save her son. It wouldn't be an option she would risk giving up. She's going to try, just like she always did.

She snatches the keys out of the air as she passes by me. 'Look after him while I'm gone,' she whispers.

'Always,' I tell her.

'What if Andrew being in this accident needs to always happen? You said that the big things always happen for a reason. So, did we just send her into the past, knowing that she'll still forget what happened to him?'

'I don't know, but it's a possibility Audrey and Mike need to believe.' David paces between the foot of the bed and the window with his hands on his hips. 'We need to get Mike back here.'

'Isn't it too soon? He'll go after her, try to stop her.'

'That's exactly what needs to happen. We need to be behind her. Once our travels are over, we should return to the car where we left. We expected that Audrey was only ever gone from this timeline for a leap second, we can help her after the crash. No one else will expect it. There will be panic.'

'She's going to get hurt.' I say. 'Was it bad?'

'From what we seen over the years, he head injury was pretty bad. When she appeared to us the last time . . .'
He gulps.

'That's what Liam's supposed to do, be there to help you guys.' I take a step towards him and dip my hand into his jeans pocket, pulling out his phone. I find Mike's contact info and hit the call button, handing it over to David. I pull a chair over to the side of the bed, staring at Andrew sleeping. My heart tightens and I force a breath out. *Please, just make sure everyone comes back from this,* I pray.

'It's done. Stella and I have told Audrey everything she needs to know.' I hear David choke into the phone.

He glances at me and Andrew, still on the call to Mike. 'There has to be a reason for all of this, Mike. We have to play our part.' He sits on the chair at the opposite side of the bed, and takes Andrew's hand in his, stroking the top with his thumb. He drops his phone from the side of his ear and lays it on the bed.

It takes a few minutes before the door is flung open. Mike's been running. Of course he ran. He knew exactly what was about to happen to the woman he loves, and he would do everything to stop it. Unlike me, I'm sending the man I love off to the unknown so he can save me and my son. It's selfish. It breaks my heart. But I need him to save Max.

'Audrey's gone,' I tell Mike. 'She took my car.'

He punches the door frame and I'm glad it wasn't my face. I would've deserved it. I know exactly how it feels to watch the person you love disappear every year. 'You drive a fuckin' mini.' He spins to David, screaming, 'If you want to give her a chance of surviving this, you could have given her your bloody jeep.'

'We can't change anything. Remember when I told you not to set anything up with the charity? I was trying to see if I could change the timeline. I already knew you were her husband and thought if I could delay the charity setup until after you met Audrey, we would have a chance at changing other things in the time line. You wanted to change it too. But because you didn't have all the information, you ended up doing the exact same thing you always did. Liam's been trying to change things ever since he got here, and he can't do it. Even the fake info you gave Audrey about moving to New York, or that fake first movie you shot in college, it was always misinformation. We can't change anything, ' David tells him. 'You are one of the important people, Mike. We can't change your life or the effects on everyone else would be too great.'

'Audrey wanted to try and save him,' I point to Andrew in the bed. 'She had to do whatever it takes to protect her son.' We both do.

'Stay with Andrew,' Mike spits at me.

'Mike, wait,' David calls, following him out. The door closes behind them both and I pull my knees to my chest, the pain flowing through my blood, infecting every part of me each time I take a breath and push the guilt around my body.

I rock back and forth. There isn't time to allow myself the release of my pain through tears. I have to pray and think positive. I have to know that the outcome will be okay. That it's already happened, and it's already worked out, that they're already back. I continue to rock in the chair for what feels like hours, but as the minutes tick over on the clock at the side of Andrew's bed, the five minutes that have passed are the longest in any of our lives. Without realising it, tears are flowing down my face slowly and sporadically.

There's a soft knock on the door and I turn to see Ethan and Max tiptoe in.

The tears push out of my eyes and I sob, covering my face with my hands. Max comes to my side. 'Ma, he's going to be okay.'

'I have to speak to you alone.' Ethan stands before me.

Max faces Ethan, toe to toe. 'What's with the tone, Bennett?'

'It's okay.' I stand next to Max and touch his arm in reassurance. 'Sit with Andrew, will you? I promised Audrey I'd look after him.'

Max nods. 'Of course. Gran came with us. She's parking the car. Abigail is with the girls. They were getting up when I left.'

I follow Ethan out to the hallway. 'Is everyone okay?'

'I'm not sure yet. But something happened after David wrote that letter, and he made me promise to wait until now.'

He hands me a worn sheet of paper. 'This was enclosed with the letter we opened last September. David told me I could give it to you after he left this morning. So you'd know why he did it.'

'Did what?'

'Honestly, I'm surprised you never recognised him. I know you said it was dark that night, but I thought for sure you would have recognised him right away from the composite the media used to try and identify him.'

'What?'

'I wanted to come forward so many times to claim him that day. To put a name to what was left behind, let people know what he did for you. To let people know that he was an angel and not some unknown bar fight victim. But then his body was just gone.'

I open the sheet of paper, written on the same yellow paper as the one that made me confess to a lifetime of visits from DD. It's short, like the last one.

In every version of reality that the universe takes us—in every time line and alternative future—I take the memories of Stella with me. Nothing is real without her. I'd die for her, right here and now and in every fucking version of reality. What did you do that was serious enough to get you lost? You died for her.

DD.

I search my memory for images of Nathan pulling the man out of the car and knifing him in the stomach. Trying to recall any detail I can to tell me that Ethan's mistaken. That it wasn't David, but I know before I even search those visions, that I never clearly saw who it was. I can't even think of what clothes Bathroom Guy was wearing in the bar. My hands shake as I pull my phone out of my pocket. The trembling causes it to catch at the edge of the fabric of my jeans. I input the pass-code wrongly before I take a deep breath and hit each number slowly and methodically.

I swipe past the purple Internet browser icon and steady my hand to slide left. I hit the search engine and type in the date of the night I saw Nathan kill someone along with the words *unidentified male facial composite*. The Internet reception is faster in the hospital than I would like and the search returns to the first page in a second. I click on the *image* tab option at the top and swallow the pain in my throat as the image loads an ID sketch of David. 'No.' My body wracks in sobs as the smallest of words struggles to come out coherently.

'He's been dead this whole time,' I cry.

I dart the tears from my face and close down the browser, dismissing David's face from my history, and scroll through my contact list.

I push Ethan out of the way as I make for the elevator.

'You're forgetting why I'm here, Stella.'

'What?' I scream.

'We can fix this,' he says.

Liam and Pamela meet me at the bottom of the stairs and we walk around to a curtained off ER bed.

'Sorry I took so long.'

He nods. 'They brought David in about ten minutes ago,' Liam says. 'He's unresponsive. I can't figure out why. Audrey's travels were over so quickly for us in this timeline, she couldn't have been unconscious more than a few minutes.'

Mike's voice approaches down the hallway before he turns the corner and Audrey, lying on a gurney, is manoeuvred into the curtain area next to ours. Slowly Mike is forced farther out of the way while people tend to his wife. When he turns, he notices us standing next to him.

'How did you know where we would be?' Mike asks. 'Who's with Andrew?'

Mike stares at me. He must see my red eyes and dishevelled face, but he can't realise I've been going through my own agony. I sent his best friend away to die.

'Max is with him. But there's a problem,' I tell him.

'Is he okay?'

I slide the curtain in front of us back. 'The problem is David.'

When my dad was in his coffin, I could see his soul had already gone. All that was left was a body. David looks like that now. Lying in bed, hooked up to machines, a nurse bent over him. 'He got here ten minutes ago,' I tell Mike. 'They can't wake him up.'

Pamela steps to the side. 'I'm going to check on Andrew and Max and I'll be back soon, okay?' She squeezes Mike's arm on the way past.

'David travelled in the crash, just like Audrey did,' I say when everyone else is out of earshot.

'He never told me,' Mike says.

'He only found out a few months ago. By then, it was too late. So much was already in play, he didn't want to risk changing anything.'

Liam flicks through his chart. 'David's in a coma of sorts.'

'He's dead.' I clutch the faded letter in my hand. 'He's the one Nathan killed in the bar fight. I never realised it was him. It all happened before I ever met him.'

'He's not dead here.' Liam closes the chart. 'He's stuck.'

'Are you saying we can save him?' Mike asks.

Liam shrugs.

'Stay with Audrey,' I tell Mike. 'If we need you, we'll send Pamela down for you.'

Mike nods. 'Keep me updated.' His face is stoic.

'Where are we going?' Liam asks when I step out to the hall with him.

'Your father has a lot of explaining to do.'

CHAPTER
Thirty-Nine

Ethan looks nervous when we enter the family room.

'What's going on?' Liam asks.

'Ethan knew this would happen,' I tell Liam.

'You knew David was going to die in the past?' Liam's eyes nearly pop out of his head.

Ethan holds his hands up in defence. 'After DD wrote his letter, he borrowed my car and some money. He gave me a time and location and told me to meet him. By the time I got there, he was already lying on the side of the road.'

'Why didn't you help him?' I hiss.

'Of course I helped him. I called an ambulance. I tried to keep him conscious, but he made me promise never to tell anyone about it. He said the important things were in his letter, and this was something that had to happen. That Stella needed this to be safe. If I tried to save him, then others would have died. I didn't even know who Stella was back then. DD told me to let him do everything in our timeline the exact way it was. He saved you so many times. If we tried to change his travels, we might end up killing you instead. He died, right there in the dirt because he chose to save you instead.'

'But he's not dead here,' I argue. 'They said he was in a coma.'

'By the time the ambulance got to us, he was dead,' Ethan says. 'Believe me, Stella, I tried to save him. I'm not sure how he's still alive here.'

'Once he died, the universe snapped his body back here, to us,' Liam says.

'But his body was in the past for a whole day before it went missing from the morgue,' I tell them. 'DD only ever left once I was safe. Maybe for some strange fucked up reason I needed him to be dead. I needed DD to be found dead, to have enough of a bargaining tool to keep Nathan away. Even after DD died, his universe kept helping me.'

'Perhaps if you die in the past, you still get reset during the shift to your own timeline. Sort of like a pass.' Liam says.

'What good is that if you never wake up in your own time? Is David going to be in a coma forever?' I ask.

'I'm not sure,' Ethan says. 'But it explains how the body disappeared from the morgue.'

'*Humph*,' I shrug. 'I knew Nathan was never clever enough to steal a body.'

Ethan stands and clasps his hands in front of him. 'There's a theory that could fit these circumstances.'

'What theory?' I clench my teeth together to stop the screams.

'We stole his body,' Liam says like the realisation has just hit him.

'Did you?' I ask.

'Not in the past, no. But we still could. Time travel, remember?' Liam grins.

'Or it might not be as dramatic as that. Perhaps something we influenced brings his body back, and that's why there was a delay. I thought it might have been time travel related that caused his body to disappear, but I couldn't figure it out,' Ethan explains. 'Unless someone else managed to travel into the morgue and take his body back when they travelled. But we never knew who would do that. I speculated that it might have been us in the future, to try and get him back to where he was supposed to be. And now, it kind of feels like it might be something we do.'

'But someone did it. His body is here, so we don't need to worry about it, right?' I ask.

'Perhaps.' Liam stands and paces the room. 'But we need to look into who brought him here, back to 2016. If it was us, we still need to make sure we put those steps in place and make it happen, otherwise it never will. And if we find out that it was something else—'

'Can we save him?' I ask. 'Perhaps we can try and go farther back before he died. He's not dead yet, he's just—'

'Lost?' Ethan said. 'Perhaps we're wrong. Maybe if you die in the wrong time line or wrong version of reality, you just get lost in the cosmic world.'

'Knock, knock,' Mike calls from the edge of the doorway, Audrey next to him.

There's a collective sound of gushes and hello's as everyone reaches to pull Audrey into an embrace. She's still wearing her clothes she's travelled to us in all these years, but she looks a little dishevelled. I guess being cut out of a car will do that to you. She's walking and talking and has a bandage on the side of her head.

When I reach Audrey, she wraps her arms around me and squeezes me extra-long.

'Hi,' I tell her.

'We need to clear out of here in a few minutes,' Mike says. 'Audrey's being admitted and she should be resting already, but they're going to set a bed up next to Andrew so they can be in the same room.'

'I'm okay,' she tells us. 'I still feel a little weird, like this isn't real, but they said that's normal with head injuries. I'm so sorry about David. Mike told me what happened.'

I nod. 'Andrew's going to be okay? We're just waiting on him to wake up, right?'

Audrey swallows thickly. 'The doctor says a lot of his recovery will be due to the fact Mike and Dave got him out of the water so quickly to start CPR. I just wish I remembered more to warn you fully.' She chuckles. 'It was always weighing with me, but it was like I couldn't get my brain to catch up with what was happening. I had the feelings and emotions of knowing what had happened. I was scared, but I couldn't warn you guys. That bloody pool gate. At least I remembered you renovated the kitchen knocked out the back wall and replaced it with the glass doors,' she tells Mike.

Mike's face falls. 'Quicker access to the garden, you told me.'

Audrey freezes. 'Yes, I guess I did.'

'Do you know anything that can help us wake David up?' I ask.

She shakes her head. 'I really don't. I didn't know much right before I left, and everything I figured out along the way I told you guys while I was in the past.'

I sink against the back wall. 'He told me he was coming back, and that we'd be okay. After everything we went through'—my hand falls to my stomach—'he was finally going to understand.'

After a pause, Audrey releases Mike and wraps her arms around Liam. 'How was the honeymoon?'

No one answers her. She pulls back and looks at Liam. 'That good, eh?' She laughs.

'What are you talking about?' Liam asks her.

'Your around-the-equator trip? Not exactly my kind of romantic honeymoon, but you always did have Caitlyn eating out of your palm. Oh, gross, that sounds so bad when talking about someone's honeymoon.' She covers her mouth.

'Audrey, are you feeling okay?' Mike asks her.

'Oh, don't be such a baby. I'm okay, Mike. I know you don't want to hear the details about their hanky-panky honeymoon, but it started as an honest question.'

Liam steps forward. 'Audrey, something's not right.'

'Okay, I'm sorry. Jeez, you guys aren't usually wound so tight.' Audrey looks at me leaning against the wall. 'Oh, Stella, I'm sorry. I know I shouldn't be making jokes right now—'

'No,' Liam cuts her off. 'Where was I? When did I leave and when did I get back?'

He holds his hand up to Mike to halt him in his approach to Audrey.

She must sense his tone and answers his questions. 'Caitlyn wanted to finish off the trip she came home early from last year. You said you always wanted to take a trip along the equator line too. Stop in as many places you could. Fly over the equator zones. Caitlyn organised it, the stops and the accommodation. Mike paid for it as our wedding gift to you guys. You got back this morning.'

Holy shit.

Mike's face has fallen and he pinches the bridge of his nose. I can see him trying to hold back his emotions.

'What's wrong?' Audrey asks.

'Who's Caitlyn?' Liam's gaze doesn't leave Audrey.

'My sister,' Mike whispers.

'Your wife,' Audrey tells Liam.

Liam shakes his head. 'I don't have a wife.'

My mouth tightens and I dart my eyes to Mike. Why doesn't Audrey remember this?

'Audrey,' Mike soothes. 'Caitlyn died years ago while she was backpacking in South America.'

CHAPTER
Forty

'**This is why I** feel like things aren't real,' Audrey whispers. 'I'm not home.' She sits on the corner of the bed that's been set up for her in Andrew's room, and Mike catches her as she staggers at the edge. 'If I'm not home then neither is David. We're somewhere else. We're . . . '

'In an alternate future?' I ask. 'If we all remember Caitlyn dying, does that mean we're all somewhere else?'

'We need to get you in bed.' Mike crouches and sweeps Audrey into his arms.

Audrey buries her head into Mike's' shoulder. 'Your sister's not dead, Mike,' she cries. 'I swear, she's okay, and when David wakes up, he's going to help us get her back.' She turns her head and reaches out for Liam, forcing Mike to stop in his tracks. 'Do you remember her?'

Liam shakes his head. 'I never met her.'

Audrey's chin quivers and she purses her lips. 'She's your wife, Liam. So while David is still gone, you're going to have to do everything you can to get her back.'

Liam pulls the sheets back, and Mike places Audrey into the bed and climbs in behind her. She reaches over and they both hold Andrew's hand in the bed next to them.

I place my hand on Liam's arm, and he flinches. 'We should let Audrey rest,' I tell everyone.

'What the hell did David change?' Liam asks as we get caught in a bottle neck with Ethan leaving the room.

'Let's give Audrey time to get settled, then we can go over everything with her.' Ethan rests his elbow on the wall rail outside their room.

'Do you think Audrey's right, and this isn't real? We're all in some other reality?'

Ethan shrugs his shoulders. 'Perhaps.'

'What do you remember happening to Caitlyn?' Liam asks.

I take a deep breath. 'She moved here after graduating in 1999 and worked for a couple of years. She was really bad at being Mike's assistant. Her head was always somewhere else. She said she wanted to travel and had a trip planned to travel the equator line. She convinced Mike to lend her the money. First stop was Ecuador, and she went missing. Mike and his parents had to fight so hard to convince the local police she hadn't run away and hired their own investigators to help locate her. Mike had given Caitlyn a chunk of cash to spend and set up her credit cards if she got into trouble. So the police were working with the theory that she may have taken the cash and left. Mike had to prove that she didn't need to steal it, that he was giving her the money anyway. That she would want to come home. After a year, she moved from missing to presumed dead. Another year later, she was officially declared dead. They issued a death certificate and everything.'

'When was this exactly?' Liam pulls out his phone and starts to take notes.

'Twelve years ago today. She went missing in 2004 on Mike's twenty-eighth birthday.'

'The same day Audrey used to appear and disappear? No one thought it was a coincidence that Mike's sister disappeared on a leap year, on his birthday, when his wife used to do the same thing?' Liam raises his eyebrows in disbelief.

My heart skips a beat. 'No. But neither did you.'

'I didn't know much about what happened. No one kept us in the loop. We thought Mike's sister died on vacation. That was always the speculation. We never knew any other details to tie it to time travel.'

'You were supposed to be documenting things from Mike's life. How could you miss this?'

'I don't know!' Liam screams.

I flinch and keep my voice low. 'What does this mean?'

'It means that maybe Audrey is right, and Caitlyn is alive. That she only disappeared somewhere because David changed something. That this version of reality is wrong. That where Audrey came from—where Caitlyn is alive and well—might be the place we need to get back to,' Ethan says.

'And David?' I ask. 'Will he be in that version too?'

'I hope so. We'll never know because Audrey isn't from a time beyond this point. She can't tell us if it's the way it's supposed to be or not,' Liam says.

'You need to be prepared for the fact that sometimes, people we love just die.' Ethan narrows his eyes. 'And we can wish they didn't. We can curse the universe and dream about a different reality where they're still with us, but we can't change it. No matter how much it hurts. This is real life and everyone's happy-ever-after ends one day.'

I place my hand over my belly before I even realise I've moved. 'I know,' I choke.

'Why can't we get a reality where we are all okay?' Audrey walks around her living room, analysing the family pictures adorning the walls. 'Everything's the same, but there are little things off-kilter.'

'Like what?' Liam asks.

'This picture.' She taps on the glass of one of the frames. 'We met Caitlyn in Brazil one summer Mike was working. She took the picture, but the sun was shining too bright from where she was standing and the glare took up half the shot.'

We all gather around the picture of Audrey and Mike on a picnic blanket with their four kids.

'Mike hung it anyway. Said it was like having part of her in the picture.'

'There's no glare here,' I say.

'No,' Mike says. 'Someone in the park took the picture for us. I'm going to check on Andrew and the girls.' He kisses Audrey on the forehead. 'I want you to sit down and rest. Discharging yourself isn't something I'm happy about.'

'I wasn't about to let Andrew come home without me,' she says.

Mike nods in understanding, then jogs up the stairs while the rest of us settle around the coffee table.

'I've been going through some boxes I had in storage based on what you told me about my relationship with Caitlyn.' Liam places a box on the table and digs through it while I make everyone coffee and tea.

'We went to Ecuador on our honeymoon?' Liam asks.

Audrey nods into her mug of tea.

Liam spreads a map of the earth across the table, which has faded notes around the equator line. 'It was my original research basis for anchorage. The centre of the earth might have a relationship to time travel. Do you think Caitlyn might have gone there to look for something relating to the time travel?'

'That's where she went missing,' Mike speaks from the doorway.

Audrey shakes her head. 'No. She went there first on a long list of places she travelled, but she was always okay. She called every Sunday afternoon, like clockwork. You always booked her airfares and she worked from town to town to cover her bills. She only ever needed hotel money once when someone she was working for never gave her last paycheck. She came home at the end of last year. She met Liam and the two of them hit it off quick.' She looks Liam in the eye. 'It's like you were made for each other.'

'Why don't we remember any of this?' I look at Ethan and Liam.

'Do you think if I get back to my real home, that Andrew will still be okay there?' Audrey takes hold of Mike's hand and he sits in the chair next to her.

Ethan clears his throat. 'Audrey, I think you are home. There is nothing to prove that a person can skip from one version of reality to another.'

'Except DD. He was stuck in an alternate reality when he travelled. He managed to get out and go back to save me. Perhaps with him skipping to an alternate, we all skipped as well.'

'An alternate future,' Ethan corrects me. 'Not an alternate reality. There is a difference.'

'How so?' Mike asks.

'Our research has so far shown us that when choices are made that can affect the future, like the butterfly effect or whatever you want to call it, the alternative future merely ceases to exist.' Liam rolls his map up. 'It's not as simple as jumping from one version of reality to an alternative. Everyone and everything in the whole universe skips to the alternative future with us. It's not as simple as getting Audrey and David back to their origin, it's getting the whole universe back to the right reality.

'The solution could be simple, though.' Ethan suggests. 'When David was travelling to save Stella and Max, he found himself in a different future. Much like Audrey has found herself here with us. David was able to travel again and change the past, to alter his version of the future. When Mike made the wish on his twentieth birthday that first time, he was able to influence his version of his future. We are all living at the centre of our own universe, able to shape our perceptions and experiences. All we need to do is get Mike to work on the exactness of his desires. He is after all the person who started all of this.'

'We don't need the earth's core to alter our own perceptions of reality,' Liam states, like he's finally understanding. 'It can be used as an anchorage to certain places and towns, when time travellers are skipping alternatives, but using the people we love as an anchor is stronger. That's why Audrey never got lost—she was always anchored to Mike. That's what DD was always trying to tell us.'

'He said something like that to me once, that you gravitate to people,' I tell them.

Liam nods his head slowly. 'I've been concentrating on the wrong thing. Focusing on the earth and the universe.'

'What does that mean, to those of us who don't have PhDs in science fiction?' I ask.

'When David figured out how to harness the time travel to his own ability, he was able to bend his perceptions of reality to suit himself. In our lives we are the centre of our own universe. Our own perceptions of reality become reality. He was able to bend his perceptions to his own desires. To keep Stella and Max alive. He embedded himself in the circumstances so deeply, that his own universe could only help him facilitate that outcome.'

'And when he tried to save our baby?'

Ethan sighs. 'The universe was confused. David has spent so long keeping you alive, there was no way to save you both. Unfortunately, the baby, Stella, was never going to survive. For whatever reason, you only get one child in this life. By David attempting to save the baby, he continuously put your life on the line, and you always died. Because David's will to keep you alive in his universe was so strong, it allowed him to go back and try again.'

'Seventeen times,' I whisper. 'He said he'd been there seventeen times, and the outcome was always the same.'

'Each time, the version he left behind ceased to exist, and he tried again,' Ethan says.

'If we skip over to the alternative future that Audrey says is real. If we want to live in an alternative future where Caitlyn is alive, we have to take a risk? Are we willing to skip somewhere else and have *this* version of reality cease to exist? What if we get back to where Audrey says she is from, and it's worse?' Mike asks.

'What if it's better?' I ask.

Ethan nods but doesn't make eye contact with me. 'DD tried to make significant changes to his past, to alter his

330

future, but the outcome was always the same. If you try to sway too far off your intended path, the universe will throw all these things at us so we'll want to go back to the original.'

'Like Stella dying,' Mike says. 'Every time David tried to save the baby, the outcome was always worse. They both died.'

'It meant that DD was finally content to let the original design be as it was. When I found DD after Nathan stabbed him, he told me his whole universe would collapse if you weren't in it. That he chose to leave a version of his future where he got to live, but you weren't there with him. And if you tried to stop him from saving you this last time, then it would all be for nothing. That he needed you to be alive, if he was ever going to be happy, even for the short times you two had together. He needs you alive in his reality.'

'This is a good thing,' Liam tells us.

'How is David being dead so I can live a good thing?'

'Because, if he was able to influence someone living in his version of a future through time travel, we can influence it too.' Liam says. 'Whatever David did has triggered an alternative future for us.'

'So he needs to wake up before we can fix it?' I ask.

Ethan shakes his head. 'Someone is trying to blend the versions of reality. Perhaps get him, and by default us, back to the original.'

'Caitlyn?' Liam asks.

'It's a good guess. She's also missing in our reality here,' Ethan replies.

'But how would she know what to do?' Audrey asks.

'Perhaps in your reality, she knew more than she let on,' Ethan paces the floor.

'We need to get moving.' Liam stands and checks his watch. 'We don't have much of the day left.'

'You're talking about sending Audrey away again?' Mike asks from the couch. 'I'm sorry, Stella, but I just got her back. We just got Andrew back. What if we change those things?'

'Not Audrey,' Liam tells him. 'All of us.'

'We don't know the first thing about facilitating time travel.' Mike gestures from himself and Audrey and finishes with me. 'David was the one who worked on the science side of things. You guys are the ones who know what you're doing.'

'But this all started with you.' Liam says. 'What if David's version of reality is actually yours? We're all here, gathered in a country that we otherwise wouldn't have been in, discussing time travel that we wouldn't otherwise be able to, if you hadn't made that first wish. You and Audrey are the key to bringing us all together, and David advancing the research as far as he did.'

Mike puts his arm around Audrey.

'We're going back to England,' Liam says.

'What good is that going to do? You said we don't need a physical location.'

'We're going to England in 1997, when this all began.' Ethan looks at his watch. 'Metaphorically speaking, of course.' Ethan's eyes twinkle. 'It's still your birthday, Mike. It's still a leap year. Let's get this started now, before we need to wait another four years to attempt to bring Caitlyn and David back.'

CHAPTER
Forty-One

Mike sets up his dining table as close as he can to resemble the pub booth he sat at with his family on his twentieth birthday and made that first wish that changed all of our lives. The men moved all the furniture out of the room and placed the dining table against the wall, in an attempt to recreate the booth the Knights were occupying.

'Dim the lights,' Mike tells Liam. 'And light some candles at the far side of the room.' Mike takes one of the four chairs and closes his eyes when Ethan tells him to.

'Tell us how you were feeling when you made the wish,' Liam asks.

'I panicked. I was young and caught off guard. It was the first birthday since my grandad had died, and he used to put so much effort into our birthdays. I didn't want to disappoint my family by not taking it seriously like we used to. My life didn't suck, but things were tough. My parents' financial life was always hard. And they suffered more when I moved to university. I wasn't around to help in the family business, which meant things declined more rapidly than any of us imagined. I had this crazy idea that if I was going to wish for something, it might as well be big. It could be a career that people dreamt of. Being rich and famous and successful, and finally in a position to support my parents and even Caitlyn. If the B&B was suffering without me, it was going to fold when Caitlyn left for college, if she even got funding to go. I made a wish to be rich and successful, and the more and more details I went through in my head about working in the movie industry, the more excited I became. I realised it was something I might actually enjoy doing.'

'And Caitlyn, what was she doing?'

'Mostly? She was being a brat. She didn't say much. She was sixteen and I never realised she was living with my mother who was having an affair with the neighbour, and my father was living in denial. She sat with her headphones on listening to her Walkman.'

'Did anything happen around the wish that could have been significant for her? To why she might be missing in this version of the future?'

'I don't think so,' Mike tells us. 'The usual sibling banter. I told her she could be my housekeeper when I was rich.' Mike tenses. 'It was a joke. She knew I'd bring her out here when I could. And she actually looked relieved at the chance to escape. I even joked that she might meet . . .' Mike snaps his eyes open.

'Meet who?' Ethan asks.

'Liam.'

Everyone turns to Liam. 'How could you know me? It was the year before we even made contact with David.'

Mike leans forward and rests his head in his hands. 'The tapes. I tried to steal Caitlyn's Walkman and she panicked. She said *I need those*, screamed it actually. My dad said she was obsessed listening to some new singer, Liam something, and I dismissed it because I knew nothing about boybands.' Mike chuckles. 'What if it wasn't music she was listening to?'

'What else would it have been?' Audrey asks.

'Would Caitlyn always have been at your birthday dinners?' Liam interrupts.

'Of course she would have.'

'I need to see a picture of your sister,' Liam tells him.

Mike steps out of the room and returns with a frame of a picture that Caitlyn had emailed from one of her trips. 'This is the last picture we have of her.'

'She was there,' Liam says. 'At the dinner party I travelled to when I was a kid. The future version of me was with her at the table, and she disappeared. She's the one who was in trouble when everyone disappeared. I always wanted to find her. To warn her or help her figure out how to stay with you guys. I would have told her about anchoring into the earth's core, at certain locations around the earth. It's all I've been focusing on up till now. If she could figure out how to gravitate to her anchor when the light came, she'd have a chance. What if I actually took her away from the others? What if I'm the reason she's lost?'

Ethan takes the frame from Liam's hands. 'In Audrey's reality, you saved her.'

'Now we know the why and how to Caitlyn's involvement. We need to figure out where we can make the changes to bring her back,' Liam says.

'That only covers the 'how'.' Mike tells him.

'She's with David. If I knew that something might happen to me in time travel, I'd cling to those who knew what they were doing. Audrey showed up to Mike and David each year.

DD said he gravitated to me each time something in my life went wrong. If Caitlyn is in trouble, she would have tried to cling to you or Liam or David, since you guys know more than the rest of us. You and Liam are here, so the only one left that she could be with is David.'

'Do you think, they're lost out there, together?' Mike asks.

'Beats being lost on your own,' I shrug.

'So if we find David and bring him back, he should bring back Caitlyn too?' Mike asks.

'David and Caitlyn are both dead here,' Ethan states. 'But if we manage to change the course of Mike's perception of reality, to a time when they were both alive, we might be able to trigger a version of the future where they're alive.'

'And will we all get to be in this version of reality?' I ask Ethan.

'That's the goal,' he says.

'It has to work. It has to be the answer,' Audrey says. 'If anything, I *know* there's a version of the future where Caitlyn never went missing, so if we can get back to that line, maybe that's the same line that David makes it back home safe.'

'Safe,' Mike says. 'When the car crashed, time slowed down. It was weird. It was just like special effects in the movies.' Mike rolls his eyes.

'Time doesn't actually slow down,' Liam tells us. 'Our brain processes everything faster in moments of danger to try and prepare ourselves. Our perception of time slows down.'

'Well, when my *perception* of time slowed down, the car came to a stop. I unbuckled my seatbelt and wished for my family to be safe. I said something about not willing to pay the price, but I never checked to see if David was conscious. I just assumed he was okay.' Mike hangs his head.

Audrey bends next to him. 'You didn't know.'

'You made another wish,' Ethan says. 'The time of the accident was your exact birth time. The same time that sent Audrey spiralling into your past, and David along too. You made a wish for your family to be safe, and you got exactly that. Every time you make your wishes, when the circumstances are right, you get what you wish for.'

'Caitlyn's not safe. She's dead. And she's my family too.'

'Unless the universe is keeping her safe, somewhere. We just need to find her,' Liam says.

'So Mike can wish us out of this?' I ask the question that's been niggling at me. 'How do we change things to get David back? What wish do we need Mike to change or alternate the wording or whatever? And how the hell do we do that? Someone needs to go back in time and risk one of your butterfly effects to make sure Mike gets his wish correct the first time?'

'I'm sorry to do this to you, Mike,' Liam says. 'To give you hope. Caitlyn might just be dead. She might just be missing—'

'She's not,' Audrey interrupts. 'She was alive when I left. This whole time jump thing is fucking too many things up.'

'Me. I fucked too many things up,' Mike says.

'No,' Liam corrects him. 'This life was always yours. The alternate reality when Audrey never travelled to help you was also a wrong one for us. But something has been changed. When David disappeared too, he altered something.'

'He was never supposed to travel?' I ask. 'All those times he saved me were never supposed to happen?'

'If that were so, then Mike would have never had his career,' Audrey says, slipping out of her ballet pumps. 'You were always there, which means David always saved you too.'

Mike shakes his head. 'You can't give me hope of getting my sister back, but David has to die to get her back.'

Liam nods. 'The equator line. I always wanted to scour the centre of the earth. When we look at the theories of the laws of attraction, most of them come into play with the notion of *reality is perception*.'

'Your perception of reality, no matter if right or wrong, becomes your reality,' Audrey clarifies.

'And if you're standing at the centre of the world, harvesting the centre of your own universe. With everything else in play. We might just be able to manipulate things and see what happened,' Liam tells us.

'Is that what Caitlyn was doing?' Mike asks.

'I don't know. I never met her. But it's what I'd do, and it looks like her travel plans were exactly what mine would have been. She believed me, and she wanted to see for herself.'

'But how did she get lost, or whatever has happened to her?'

'I think at one point, when realities were crossing, things were changing, and she happened to be in the right place, looking in at the right time and got stuck. Wherever she was, when things reset, the anchor sucked her in and kept her.'

'You want me to travel to the equator, to see if we can get her back?'

'No, I want you to look,' Liam tells Mike. 'Your life and your perception of reality and your universe is the centre of all things that have been altered. You can tell us exactly what you know about Caitlyn's disappearance, we can tie it in with what I know about the travel plans across the centre of the earth, and Audrey can let us know what happened in her version of reality. We can see what's changed and then we can work from that.'

'Caitlyn did a trip here the morning she disappeared.' Mike's finger lands on the equator line that runs through Ecuador. 'It was in the police report. The company confirmed that she came back out of the cave, but asked to be dropped at the village nearby rather than home at her hotel. She said she had plans there and a ride home.'

'So they left her out there?' I ask.

'She's an adult. What were they supposed to do?' Mike argues.

'She went back into the caves,' Liam says.

'How do you know?' Mike asks.

'It's what I would have done. To get closer to the centre of the earth, she would have needed to go farther than the tourist trip took her.'

'Do you think something happened to her down there? Maybe she slipped or fell?'

'Or disappeared? The last place she was seen was also in David's alternate reality. I saw her there, and so did David. We both saw her disappear somewhere else when he left. So maybe, her being this close to the centre of the earth, when realities were crossing, pulled her somewhere else, like limbo,' Liam explains.

'Do you think David could be in limbo too?' I ask.

'If he is, then that means that for Caitlyn it's not somewhere physical. Her body is missing too. At least David is in a hospital with IVs and being looked after. If Caitlyn were missing with no one looking after her, her body would have died after a few days.'

'So we might find my sister, but it's going to be years too late? Why the hell don't you just bring her back to life and then kill her again for me?' Mike retorts.

'I told you this might all be bull. I never wanted you to get your hopes up.'

Audrey nods. 'I think Liam was the guy who broke her heart and the reason she came home.'

'But you said I never met her until she came home and started working for David. How could I break her heart if I never met her?'

'Oh, Liam, a girl can fall in love with someone she never met. If you were giving her information on tapes about your life's work and passions. And this fuelled her own passions for travel. It didn't matter that you two never met. She fell in love with your passions and your work, and you allowed her to be a part of something spectacular, all the time trying to save her life. It's more than a lot of people ever manage to experience even with partners they've had a long time. When she came home suddenly last year, Stella called it straight away. Some fella broke her heart and she scarpered.'

'What did she say?'

'Not a lot. Just that she was working on something for someone and in the last message he told her to give up and go home. She took it personal. Said that he thought she couldn't work through the problem so he dismissed her.'

'That doesn't sound like something I'd do,' Liam frowns.

'No, but remember, perceptions become reality.' Audrey winks.

'There are two sides to every story.'

'Actually there are three. Your side, her side, and the truth,' I chirp.

'How do we find out the truth?' Liam asks.

'Caitlyn told us,' Audrey says. 'Stella and I took her out to lunch the day after she came home. She told us what happened. That she wanted to confront him, but she realised he was right and then she felt like a fool and couldn't tell him who she was. It didn't make much sense, but now I realise it was because she'd already met you, and you two hit it off straight away.'

'So Liam saved her?' Mike asks.

Liam shakes his head. 'Not in this time line, I didn't. I never had any contact with her. How did I get tapes to her years before I met her?'

'Maybe this is the thing that needs changing. She was always listening to tapes and updating the files to her phone. Maybe you need to go back in time and record everything you know. That way she stays safe and becomes your wife, like she always was,' Audrey says.

'How does that help David?' I ask.

No one answers.

'We need everything in line and you can make one of those damn wishes,' I tell Mike.

'You want us to wait a year before we try and get my sister back? Until we have a chance to wake David up? Or what? Four years until another leap year?'

'No. We're going to try it today. Everything that's ever happened with our time travels has come from this day,' Liam says. 'There's another major shift at the end of the twenty-four hours of your birthday. The same time Audrey always disappeared. If we get the timing right, like you've somehow managed on your own all these times, we might have a chance of this working again. No point in waiting.'

'**What if I get** it wrong? What if I wish for the wrong thing or say the wrong thing, and neither of them come back?

'Today is a leap year, the strongest things are going to get. Unless you want to wait another four years?' Liam lights the candles on the cake Audrey had in the kitchen.

'There wasn't a cake and candles when I made the wish in the front seat of the car.' Mike throws out.

'We have to try and get everything right. You have to try, Mike. You have to tell him to come back to me. DD once said he felt like he gravitated towards me, and he can do that this time, to make it home. I can be the centre of his universe, his gravity force, and I can pull him to me. He only needs to hold on.'

'When David found out a few months ago that he was going to travel, he made a decision not to tell you,' Liam tells Mike.

'He didn't trust me.'

'He knew you didn't trust the universe. Not when it came to Audrey's safety. Your focus was always on Audrey and not on the bigger picture. It's why he chose to leave you behind. If you were to travel with him, you would confuse the universe. So I'm going to tell you, when you make this wish, you have to trust the world to get itself back in order. Don't obsess over your family or Audrey or the details. You try too much to figure out how it all works. Just trust that it will.'

Liam looks at his watch, and we all wait in silence. 'We're on the last minute,' He says. 'Forty seconds.'

Mike takes a deep breath 'I wish, we can all live in our happy ever after.' He blows out the candles.

The white light engulfs us, and I'm finally seeing what Audrey went through all these years ago, and what David did each time he came to save me. I place my hand over my lower belly and remember the pain at losing my baby. The pain of my marriage ending, and I make a promise to the universe that I won't be able to live without David. I waited my whole life to find my soul mate and now it's possible to have David and DD all rolled into one. To have the man with all the memories of what we've shared together. What's the point in David risking everything to keep me alive, if a chunk of me is going to die without him? If Mike and David get to ask the universe for things, then so am I. I'm going to ask for David to live in the same version of reality that I survive in. I deserve my happy ever after, otherwise what was the use of David fighting so hard? The bright light and noise is loud and scary, but once it has fully engulfed us, it's calming for a second before we're pinned down by gravity, pulled at from below while being thrust forward.

The light retreats and I'm back sitting in the hospital next to Andrew's bed, like I was when this whole alternative whatever thing started this morning. Ethan and Max come into the room and I nearly jump into Max's arms.

'It's okay Mom,' he soothes.

I look at Ethan over Max's shoulder and the crinkle around his eyes relaxes.

'Stay with Andrew,' I tell Max and run out the door and down the stairs, crashing into Liam at the bottom. I stare at him, and he at me. Nervous to ask what the hell is going on.

'I think things reset,' he tells me. 'I did it.'

'You made it back to Caitlyn at the dinner party?'

'It was strange. Things were exactly as I remembered them, but from a different perspective. Instead of the boy sitting watching them, I was me, at the table with them. When we disappeared, I went to a different time in England. I knew who she was and where to find her when she was sixteen, and

I knew what I had to do. I got everything we knew onto tapes and left them for her.'

I let out a breath. At least wherever I am, I'm not alone. Liam knows exactly what's happening. 'I remember Caitlyn coming home from her travels.'

Liam looks down at his left hand and chuckles at the ring on his finger. 'I remember her, too. We diverted our flights to Manchester on the way home from vacation because I needed her to see the pub in Blackpool. All those things she learned from my tapes and our trip saved her. It gave her the information she needed to save herself when we disappeared from that dinner party in the alternative future. This time she knew it wasn't just about the location, she needed to focus on the people around her too. To help her navigate her way home.'

'Do you think it was also enough for her to save David?' My heart thuds in my chest.

Liam looks at me from the corner of his eye. 'Maybe. We were both trying to hold onto David when we were leaving. I think the first time, Caitlyn got lost along with him, but somehow he needed to be lost to survive. With everyone bringing him back, maybe it was enough to pull him all the way back. I arrived here when things reset. Caitlyn was on her way to Mike's house to check on the girls. She must have been put back there too.'

'Call her. Tell her to turn around and come here. We need to see her. Mike and Audrey will need to see her.'

I walk to the ER entrance and wait for the ambulance to pull in with Mike and Audrey, like it did this morning.

'Do you remember when Caitlyn interrupted us a few months ago?' Liam asks. 'She said those tapes told her how to save David. I tried, Stella. I really tried to tell her everything I could think of that might help him. I remembered what you said about people being our centre and I thought of Caitlyn and David and you, and even Mike and Audrey. How we all get to be complete with each other. That she should hold onto him.'

'I was back in Andrew's room, so maybe David was put back in the car, like he was the last time.'

When an ambulance pulls up, the gurney is taken out the back, and Mike hops down, holding onto Audrey's hand as they push her through the doors.

'Mike?' I ask.

'Caitlyn's here?' he croaks. 'I remember it differently now.'

I nod. 'Two sets of memories, but this one feels stronger, like it's the right one. Why do we remember a reality that has ceased to exist? I never remembered all the times DD showed up to try and save our baby.'

'Because this time we were the ones skipping through them. We hold onto those memories and experiences.'

'Like David held onto each and every way our baby died?'

Liam breaks eye contact with me. 'Probably.'

'DD tried to save us but ended up torturing himself time and time again.'

Audrey pulls his hand closer to her chest as we follow her down the hall. 'The last time it all felt dizzy around the edges. Like a dream. Caitlyn's okay, Mike. I can feel it.'

We are pushed out of the way while people tend to Audrey and stand at the edge of the neighbouring curtain. My hands shake as I take hold of the edge, my knuckles turning white clutching at the thin layer of fabric, holding my own moment of reality together.

'You need to know something, Stella, before we step in there.' Mike lays his hand on my shoulder. 'He would never take it back. He would die for you and Max in every version that this universe throws at him, Stella. If this didn't work, it might be time to let him go.'

I pull the curtain back and David opens his eyes and blinks a few times. The fluorescent lights above must be too bright for him.

Mike and Liam flank on either side of the gurney and put their hands under David's arms to hoist him into a sitting position.

With a groan, David leans forward and reaches his hand out to me.

I intertwine my fingers with his. 'Welcome back,' I tell him.

David jerks our hands, pulling me forward, crashing into him. Mike puts his weight at David's back to help him support us both, and I let a giggle escape.

'You're my core,' David whispers through my hair. He clasps the back of my head. He pulls back and takes my face in his hands, studying me hard. 'I'm so damn sorry that I wasn't there for you.'

'You were,' I tell him.

David sighs and gives me one tight squeeze before inching to the edge of the gurney. He stands, still not releasing me. 'Audrey okay?' he asks Mike.

Mike nods. 'Yeah. And Andrew is going to wake up soon and we'll be discharged by the end of the day.'

'How do you know?'

Mike chuckles. 'Call it a hunch.'

'Are we good now?' Liam asks. 'Everyone got their happy

ever after. Three couples, and we finally get to live in a time like we should have been?'

Mike smiles sadly. 'I say we don't fuck with fate anymore, and let things play out the way they're supposed to be.'

Liam nods. 'No threat of going anywhere else, right?'

David smiles and pats Liam on the shoulder. 'You're never going to believe where I've been.'

'Where?' Mike asks.

The end.

A NOTE FROM
The Author

Did you know the best way you can support an author is to leave a review? If you enjoyed this novel, please take a few minutes to click on the AMAZON link to leave your rating. I appreciate the support!

Enjoy this story? Want FREE deleted scenes from the novel? Want Giveaways? Advanced Reader Copies? Exclusive sneak peeks of future chapters?

Click on the link below to sign up to my mailing list (I promise not to spam you) and keep up to date on future releases and claim your first FREEBIE – The first draft of David and Stella's entire 36 questions to fall in love, https://dl.bookfunnel.com/hcq4emo3dr

I use a service called BookFunnel to deliver my books. It may take a few steps depending on your reading device. If you have trouble, just tap the Help Me link at the top of the book download page.

The amount of social media platforms out there kind of scare me, but you can find me on Facebook where I know how to work it (ha, kind of!)

https://www.facebook.com/bronamillsauthor

Or my new Instagram account where I combine my two loves: food and books!

https://www.instagram.com/for_the_love_of_food_and_books/

34611278R00197

Printed in Great Britain
by Amazon